Louise Allen has been immersing herself in history for as long as she can remember, finding landscapes and places evoke powerful images of the past. Venice, Burgundy and the Greek islands are favourites. Louise lives on the Norfolk coast and spends her spare time gardening, researching family history or travelling. Please visit Louise's website, www.louiseallenregency.com, her blog, www.janeaustenslondon.com, or find her on X @LouiseRegency and on Facebook.

TEMPTED BY HER ENEMY MARQUIS

Louise Allen

MILLS & BOON

First published in Great Britain 2025
by Mills & Boon, an imprint of HarperCollins*Publishers* Ltd,
1 London Bridge Street, London, SE1 9GF

www.harpercollins.co.uk

HarperCollins*Publishers*, Macken House, 39/40 Mayor Street Upper, Dublin 1, D01 C9W8, Ireland

ISBN: 978-0-263-34501-8

01/25

Chapter One

Ravenham Hall, Hertfordshire—
September 5th, 1815

'But you are a woman,' the Marquis of Ravenham said.

'Yes, my lord.' The neat figure in front of him dropped the slightest of curtsies. Her face was composed, but he had the strong impression that she was amused.

'I do not want a woman—' Will stated, then broke off when he realised what he had just said.

This time he was certain of it. She was laughing at him.

One week before

'Something must be done. I cannot live in this chaos,' the new Marquis of Ravenham said flatly. 'I had no idea my late cousin's collecting had become quite this uncontrolled. This is not normal.'

He gestured around the ballroom of Ravenham Hall where, spread out before him, there were enough examples of statuary to furnish a large park, interspersed with packing cases, some with their lids off, straw spilling out.

'Virtually every space in this house is a lumber room of paintings, boxes and objects. The only way to navigate the library is by way of paths through the stacks of volumes.' It made him feel weary just looking at it. 'Ravenham Hall looks like an Eastern bazaar crossed with a madman's attic, not a nobleman's residence.'

Arnley, his steward, coughed apologetically. 'I fear His late Lordship's enthusiasm did tend to run away with him these past few years, my lord. Mr Townsend, his secretary, found it all too much to cope with and resigned eighteen months ago. Since then, it has become worse. His Lordship appeared to value only the acquiring of objects, then neglected them when they arrived.

'I believe His Lordship did have his own methods of recording his purchases, but what they might be...' His voice trailed away unhappily. 'He was somewhat secretive, of late. No visitors were admitted beyond the drawing room, dining room and his study.'

Which would explain why his heir had no idea of the state of things. Will Lovell was a barrister, a second cousin of the Marquis who had provided a large part of his income. All their interviews had taken place in the study and it had been made clear that he was not expected to stay in the house.

The recently deceased Randolph had used Will's services in the numerous court cases he brought. Whether it was a neighbour encroaching on his land, a tenant defaulting on his lease, a dealer he suspected of not playing fair or a threat of slander, Randolph had pursued the case relentlessly.

As head of the family Will owed him respect. As the man who had paid for his education and legal training, he owed him his loyalty and, as the provider of juicy cases to get his teeth into, he owed him his attention at all times.

There was no denying that Randolph had always been eccentric. His only passions in life had been antiquities and horses and it was the latter that had killed him, along with his heir, when they had collided in the course of a curricle race.

Will had never expected to inherit. Randolph had still been young enough to wed again after a childless first marriage and his heir presumptive had been his first cousin, already married, with two daughters and ample time to produce a son. Will was only a second cousin, sharing a great-grandfather.

'I believe you will require a librarian and someone to advise on antiquities, as well as a secretary, my lord,' Arnley ventured after they had surveyed the scene in depressed silence for another minute 'I will advertise immediately.'

'Do so.'

'Mama!' Katherine Jones erupted in to the drawing room, brandishing a copy of *The Times*. 'He is advertising for a librarian *and* an antiquary.'

Her mother steadied the small velvet bolster to which an exquisite piece of Valenciennes lace was pinned and looked up. 'To whom do you refer?' She added a pin to the piece which she was repairing and set it to one side. Her skills with valuable antique lace were in high demand and a profitable supplement to their income.

'The new Marquis of Ravenham. The swine of a lawyer who ruined Papa. Look, it cannot be anyone else.'

Mrs Jones took the paper and read aloud. '*"A skilled and experienced librarian and an antiquarian scholar with a wide range of knowledge are required to assess, catalogue and advise on the arrangement or disposal of a large collection of volumes and artefacts recently inherited by a Gentleman. Applications with full details and references should be submitted to Lovell and Foskett, Lincoln's Inn."* How do you know this is Lord Ravenham?'

'His name is William Lovell. That must be his legal practice. This is our opportunity to find what his cousin stole and to bring him to account for blackening Papa's name. I intend to apply for both positions.'

Her mother dropped the newspaper. 'But… My dear, he will never employ a female. And he will recognise the name. Besides, how can you provide references?'

'He will accept me when he realises that I am the best qualified applicant—and that he can save money by employing one person instead of two. And Lady Eversholt will give me a reference and so will some of my other clients. Miss Deben, the bluestocking, is delighted with my arrangement of her library, for one. I can choose any name that I wish and ask them to use it.'

Her mother gave a faint moan and closed her eyes. 'You are as impetuous as your father, and as stubborn. It will never succeed, although I would dearly like to see that man brought to face his just deserts.'

'Oh, so would I,' Katherine said grimly.

And I want the Borgia Ruby back, she added silently.

Precious, unique and exceedingly valuable, it had been stolen along with her father's good name and the double loss had sent him to an early grave.

'One applicant remains, my lord.' Giles Wilmott, Will's new secretary, hesitated on the threshold of his study. 'A somewhat…*unusual* candidate, applying for both posts.'

Will glanced at the last file on the desk. 'C. A. Jenson. Excellent references, I must say. Miss Deben sent an example of how her library was organised and Lady Eversholt's reply included a copy of the catalogue of her late husband's collection from his Grand Tour, with valuations and recommendations. Impressive. I have to say, the other applicants have been hopeless.'

There had been one librarian who was so vague that he made the newly retired Mr Townsend appear as sharp as a box of knives; one who wanted to impose his novel, and highly complex, system of cataloguing regardless of what Will needed; an antiquarian who clearly wanted to acquire the spoils for himself and one who was knowledgeable about statuary, but ignorant of just about everything else.

'Show him in.'

Wilmott looked as though he wanted to say something, then bowed and went out. A minute later the door opened to admit the final applicant.

Will got to his feet. 'But you are a woman!'

'Yes, my lord.' The neat figure in front of him dropped the slightest of curtsies. Her face was composed, but he had the strong impression that she was amused.

'I do not want a woman—' he stated, then broke off when he realised what he had just said.

This time he was certain of it. She was laughing at him, although not a muscle in the smooth oval of her face twitched. It was all in those hazel eyes.

'Damn it.' After a moment he got himself under control. 'I beg your pardon. Please sit down, Miss Jenson. There would appear to have been some mistake. I am advertising for a librarian and an antiquarian advisor. Not a housekeeper.'

'That is fortunate, as I have no skills as a housekeeper, my lord. As I am sure you are aware from the examples of my work I see in front of you, my talents lie elsewhere,' she said calmly. 'I have the skills and knowledge you require. It runs in the family. My father taught me. I can produce further references if you so require.'

When he remained silent, she added, 'I have some idea of your problem. The late Marquis had become notorious in the circles in which I move. I presume the place is overrun with his purchases.'

'Yes,' Will said curtly. It was useless to try to hide the facts. 'There is complete disorder.'

Miss Jenson nodded. 'As I expected. By employing me you will save on a salary. I require one hundred pounds a year, a modest suite of rooms and board and lodging for myself, my chaperon and our maid.'

'One hundred pounds? I could employ two butlers for that, Miss Jenson.'

'If you can find two butlers who can do what I am

capable of, my lord, then I recommend that you employ them,' the provoking woman said politely and folded her hands in her lap.

Will had not become a successful barrister by allowing himself to be caught on the back foot for long. He leaned back in his chair and studied her across the width of the desk. Most witnesses would have begun to shift uneasily. She stared back, unabashed.

'This is a bachelor household. Surely you have a concern for your reputation?' She was clearly a lady from her speech and the quiet good taste of her sensible clothes.

'I would have my maid with me, a formidable protection against anything I might encounter, from amorous footmen to large spiders, and my chaperon, a clergyman's widow of the utmost respectability. And I assume you employ a housekeeper and maids?'

'I do. But they are servants. You would be here in a professional capacity, much like my secretary. I would expect them, and my librarian, to dine with me often, for example.'

'My chaperon, Mrs Downe, is my cousin. She perfectly used to dining at a nobleman's table. Or an archbishop's, come to that, although I imagine those are rarely invited.' When he did not reply she added, 'I assume the London town house is also awash with items.'

'If only there *was* space here for things to be awash,

Miss Jenson,' he said grimly. 'However, my late cousin retired here during the last few years and the spoils of his collecting appear to be concentrated in this residence. The London house is relatively...normal. Come, I will show you around and you can see what you are offering to deal with.'

That should daunt her.

The Marquis ushered her out with perfect politeness. He was certain, Katherine could tell, that she would take one look at the task in front of her and flee in horror.

The study had been relatively tidy, with bookshelves on two walls containing volumes that seemed to be frequently used reference books and only a row of Roman busts on the mantel shelf to hint at the late Marquis's obsession. The hallway had statues and paintings, but not much more than the average home that had received the souvenirs of several Grand Tours, and the small reception room where she had waited was also relatively plain.

But once beyond those spaces, as they wove their way around the ground floor rooms, they entered a world of packing cases, of statues jostling for space, of mysterious cabinets with many drawers and paintings stacked against walls.

Somewhere was the ruby, but it did not call to her as she had felt it would. Perhaps she was being foolishly superstitious, thinking that she would sense something that had brought such grief to her family in its wake.

'What is your priority, my lord?'

'The library,' he said without hesitation. 'I want an organised collection where I can find what I want quickly.'

Of course, as a lawyer he was used to laying his hands on stacks of familiar legal tomes and the outcome of a case might depend on finding just the right one, and fast. Information and organisation would be a priority for him.

'And how do you want it ordered?'

'Logically,' he said with a look down his high-bridged nose that said he should not have to state the obvious.

'Your idea of logic may not be mine, my lord.'

'That, I imagine, is very true,' he retorted in a tone clearly intended to put her in her place.

Katherine directed a grimace at the broad shoulders in front of her. Insufferable man. But she knew that already. He was a ruthless bully, ready to crush a man simply because his lord and master directed it.

But he was a handsome bully, she had to concede. Glaring at him was no hardship on the eyes. Tall, dark and, judging by his flat stomach and narrow hips, a man who kept himself in trim and did not spend his time hunched over his law books or devouring vast dinners at the Inns of Court.

The Marquis opened a door, turning as he did so to show her in, and she looked away from the penetrating dark blue eyes. He saw too much and he would recognise dislike when it was staring at him.

'My goodness, what a very fine room.' She needed no excuse to move away from him; the library deserved admiration, or it would have done if it were not in such a state of disorder. She needed to take the upper hand, demonstrate competence now, before he made up his mind to show her the door.

'My plan would be to organise all the volumes into subjects and by author and to catalogue them by both. You can then decide which you wish to keep and which are to be disposed of. I will clean and make basic repairs as I go and make an estimate of value. I will require maids for cleaning, footmen for moving things around, ladders and trestle tables for sorting.'

She had struck a chord with him, Katherine could tell. That was what he had wanted, even if he had not put it into words, and he was a man who, professionally, had been able to turn his tactics on an instant as things changed.

'Yes,' he said. 'Very well. I will take you on a month's trial and meet your conditions.'

'Thank you, my lord. And the London house and any other properties?'

'One thing at a time. I have to be here to manage business.' For a moment she thought he looked weary, then he smiled grimly. 'It is not only the library that needs attention. When can you begin?'

'This afternoon, my lord. Mrs Downe, my maid, Jeannie, and my baggage are in a carriage outside.'

One eyebrow rose with an ease that made her want to kick him and surprise the arrogance off his face. 'You were very confident, Miss Jenson.'

'I would not travel out from London without my chaperon and maid. If you had failed to employ me, then all that would have been lost was the time spent packing my belongings. If your housekeeper can show us to our rooms and provide us with something for luncheon, I will begin work this afternoon.'

Lord Ravenham regarded her for a long moment. 'Are you confident or arrogant? Well, we shall see. Come with me, Miss Jenson.'

Katherine walked behind, not attempting to match his long-legged stride. She hid her smile when he realised he had lost her and came back down the maze of passages, his mouth set in a hard line. It might take His Lordship a while to discover that she would not dance to his piping, but she had better make certain that he found her indispensable before she irritated him too much.

There were two men waiting when they reached the hallway, one of whom she had already met.

'Miss Jenson, Mr Wilmott, my secretary, and Arnley, my steward. Arnley, Miss Jenson, her companion and her maid require accommodation. A suite with two bedchambers, a dressing room with a bed for the maid and an adjoining sitting room should answer, if you can identify such a thing in this place. They will also require luncheon, if you would be so good as to inform Cook and Mrs Goodman. My housekeeper,' he added aside to Katherine.

'Miss Jenson will begin work on the library this afternoon. I am certain she will have no difficulty in informing you both of her requirements.' With that he stalked off towards the study where he had interviewed her.

Katherine returned the secretary's quizzical look with a bland smile. 'Mr Wilmott.'

'Miss Jenson. If you could follow me, I will introduce you to Mrs Goodman.'

'Thank you. Perhaps somebody could fetch my companion and maid and our luggage from the carriage?'

'Of course.' Mr Arnley bowed and hurried off.

Mr Wilmott hesitated, then said, 'You will become used to His Lordship's manner very soon, I am certain. He is used to running a tight ship, as they say in the Navy, and the degree of disorder he has found here does not suit his temper.'

'Please do not concern yourself about me, Mr Wilmott. I am as used to creating order as Lord Ravenham is of managing it.'

And I am just as stubborn as he is, she added under her breath as the secretary showed her the way.

An hour later, a very pleasant luncheon consumed, she stood with her cousin, Elspeth Downe, and her maid, Jeannie, and surveyed the suite they had been allocated.

'I doubt it has been redecorated in ten years,' Elspeth said, eyeing the dull crimson curtains.

'It is clean, though,' Jeannie said, running her finger over the table top in the sitting room. 'And well aired.'

'I should imagine that the housekeeper was glad to find some rooms that she *could* clean,' Elspeth said tartly. 'It must be like living in a very badly organised museum. And surely those were not coffins I saw on the first landing?'

'Sarcophagi,' Katherine said, pushing the curtains aside and opening the widow. 'Ancient Egyptian.'

She would not mention the possibility that they contained mummified remains or Lord Ravenham would find himself on the receiving end of a lecture from the dean's widow on the impropriety of keeping them unburied.

Jeannie went to help the maids who were making up beds and Elspeth settled in one of the armchairs. 'Comfortable enough,' she conceded. 'And are you intent on making Lord Ravenham as *un*comfortable as possible?'

She knew that the Marquis had been responsible in some way for Katherine's father's disgrace and, after a token protest about the virtues of forgiveness, had conceded that he should be made to acknowledge the error of his ways, but Katherine and her mother had never been able to talk about what lay behind the scandal. Sooner or later, she told herself, she would have to tell Elspeth the whole story—and explain why she would be grateful for some very lax chaperonage.

'Certainly not,' Katherine said, watching as a black-clad figure on a grey horse cantered across the park in front of the window. 'I have every intention of being amiable, indispensable and of lulling Ravenham into regarding me as nothing more than an innocuous part of the household.'

Until it suits me to deliver what he is due.

Chapter Two

Katherine stood in the middle of the library and directed the footmen who were erecting three trestle tables in as near a straight line as they could find space for. Another had set the rolling library steps against the first bay of shelving and was passing books down to a man who ferried them across to a desk where Katherine had set out notebooks, small rectangles of paper, pencils, pen and ink, soft brushes and a stack of coloured slips.

A maid came up and bobbed a curtsy.

'I need clean cloths for dusting, if you please,' Katherine said.

'Yes, Miss. I have a message from Mrs Goodman. She says His Lordship has requested that you and Mrs Downe join him for dinner. At eight o'clock, Miss.'

'Of course. Thank Mrs Goodman and tell Mrs Downe—after you have found me the cloths.'

Katherine took her seat at one end of the trestle tables and opened the case of her little travelling clock, setting it to chime the hours. She was perfectly capable of getting so carried away with her work that she would forget the time and she had every intention of sitting down to dinner punctually and looking the perfect—and perfectly innocuous—librarian.

She already had her labels ready—Religion, Philosophy, Natural Philosophy, History and so on—and handed them to one of the men who had finished with the trestles. 'Lay these out along the front edge of the tables in the order they are now, please. Then finish emptying the first bay of shelving so that the maids can clean it.'

She reached for the nearest book, dusted it off and opened the cover. Number one of several thousand. If it were not for the thought of what she was really here to achieve, she would be enjoying herself.

At half past seven Katherine entered the drawing room with Elspeth. She was wearing a gown of dark blue silk ornamented by a frill of lace at the neck and sleeves. Her chestnut-brown hair was up and her only ornaments were cameo earrings, a cameo pendant and a bracelet of twisted gold. But the lace was antique, the cameos Roman and the gown would tell anyone who knew about such things that the simplicity was due to choice, not poverty.

Elspeth wore black with jet and silver jewellery and

a small lace cap on her dark blonde hair. 'It seems we are the first down,' she remarked as they entered.

'Who are you?' A lady rose from a chair with its back to them and regarded them with narrowed eyes.

Katherine heard the sharp hiss of indrawn breath beside her, but continued into the room, revising her first impression.

Perhaps not quite a lady...

'Miss Jenson, Lord Ravenham's librarian, and my companion, Mrs Downe. Who do we have the pleasure of addressing?'

It was quite clear that if any pleasure was involved, it was entirely one-sided. 'I am Mrs de Frayne. A guest here.' She sank down into her chair again in a rustle of expensive fabric.

Katherine looked at Elspeth and raised her eyebrows. Unless she was very much mistaken, they were in the company of His Lordship's mistress. Elspeth pursed her lips, but Katherine sailed into the room and sat down on the sofa at right angles to Mrs de Frayne.

Jet-black hair, fine brown eyes, dark brows and lashes and a figure that could best be described as lavish were set off by deep red satin and diamonds. Rather fine diamonds, if Katherine was any judge. They gleamed in her hair, at her ears, at her throat and on her bosom.

An expensive *mistress,* Katherine amended.

'But you are a woman.'

'Yes, I know. That is the second time today someone has pointed it out to me,' Katherine said.

'You are an employee.'

'We all have to earn our living in one way or another, do we not?'

Two red spots appeared on Mrs de Frayne's cheeks. She moved, a sharp twist of her body that set the folds of her gown rustling angrily and, for a moment, it seemed she would surge to her feet.

Katherine braced herself, then relaxed as the door opened and Lord Ravenham and his secretary entered.

She and Elspeth rose and curtsied. 'Good evening, my lord. Good evening, Mr Wilmott.'

'Good evening.' The Marquis took a chair opposite Mrs de Frayne, Mr Wilmott sat beside Elspeth. 'You have met Mrs de Frayne, I see.'

'Only just,' Katherine said, smiling at him. 'We have hardly begun to become acquainted.'

'I doubt you have much in common,' Lord Ravenham said.

'So do I, but that lends spice to life, do you not think? Encounters with the unfamiliar and exotic?'

The satin rustled angrily again as Mrs de Frayne turned her shoulder to Katherine and said huskily, 'My suite is draughty, my lord.'

'They probably all are, Delphine,' he said. 'There is very little choice, unless you wish to share one with an Egyptian mummy or a stack of packing cases.'

'I shall catch a chill. I should return to London,' she said petulantly. 'But I have nowhere to go. You must find me a house, William, or refurbish my suite here.' She regarded him from beneath lowered lashes. 'Or I could return and find something myself.'

'If you wish,' he said indifferently. 'Giles, make a note to have the estate carpenter see what he can do about the draughts.'

'Yes, sir.'

Well, His Lordship was certainly not besotted, Katherine thought. He has an exceedingly demanding woman on his hands and has the sense not to let her loose in London to spend his money. She must be very wearing, but presumably he found there were compensations.

Elspeth was making conversation with Giles Wilmott; Mrs de Frayne was smouldering at Lord Ravenham and he had the air of a man who very much wished himself in his London club.

'We have made a good start on the library, my lord,' she said, unable to think of a single topic of polite conversation which might engage the other woman, so turning to him instead.

'Call me Lovell,' he said abruptly. 'My family name. This incessant *my lording* makes every exchange twice as long as it need be.'

'But that is very familiar for a servant,' Mrs de Frayne drawled.

'So it would be,' Katherine agreed, 'but I am a professional. Like a doctor. Or a lawyer. Is that not so, my lord? Lovell, I should say.'

He looked at her, clearly trying to decide whether she had intended that as a jibe at his own professional standing before he had inherited. She met his gaze, thinking that the colour of his eyes was a very good match for her gown and trying not to let the frisson of awareness he provoked show on her face.

He was a very handsome man, the possessor of a fit, lithe frame and, most attractive to her, a penetrating intelligence. The fact that she thought him a ruthlessly devoid of conscience did not, for some reason, stop that little internal quiver of recognition that here was a man and that she was a woman.

'Exactly, Miss Jenson,' he said, just as the butler came in.

'Dinner is served, my lord.'

Lord Ravenham offered his arm to Mrs de Frayne and, after a moment's dithering, Giles Wilmott recollected that he should escort the married lady rather than the unmarried one and took Elspeth in. Katherine followed behind, doing her best to appear demure. It was something of a strain.

With two men and three women the table was unbalanced. She suspected that it could be extended to seat at least twenty, but all the extra leaves had been removed and now was small enough to permit conversation. Lord Ravenham sat at the head with Elspeth on his right and Katherine on his left. Mrs de Frayne was at the foot and Mr Wilmott took the seat between her and Elspeth.

Lovell was, very correctly, making conversation with his right-hand partner. Delphine de Frayne clearly did not feel she had any obligation to make conversation with anyone and ignored the secretary. She snapped her fingers at the footman who was approaching with the wine, then sat twisting the stem of her glass between her fingers and taking frequent sips.

I refuse to believe in Delphine de Frayne as a name, Katherine thought.

Was she an actress or a singer? An actress, she suspected, given the lady's flair for the dramatic.

She smiled at Giles Wilmott. 'In the absence of anything in the middle of the table, we can converse across it, I am sure,' she said. 'Were you here with the late Marquis?'

'I was working at the chambers of Lovell and Foskett.' He cast a nervous glance in the direction of Mrs de Frayne, who ignored both him and their breach of etiquette. 'I did not find the law suited me and I had decided to apply for a position as a private secretary when His Lordship inherited.'

'It must be very interesting, helping to set all to rights after a somewhat chaotic period. I suspect the late Marquis was not overly concerned with his estates.'

'It certainly seems it was not an interest of his. Fortunately, he appears to have spent all his time here and the other estates are in the hands of capable stewards, so matters are not quite as bad as they might be.'

That was interesting and useful. It was unlikely that the ruby would be anywhere but in this house or, just possibly, at the London one, if that was the case.

Delphine de Frayne was crumbling a bread roll, ignoring her soup and already on her second glass of wine. Lovell seemed deep in conversation with Elspeth about her late husband's position as a dean at Westchester Cathedral, so Katherine risked probing some more.

'I hope that you are not expected to delve into all those packing cases, Mr Wilmott.'

'Fortunately, no. There is more than enough to be done trying to create order out of the papers. I am sure the late Marquis had a method, if only we could work out what it was,' he said with a rueful laugh. 'At the moment it eludes me.'

Katherine guessed that he was a younger son of a good family, expected to make his own way in the world, unlike the heir to whom everything would be entailed. The law would have been considered very suitable, but a post as secretary to a nobleman was also a sought-after position, perhaps leading to a political career with the influence of his former employer behind him.

They fell silent as the soup plates were removed and the entrée served. Wilmott turned to speak to Elspeth and Katherine to the Marquis.

'Have you made any progress, Miss Jenson?'

'I have made a start, but I would hardly call it progress. Your cousin does not appear to have been a great reader, which means that most of the volumes are in good condition, although very dusty. I am working through by going around the room, but if you would prefer me to identify all the books on one subject and deal with that first, I can do so.'

It was not the most logical way to proceed, but she wanted to please him with her work to the extent that he had no qualms about keeping her on.

'No, continue as you are, Miss Jenson. I want a usable library as soon as possible. In fact—'

'William, what are we doing tomorrow?'

'You may do as you please, Delphine. Wilmott, Miss Jenson and I will all be exceedingly occupied.'

'But I am bored.'

'I did warn you how dull it would be here. You can see for yourself that the house is in not fit state for entertaining. You could ride, or drive yourself. Or one of the grooms could accompany you. Go for a walk or have the coachman take you in to St Albans.' He turned to Elspeth. 'Please feel free to ride, drive or be driven, Mrs Downe. Or walk about the estate as you prefer.'

'Why, thank you, my—'

'St Albans is certain to be insufferably provincial.' Mrs de Frayne pushed her plate away, the food virtually untouched.

'That is the nature of the provinces, Delphine,' Lovell said so drily that Katherine almost choked, trying to stifle a laugh.

'I might drive into St Albans one day, if I may borrow a gig. I believe it to be an interesting city of some antiquity,' Elspeth said. 'I could take you up, Mrs de Frayne, if you would care for the outing.'

'In a *gig*? Like some farmer's wife? Certainly not.'

Katherine hastily asked a question about the neighbouring towns and villages and whether there were any local features of interest.

That occupied the three of them who were conversing until the arrival of the dessert course when it became apparent that, as well as diamonds, the Marquis's mistress greatly enjoyed sugary things. Katherine wondered if the syllabubs and bonbons would improve her temper.

One glance told her that it was unlikely and, when the table had been cleared, she exchanged glances with Elspeth and said, 'If you will excuse us, Lovell, I think we must retire. It has been a long day.'

He and Wilmott rose and bowed slightly as they

left. There was no response from Mrs de Frayne to their, 'Good night.'

'That was a most uncomfortable meal,' Elspeth remarked, low-voiced, as they climbed the stairs. 'What a frightful creature. It must be like keeping a leopard in the house and one with an evil temper, at that.'

'No doubt he finds there are compensations,' Katherine said, earning herself a reproving look. 'Perhaps Lovell enjoys danger. I wonder how long he has had her in keeping?'

'And how much longer it will last,' Elspeth said as she closed the door of their sitting room behind them.

'What do you want her for, that dowdy little sparrow?'

Will closed the door of his bedchamber behind him and sighed. He really did not need this now.

Delphine had provided several months of highly enjoyable diversion, but he had begun to feel that, despite her enthusiastic participation in bed sport, her sulks and tantrums outweighed the pleasure.

As a lawyer he had not gone to the lengths of setting her up as his mistress in her own establishment and had been on the point of bidding farewell with a generous present to sweeten the parting when the news of his cousins' deaths had reached him.

'Miss Jenson is a librarian and antiquarian, Delphine. One glance at the state of this house should tell you what I want her for.' He unpinned the sapphire from his neckcloth and began to unwind the strip of starched muslin.

Delphine was lying across the bottom of his bed, her chin cupped in her hands, her feet, bare of slippers, in the air. 'Why won't you buy me a house in town?' she said, returning to her usual complaint.

'Because I am here and will be for the foreseeable future.'

And because I do not see why I should pay for you to use my money, or my house, to amuse yourself with other lovers.

He had no illusions about Delphine.

He shrugged off his coat and draped it over the back of a chair. His valet knew better than to appear when Mrs de Frayne was upstairs.

She was sulky, provoking—and, despite that, damnably provocative, especially to a man who knew just where her talents lay.

'Surely you are not jealous of a spinster librarian with a clergyman's widow as a companion?' he asked as he emerged from the folds of the shirt he was pulling off over his head.

'She's a little pretty, I suppose,' Delphine said with a pout.

'Pretty? I hardly think so.' Will was tired and harassed, but he knew how to take his mind off that and how to stop Delphine's sulks. 'And we are both wearing far too much clothing, my dear.'

Chapter Three

Breakfast was brought to Katherine and Elspeth in their sitting room by Jeannie who had already, she reported, got her feet comfortably under the table in the servants' hall.

'They're all right,' she said, pouring tea. 'I thought they'd be all stuck up, being a marquis's household, but it seems a pretty ramshackle place, if you ask me. Mr Grigson the butler's a bit strict, but Mrs Goodman's nice enough and Cook's ready for a laugh. The other girls are all friendly and cheerful, and the lads, too.

'I'm glad to have my own bed in the dressing room, though. They say it's like a lumber room up on the top floor and they're jammed in with all kinds of odd stuff.' She straightened the toast rack. 'They're happy to have His new Lordship here, even if it does make more work for them.'

She unloaded her tray and bustled out.

Katherine passed Elspeth the toast. 'Did you sleep well?'

'Remarkably so. Now, tell me, what is your plan?'

'I must make a good start on the library,' Katherine said, buttering her slice. 'That is what Lovell most wants and it will lull him into ignoring me if I do that. Then, after a week, say, I will begin exploring the rest of the house. If I am challenged, then I will say I am looking for stray volumes and assessing the antiquities.' She hesitated. 'Elspeth, it would be helpful if your chaperonage was rather…lax. I want to be as unfettered as possible as I search for the ruby. The fact that you are here at all gives the impression of respectability and I think that is all that is necessary.'

Katherine lifted a silver dome and surveyed the platter while she waited for a response. 'They do not intend us to starve.'

'No, indeed.' Elspeth helped herself to bacon, egg and a sausage. 'I understand what you are saying and it does appear—if one leaves aside the presence of that woman in the house—that it is a safe place for a young lady to be. I believe we will be comfortable here, provided we can avoid that Mrs de Frayne, although what your mama would say if she knew you are in the same house as a woman of that kind, I shudder to think.'

'So do I,' Katherine said. 'But I do wonder just what kind of life she has had to send her down the path of becoming a kept woman. She is appallingly rude, but I shall do my best to ignore her. Annoying her hardly adds to the domestic harmony and it is in my interest to keep Lovell in a good temper.'

'So, if you are happy alone, I shall take up His Lordship's permission to take out a gig and go and explore St Albans, if you will spare Jeannie to me. Is there any shopping I can do for you?'

Katherine found her team of maids and footmen already waiting for her and looking quite happy to be involved, despite their hard work the previous afternoon, although their faces fell when she explained that she did not require the maids until the next bay was emptied and that only one footman was necessary for a while.

She picked out the one who had seemed the most interested the day before and asked his name.

'Peter, Miss.'

'Let me show you how I need to sort the books.' She led him along the trestle tables, pointing to the labels that were already there. 'As I decide which subject to place a book in, I need you it put behind the correct label and, as the sections fill up, they may need moving about to make room, but keeping together. Do you understand?'

'Yes, Miss. You don't want them getting muddled again.'

'Exactly. How accurate do you think you would be putting books into alphabetical order by their author?'

'By their surname, Miss? All the ones beginning with A together and so on? Yes, I can do that.'

He proved as good as his word and they worked steadily through several piles of books, even faster when he offered to dust them before passing them on to Katherine.

When her little clock struck half past ten she sent him off to have a cup of tea, or a glass of ale or whatever refreshment he could extract from Cook. 'And please bring me some coffee when you return,' she called as he went out.

Katherine pushed back her chair and surveyed the room. She had virtually finished the books from the first bay.

If they cleared another one, she could then see if Peter could sort some of the piles of books that sat about the room—on the floor, on the atlas stands, on the chairs—into subjects himself, dusting as he went. Then he could feed them through to her. It might speed things up, or it might cause more chaos, she wasn't sure, but she would see what was on that next set of shelves first.

The tall library steps were on wheels, with a railed platform at the top and a braking device that stopped one of the wheels moving when it was pushed down.

It was stiff and she broke a fingernail freeing it, but the wheels ran easily when it was unlocked and she trod on the brake when she had the steps in position in front of the second bay of shelves.

The top shelf all appeared to be concerned with religion, which was helpful. She lifted down those she could reach and set them on the platform at her feet, then the remaining half-dozen volumes fell sideways and by stretching she could pull them towards her.

Something red fluttered at the end of the shelf and she could see a small box, tied with ribbon, at the far end. Katherine stretched and her fingertip just touched it. She could get down, of course, and move the ladder, but if she just stood on the lower rail enclosing the platform she might manage. A small box hidden—if, by great good chance, it concealed the ruby then the first part of her mission was at an end.

She climbed up, both feet on the rail, the top bar against her thighs. Her fingers closed around the ribbon, she tugged and the whole stepladder shot forward. Katherine jumped down from the rail, her feet stumbling over the heap of theological tomes, then she found herself tumbling backwards, a shower of small, hard objects hitting her as she went.

The alarming thought that the library floor was solid oak planks went through her mind in the second after she fell. Then she hit something rather softer.

It went '*ough*' as it caught her, held her and set her on her feet.

That poor footman, she thought, turning, expecting to see Peter and instead finding herself almost nose to nose with the Marquis.

'Thank you,' Katherine said. She tried to step back and stumbled on fallen books.

He reached out, caught her by her upper arms and pulled her upright again. 'I thought you were a librarian.'

'I am. I fell off the ladder—the brake does not work very well.'

'Surely familiarity with library steps and an ability not to throw volumes all over the floor are basic requirements of your profession?'

'Accidents do happen, Lovell,' Katherine snapped. 'And it is your equipment that is faulty.'

He was still holding her and that was decidedly unsettling. Not that he was gripping hard, or attempting to grope, but it was just…unsettling. And warm. And, frankly, there was nothing wrong with his equipment that she was aware of.

'You may release me now.'

He did so, very readily. Yes, she had no need to fear that her employer would be free with his hands.

'Thank you.' She tried for a more moderate tone, stepped sideways and promptly turned her foot on something small. 'Ouch.'

'What on earth?'

They both looked down at where they stood in a scatter of colourful stones. Blood red, blue, purple, white, green—the ovals gleamed against the old oak.

As one they crouched, banged heads and tumbled into a heap.

'Oh, for goodness sake!' Katherine flailed in an effort to right herself and ended up with her hands around Lovell's neck, at which point, with horrible inevitability, the door opened.

There was a shriek of fury and Katherine threw up her arms to protect her head as something slapped down on it.

'I knew it! You are a *beast*, Ravenham. You are a liar and I am going back to London this moment and you can keep your plain little miss. Librarian? *Pah*.'

Delphine de Frayne swept out, dropping the copy of *La Belle Assemblée* that she had been belabouring them with as she went.

'I am quite all right, but you had better go and explain,' Katherine said, uncurling herself. How it had happened she had no idea, but somehow, she had become thoroughly entangled with Lovell and her skirts were up to her knees.

'I don't think so.' Lovell got to his feet and extended a hand to haul her to hers. He showed not the slightest interest in the expanse of calf and ankle that was exposed.

No doubt, she thought, her very ordinary legs in their cotton stockings bore little resemblance to a courtesan's silk-clad limbs.

When Peter appeared a moment later, a tray with a cup of coffee on it in one hand, Lovell took it from him.

'Tell the stables to have a carriage ready to convey Mrs de Frayne to London, send her woman to her to pack and inform Mr Wilmott that I would be obliged if he would provide the necessary expenses for her journey, to be given to her with my compliments. And the blue Morocco case from the safe.'

'What?' he demanded as the footman hurried out and he turned to put down the tray.

'You are very ruthless in disposing of your—er, I mean I am sure she would understand if it was explained.'

'I do not appreciate being called a liar, I do not tolerate anyone abusing my staff and I did not invite her here in the first place. She *was* my *er*,' he added with a sardonic smile for her evasion. 'She is no longer.'

Unable to find any satisfactory reply to that, other than, *Of course you are a liar. You are a lawyer, I have heard you in court,* Katherine drank her coffee in one quick gulp.

'And what the devil are these?' He crouched down again and began to gather up the confetti of fallen stones. 'Intaglios.'

'Oh, lovely.' Katherine joined him on hands and knees with the box, carefully checking each engraved oval for chips before she put it back. 'They are a mixture, I think. Some are Roman and some later. Renaissance, perhaps. I need to see them with a magnifying glass in good light. I don't think any are damaged.'

'Where were they?' He looked up when she pointed to the shelf. 'Are they of any value?'

'To collectors, yes. The Renaissance ones more so, because they are often very fine work and, of course, they are semi-precious and precious stones. They could be set in jewellery or displayed under glass. Where would you like me to put small valuable items that I come across?'

'Give them to Wilmott.' Lovell stood up. 'He can use the strongroom.' He looked at her, his face expressionless, although Katherine had the strong impression that he was angry. 'I apologise for Mrs de Frayne's personal remarks and for her insinuations about your character.'

'I do not regard it,' Katherine said as she tied the ribbon on the box.

It was disconcerting to find that this man whom she despised recognised that an employee had feelings, let alone that it mattered if they were hurt. Although, of course, she thought as he walked away without another word, he, too, had once been employed.

'Please pick up the fallen books, Peter,' she said

when the footman returned. 'Where is the strong-room?'

'In the basement, Miss, next to the silver safe and the butler's room.' He straightened up with an armful of books. 'I don't think there's any damage to these.'

'Oh, good,' Katherine said absently.

Why hadn't she thought of a strongroom? The late Marquis had fought through the courts to retain his hold on the ruby and it was logical that he would protect it.

She would have to let Mr Wilmott become used to her coming and going until he left her alone in the room and she could search. She could hardly ignore Lovell's direct order to begin on the library in order to pretend to catalogue the small valuables. If he could dismiss his mistress so abruptly, he was not going to forgive a mere employee for disregarding his orders.

Best to become indispensable first, she concluded, whisking a soft brush over a commentary on the early Church Fathers, then she might expect more flexibility from him.

He had certainly been flexible when he had caught her, she mused, her mind wandering. And when they had ended up in that undignified tangle on the floor. Strong and flexible—

Katherine pulled herself together with a muttered curse. The Marquis was an unscrupulous bully and the fact that he was good to look at—*and to feel,* a treacherous little inner voice murmured—did not make him any less the enemy.

He had looked imposing in court, too, his face stern and unyielding under his lawyer's wig, the black gown swirling around him as he paced in front of judge and jury. The occasional flashes of humour were as nothing in mitigation, either.

Elspeth returned from St Albans, full of interesting facts about the abbey—'Sadly tumbledown, I fear'—the quality of the shops—'Very good. Rather too good, in fact. I allowed myself to be tempted into buying some lace, some soap and a pair of gloves'—and the attractiveness of the countryside.

'Not that I expect you will have much time spare to drive about,' she said, clearing some books off a chair and dusting it with her handkerchief before sitting down and surveying the library. '*What* a mess.'

'It is at the *getting worse before it can get any better* stage,' Katherine said.

In fact, she was rather pleased with progress. Peter was proving a helpful assistant and she had hopes of having everything in a preliminary order by the end of the week. Then she could write up the catalogue in the evenings and, hopefully, start searching through the small boxes.

Perhaps she could persuade Lovell that it would be a good idea to locate and deal with anything portable and of value before worrying about statues and sarcophagi.

'But you missed all the excitement,' she reported. 'Mrs de Frayne has taken herself off to London in a huff, with Lovell's parting gift in her baggage.'

'Excellent. The woman created a tension and un-pleasantness wherever she was. What caused the rift, do you know?'

'I did,' Katherine said ruefully, checking that the door was closed and Peter still off searching for more black ink. 'I fell from the ladder, was caught by Lovell, we ended up on the floor somewhat entangled and me with my skirts up to my knees, and in walked Del-phine. She put the worst possible interpretation on the scene, belaboured us with a copy of a fashionable journal—painfully—and stormed off.'

'My goodness.' Elspeth was wide-eyed. 'How em-barrassing for you. The Marquis did not—that is, I hope he…'

'He behaved like a perfect gentleman. I was of about as much interest to him as the sack of potatoes I fear I resembled. Our instincts about there being no need for me to be closely chaperoned were quite correct, it seems.'

The more she thought about it, the more insulting it was. *Of course* she hadn't wanted him to take advan-tage of the situation, that would have been appalling, but she had to admit it would have been gratifying to see a gleam of interest, or to gain the impression that he was tempted by her loveliness and manfully restraining himself.

'Excellent,' Elspeth said briskly. 'I can see I need have no qualms about leaving you.'

'None whatsoever.' The door opened to admit the footman carrying a bottle of ink. 'I must get on. Do you think you can find out whether we are expected to dine with the Marquis tonight, Elspeth?'

'Mrs Goodman and Grigson believe we are expected to dine every evening, unless told otherwise,' Elspeth said several hours later when they were in their sitting room drinking tea. 'Jeannie!'

'Yes, ma'am?' The maid emerged from the dressing room where she was putting away Elspeth's purchases.

'It seems we will be dining formally every evening, Jeannie. Have we enough gowns, do you think?'

'Only two each.' She frowned in thought. 'But we can add and take away lace collars and trims and there is the net over-skirt to Miss Katherine's blue gown. That could go with your amber-coloured one, ma'am. With different shawls we could make it seem more varied.'

'I did see a dressmaker's shop with some elegant but simple gowns on display in the window when I was in St Albans,' Elspeth said. 'I went in and enquired—one never knows when one might need a reliable seamstress—and I have their card. The terms seemed reasonable.'

'I'll order something,' Katherine decided. 'In the meantime your ideas are excellent, thank you, Jeannie.'

When the door closed behind the maid Katherine said, 'I do not know why I am so concerned. It will just be the two gentlemen every evening and I am certain neither of them is fretting over boring us with the same waistcoat night after night. Besides, I doubt whether Lovell would notice if we were in full dress or bathing costumes.'

'I doubt he is quite that unobservant,' Elspeth said and they both gave way to a fit of the giggles.

Chapter Four

The two women were in high spirits Will noticed as he joined them in the drawing room. He could almost believe they were laughing at *him*, but that was probably because his own mood was so foul he was prepared to think he was bring mocked.

The departure of Delphine had been accompanied, so Giles informed him, by a great deal of flouncing and her absence, along with her moods and dramatics, was a relief in many ways.

On the other hand, she had been spectacular in bed and he was going to miss that. In fact, he already was, which did nothing for his temper, already provoked by having to spend all day wrestling with paperwork.

The sight of Miss Jenson, cheeks pink, eyes sparkling with suppressed laughter, brought back the memory of her body hitting his and the feel of warm, yielding femininity under his hands.

She is not a beauty, he told himself now. *Not even pretty. An ordinary oval face, ordinary hazel eyes, ordinary brown hair, not quite chestnut. And she is a respectable young woman which means I should not even be thinking about her in that way.*

Giles, who was talking to Mrs Downe, pushed away from the mantel shelf where he was leaning as Will entered and the ladies made as though to rise, then sank back as he gestured for them to stay sitting.

They were ladies, he thought irritably, even though one was an employee. Ladies had not stood for him when he was plain William Lovell and he saw no reason for them to do so for the Marquis of Ravenham.

'You have no ill effects from your fall, Miss Jenson?' He stood on the other end of the empty hearth from Giles, one foot on the fender. 'The locking mechanism on the library steps has been repaired, I understand.'

'I am quite unharmed, thank you.' The laughter was still in her eyes and he thought he understood why when she added, 'I had quite a soft landing.'

Was she implying that he was flabby? Will pulled in his already perfectly flat stomach and managed not to glower. Confound it, he knew full well he was in good trim. Lawyers risked becoming stooped and weak from hours spent at their desks, but he had always taken care to ride daily, to spar at one of the capital's boxing salons and to keep up his fencing practice. This bright-eyed female was making him self-conscious and that was a novel and unsettling feeling.

He did what he always did when he sensed a threat, he went on the attack. 'It would be as well if you kept off ladders in future, Miss Jenson. That is what footmen are for.'

'Librarians climb ladders of necessity,' she said composedly. 'However, I will check the brake on any others I ascend in future.'

And that was supposed to be an acceptable answer to a direct order?

'Dinner is served, my lord.'

Will bit back the words he had been about to utter. 'Thank you, Grigson. Mrs Downe?' He offered his arm and she rose to take it.

'Thank you, my lord.'

'Lovell,' he reminded her, aware of Miss Jenson's voice behind him, speaking to Giles. Why was it that he sensed hostility under her calm words to himself and yet there was none there when she spoke to his secretary? Imagination, obviously. She had no reason to resent him: he had, after all, agreed to everything she had requested.

Perhaps she found dealing with a marquis intimidating and was unable to truly relax around him. Will smiled wryly to himself, still not quite able to comprehend his sudden rise in status.

He seated Mrs Downe on his right and gestured to Giles to take the foot of the table which had now been reduced to a smaller rectangle. That put Miss

Jenson on his left, to be conversed with during the second remove.

He should have known better than to rely on her to observe the formalities.

'Have you found any papers relating to the collections, Lovell?' she asked as soon as they were seated. 'Some provenance and an indication of the price paid for each item would be very useful.'

'We have discovered little and what there is has been put to one side unexamined,' he said. 'There is too much else to deal with. The estate here has been badly neglected, Mawson at Home Farm tells me he despaired of being given any clear direction, the tenants' cottages are in poor repair—no doubt you can imagine the problems.'

'At least you have the experience in handling large numbers of facts, of sifting through documents and creating order from them,' she said as a footman placed a bowl of soup in front of her.

'Close attention to documents is not a problem. In many ways my career in the law relied upon it, but now I have to learn an entirely new language, that of estate management,' Will admitted.

'If I come across anything relating to the subject I will inform Mr Wilmott. I saw map cabinets behind some of the piles of books. If there are any estate plans in there, shall I have them brought down to you?'

She was thinking like one of his clerks, he realised.

Anticipating his needs, planning to satisfy them. As he thought it, she smiled suddenly at Giles who had passed her the bread rolls and Will caught his breath.

He was, he knew, a man of strong appetites, but he had never failed to keep them under control as a gentleman should. Mistresses had come and gone over the years, usually with far less drama than Delphine had provided. They expected, and received at his hands, respect, maintenance and, at the end of a relationship, a civilised parting gift. He had experienced a number of perfectly satisfactory liaisons in the nine years since he had first been able, at the age of twenty, to afford such a luxury.

Wives and families involved a considerable investment for an ambitious lawyer—a respectable town house, more servants, a carriage, large bills from modistes and milliners.

It would be time to take a wife when he was thirty, Will had decided. He had a year to that deadline and in the meantime had felt no need to flirt with respectable young ladies beyond what was expected in polite society.

It was a shock to discover that the thought of Miss Jenson satisfying his needs, combined with that smile, should be so arousing. Will rearranged the napkin on his lap with some force and told himself that men who lusted after those in their employ were no gentlemen.

Besides, now that Miss Jenson had ceased smiling and was regarding him with the air of someone about to ask a difficult question, the heat of desire ebbed away.

'Yes?'

She blinked a little, deliberately as a reproof for his abruptness, he was certain. 'I expect to have made the library usable, although not completed, by the end of the week,' she said coolly. 'I could then divide my time between completing it in every detail and, for example, directing the clearance of any other room you wish to have in use. Or I could scour the house for small, portable items of value, such as those intaglios, and ensure they are safely locked away.'

'You distrust the staff here?'

'I have no reason to, although I do not think it right to leave temptation in front of them. You have no idea what you have, or where it is. And this is a large, rambling house. Anyone could get in and pillage it to their heart's content, I imagine.'

The fact that she was perfectly correct, and it was not fair on the staff to put them in such a position, did nothing to soften his mood.

'Very well,' Will said shortly. 'From tomorrow spend half the day on the library and the rest searching for anything portable and valuable. Giles, I assume there is space in the strongroom?'

'Sir?' Wilmott had been deep in conversation with Mrs Downe.

Interrupting the lady was bad mannered and he forced himself to apologise. 'I beg your pardon, ma'am.'

She sent him a sunny smile of forgiveness. 'Not at all, Lovell.'

Now he felt a boor as well as a libertine. He must have been mad to employ a female, let alone saddle himself with two respectable ladies living in his house.

Before they had arrived he had merely felt harassed by a deluge of demands that required knowledge and skills he did not yet possess and resentful of his cousins for being such confounded fools and getting themselves killed. No doubt the rest of the world considered the inheritance of a title, lands and wealth as an astonishing windfall, Will could only feel aggrieved.

Common sense told him that eventually he would have all this under control and could begin to enjoy his privileged position, but just now he felt that he was having to work harder than he ever had in his entire life.

With an effort that felt almost physical he enquired, 'And did you have an interesting visit to St Albans, Mrs Downe?'

Although it was very satisfying to observe that the Marquis did not appear to be enjoying his elevation to the peerage and it was tempting to tease him a little more, Katherine decided that an early night might be strategically sensible. She had no wish to irritate him to the extent of sending her packing.

'Lovell is not a happy man,' Elspeth observed as she poured tea in the privacy of their sitting room. 'One would think that the departure of that woman might have improved his temper.'

'Not if he is missing the, er, benefits she provided.' Katherine dropped a slice of lemon into her cup and resisted adding a small lump of sugar.

'True, although she is hardly out of the door— surely he cannot be missing her already.' Elspeth gave a little shake of her head. 'What an improper conversation for an unmarried lady to be having. Stop speculating about his private life, Katherine, and explain more about this ruby you are hunting and why you hate him so much. I know he was perfectly dreadful to your poor father in court, but I never quite understood what it was all about.'

'There is this jewel made in the sixteenth century— a large cabochon ruby in a wonderful gold mount and with three baroque pearls—those twisted freshwater kind—hanging below. There is a portrait of Lucrezia Borgia wearing it, which is why it is known as the Borgia Ruby.'

'She was the natural daughter of one of the popes, wasn't she?'

'Yes, Alexander VI, and she has a reputation as a poisoner, which I'm not sure I believe. I have always suspected it was a question of putting blame on any attractive young woman.

'Anyway, this wonderful thing disappeared for a while, then there were reports of it being in Venice, the possession of a great courtesan and mistress of the Doge in the early seventeen hundreds. It vanished from sight again and then the Venetian Republic was overthrown by Napoleon in 1797.'

Katherine refilled her teacup and drank while she got the rest of the story in order. 'Then Papa heard a rumour that it had been looted by a French army officer, lost in a game of cards and had ended up in the possession of a dealer in Lyon. That was in the April of 1814, just before Napoleon abdicated. The war was over, everyone thought, and it was possible to travel in France, so he went and found the dealer.'

'How on earth could he afford such a valuable item?' Elspeth asked. 'I know your father did some buying and selling, but mainly he was employed for his scholarly knowledge, was he not?'

Katherine nodded. 'He scraped together everything he had and, when he found the man, discovered that he was in fear of his life. He had made many Royalist enemies who were out for his blood now the monarchy was being restored. He agreed to a very reasonable price if Papa could get him safely out of France, which he did.'

'So, your father was back in London with the jewel. How did the late Lord Ravenham become involved?'

'Papa needed to recoup his investment and Ravenham was the collector most likely to buy it. The Marquis was interested, but said he wanted his own jewellers to assess it. Papa was reluctant to leave it with him, so Ravenham paid him two hundred pounds as a surety and Papa signed the receipt.'

'Oh, I can guess what happened then. Ravenham maintained it was an outright sale and kept it.'

'Exactly. It is worth perhaps ten times that, perhaps more, if handled with the right publicity, although Papa had no hope of achieving that figure. He asked for six hundred and when Ravenham refused to either pay the difference or return the ruby, he took him to court.'

Elspeth put down her cup with a rattle. 'Of course he did, it was theft.'

'He might have had a chance,' Katherine said, 'but William Lovell, then Ravenham's lawyer, defended his cousin, made out that Papa had obtained it in France through dubious means and that it was probably not the real Borgia Ruby in any case. Papa was branded a liar and a fraudster and, even worse, someone who traded with a supporter of Napoleon.

'The two hundred was what he had paid the Frenchman, so he did not lose that, only the costs of his travel and getting the man out of France safely, but the money hardly mattered. Nobody would employ him again. There were even rumours, after Lovell's very strong hints in court, that Papa had been a spy during the war and had been in league with the man then. The disgrace killed him.'

'Do you believe that William Lovell knew that his cousin had, in effect, stolen the jewel?'

'I have no idea. But lawyers don't care, do they? It is their job to defend their client regardless, even on a murder charge. It must have been he who discovered that the man from whom Papa bought it was a Bonapartist and that he had smuggled him out of France. I imagine that employment for a marquis must be very well paid,' she said bitterly.

'It is terrible,' Elspeth said hotly. 'No wonder you are so determined to retrieve it. Lovell and his cousin ruined your poor father's name, took his livelihood, sent him to an early grave and now your mother must trade in lace and you seek employment.'

'It is fortunate that both of us enjoy what we do and are able to support ourselves by it. Not that it would make any difference to Lovell if we hated it and were poverty-stricken. But at least the one thing he could not do was ruin us financially.'

'But what can you do about it?' Elspeth said. 'The man's a marquis and possession is nine-tenths of the law, even without a court finding in his favour. You certainly can't steal it back—that would be a hanging offence, taking a gem of that value.'

'I know.' Katherine reached for the teapot again. 'I am attempting to get him used to me as a vaguely irritating, but useful, presence. He already seems able to accept me as more than a servant. Soon, I hope to have the free run of the house and be able to pry into files and documents. Somewhere there might be the original correspondence between the late Marquis and Papa and the genuine receipt. When I have those, I can prove my ownership, bring him to court or use the evidence to make a public scandal of the way Papa was treated.'

'I wonder that you manage to be so pleasant to the man. I am not certain that I will be able to, not now I know the whole story.'

'Please try, Elspeth. As for me, I would smile and be pleasant to the Devil himself, if necessary.'

'You know what they say about taking a long spoon if you wish to sup with *that* gentleman,' Elspeth warned.

'I will take care, but I *will* have Papa's good name restored, I *will* expose Lovell for the lies that he told, I *will* claim the ruby—and William Lovell can go to the Devil himself.'

Chapter Five

There was one problem with Katherine's plan, she acknowledged to herself, and that was the fact that she found the Marquis of Ravenham attractive. Not his personality, of course, that was beyond forgiveness, but his looks.

She was resigned to spinsterhood unless, improbably, she found a reclusive antiquarian to fall in love with. Anyone else would shun an alliance with the daughter of the disgraced Arnold Jones. And she knew who to blame for that.

Although it was possible that she might encounter such a person, it did seem unlikely that he would be her soulmate and would love her in return and she was not given to hopeless daydreams, although it was not always so easy not to yearn, just a little, whatever common sense told her.

But she was twenty-six years old, a healthy female, and whatever her brain was telling her, the rest of her body was informing her that it was in the presence of an attractive specimen of the opposite sex. It asked, quite insistently, what she was going to do about this because, it kept reminding her, it had very much enjoyed landing in his arms and being entangled with him on the library floor. It even made suggestions by means of dreams about how it would like matters to proceed.

The answer, that she would do nothing, was not helping Katherine's sleep and, for the second night in a row, she found herself at three in the morning wondering why Giles Wilmott wasn't filling her dreams instead of his employer. He was a nice man: intelligent, kind and perfectly pleasant to look at, being tall, slim and possessed of a pair of kind brown eyes and a head of thick blond hair, yet he did not arouse the slightest flicker of an improper thought in her mind.

It had never occurred to her that it would be possible to find someone she hated attractive and it was not a pleasant realisation. Clearly, she had very poor taste and it was fortunate that William Lovell appeared quite impervious to whatever charms she possessed.

That was not surprising, Katherine had to admit. Her looks, she considered, were perfectly pleasant. Brown hair tending towards chestnut, an oval face, hazel eyes and nothing objectionable about her nose, chin or figure. There were thousands of women as ordinary as she was and none of them, unless they had a vast dowry or near-royal bloodlines, would be of any interest to a marquis.

At which point she pummelled her pillows, pulled up the covers, reminded herself that the said nobleman was the enemy and attempted to sleep by counting as many authors of commentaries on the Bible as she could recall.

Katherine was in no mood at seven the next morning to exchange bantering conversation with Lovell over the breakfast table, which was fortunate, as he barely acknowledged her presence beyond half rising, before burying himself again in a pile of correspondence.

On the other hand, she needed to be certain he was still in agreement with the programme she had outlined the previous evening.

'I will be working in the library this morning, Lovell,' she said, reaching for the toast.

'Indeed?' He did not look up, allowing her to observe that he had a full head of hair with no sign of thinning on top.

'I will see what estate maps I can find.'

'Good.' He tossed the letter on to a pile on his left hand and reached for another.

'And this afternoon I will begin searching for small valuable items to put into the strongroom, as agreed.'

'Yes.' That letter went to the right and he opened another.

Giles Wilmott came in, greeted her and apologised to Lovell for being late.

'As long as you are in the study at half past, the time you eat your breakfast is of no concern to me, Wilmott.'

Katherine caught the secretary's eye and pulled a wry face. He grinned back. Yes, a very pleasant gentleman and when she looked at him her heart remained as steady as a metronome.

She decided she would take a day or two bringing him items for the strongroom. Then, when that had become routine, she would innocently enquire where the paperwork relating to them might be and offer to search for it herself—in a spirit of pure helpfulness, of course. If the late Marquis had kept records about such *objets de virtu,* then the papers relating to the ruby might be with them.

Lovell looked up, his gaze locking with hers. Katherine controlled the instinct to look away and he broke the contact first, returning to his scrutiny of the correspondence in front of him. If it were possible to shrug with the eyes, she thought, he had just done so.

That indifference was excellent, of course. He clearly regarded her as of much interest as his footman, which meant he detected nothing amiss, no threat to himself.

And of no interest as a woman, a small, resentful voice murmured in her thoughts.

'Is there anyone in charge of the woodlands?' Will asked, looking up from the account books spread on his desk. 'I haven't seen anything relating to timber sales and we are surrounded by beech woods. I can recall suing a Mr Atherton to the east over forestry boundaries several years ago.'

'I have seen nothing in the wages books for a forester or a wood reeve, as I believe they are called in some parts, sir.' Wilmott gestured towards the stack of ledgers on a side table. 'If the late Marquis was concerned enough about his boundaries, you would expect him to take equal care of the actual property.'

Will shook his head. 'It was all about ownership. He had to *have,* but once he possessed something, he lost interest. Ask the outside staff later, will you, Giles? If you are correct and nobody is employed, then we will advertise. Timber is a valuable asset. Have you seen any maps that show the extent of the woods? There must be something somewhere or I'd not have been able to prepare that case.'

'Nothing here, sir. The only estate plans we have found so far are the grounds around the house. Perhaps Miss Jenson has unearthed something in the library—she did say she would look.'

Will pushed back his chair. 'I will go and see and

make sure while I'm there that the confounded woman isn't lying on the floor with a broken neck after clambering up the map stand.'

He ignored the muffled snort of laughter behind him and strode off down the corridor, his progress impeded the further he went by statues and packing cases.

The library, when he reached it, was a scene of well-ordered chaos. The piles of books he recalled were still there, but neatly stacked. Trestle tables held even more volumes, bristling with paper tags, and George, one of the footmen, dodged back and forth between the desk, where Miss Jenson sat, and the trestles.

Two maids were dusting empty shelves and Peter, instead of working with his colleague, was seated and appeared to be sorting more slips of paper.

Will cleared his throat and, like a game of Statues, everyone froze. Except of course, Miss Jenson, who finished the line she was writing, put down her pen with care and then looked up.

'Lord Ravenham.' She rose to her feet. 'Good morning. We have beaten a path to the map cabinets, but I have not investigated their contents yet. Peter, could you remove anything that looks like an estate map to that empty trestle for His Lordship?'

Will approached the desk as the man threaded his way to the back of the room. 'You have acquired yourself a secretary, I see.'

'An assistant, certainly.' Miss Jenson lowered her voice as she sat again. 'He is an intelligent young man and ought to be aspiring to something more. A clerkship in a legal firm, for example.'

'He can rise where he is, if he has the ability.' Was the confounded woman equating his own legal training with what a footman could achieve?

'He is the fourth footman, I believe. This is not the army where one can expect those above you to be killed off on a regular basis. Unless, of course, there are more hazards in this house, like those library steps.'

His retort was cut short by Peter coming back. 'I have laid them out on the table, my lord. Do you wish me to carry out a preliminary sorting?'

What on earth had she been teaching the lad? 'Thank you, no. I will look for myself.' He made himself smile at the footman. It would not do to take out his temper on an innocent party when the cause of his irritation was sitting right next to him.

And the very fact that she was irritating him was an annoyance in itself. He had wanted access to the plans and Miss Jenson had given him that, speedily and efficiently. Will gave her a brisk nod of acknowledgment and went to look at what Peter had laid out.

As he sat down and began to unroll the first, someone put something down on the table. He looked up and saw her, hands full of small bulging objects. She set some more beside him.

'Weights. They will hold down the rolled-up maps without damaging them.'

She turned and went back to her place before he could thank her. Will stared at the innocuous pale brown lumps, each about the size of a child's fist, then picked one up. It was heavy, made of a close-woven cotton, tightly stitched in dark red and with KJ embroidered on the side.

Thoughtfully he unrolled the first map, weighting its corners. Miss Jenson was obliging, efficient, polite and good-humoured. She even engaged in light banter on occasions. So why did he sense something else behind that pleasant smile? Dislike? Or something even darker?

That was ridiculous, unless of course she was of a radical disposition, inclined to hate those possessing power, privilege and wealth on principle. He re-rolled the map which showed the park and reached for another, giving a mental shrug while he was about it. Even if Miss Jenson did hate him, it was of no matter, provided she did her work and did not attempt to poison his tea.

In his career as a lawyer he had often been hated by those he opposed and, on a few occasions when he had failed to achieve what a client wanted, had received blustering threats. He ignored them all—they were part of the cut and thrust of the legal process. If a lawyer allowed himself to be intimidated by them, then he would never last long in the courts.

But Miss Jenson was a puzzle. He had done nothing to thwart her, so either she had a general dislike of aristocrats, she objected to something about his person or, more likely, he was imagining things.

The map in front of him dragged his attention back to where it should be. The whole estate lay before him, the blocks of woodland shown in green. Yes, he definitely did need a wood reeve to manage this significant resource. The estate was going to cost a great deal to set right, but there was every indication that, properly managed, it could pay for itself.

Will rolled the map up, tucked it under his arm and began to walk out.

'One moment if you please, Lovell.'

He stopped by Miss Jenson's desk and raised an eyebrow as she held out a hand for the map.

She took it with a nod of acknowledgement, unrolled it enough to see the title and date in one corner, made a note on a slip and handed it back.

'Am I not allowed to take my own property without permission?' he enquired acidly.

'Of course, my lord. But that has not been catalogued. Now I know what it is and where it has gone.'

She looked back at him with a hint of challenge in her eyes.

Go on, that look seemed to say. *Argue and we'll see who wins.*

'Excellent, Miss Jenson. A most sensible idea,' Will said with a condescending smile calculated to make any right-thinking woman wish to slap him. 'Carry on.'

'Oh, I will, my lord,' she said, perfectly composed.

Now, who won that round, I wonder? he thought as he closed the library door with a gentle *snick* of the catch.

After luncheon with Elspeth, who had spent her morning exploring the overgrown and neglected gardens in front of the house, Katherine left Peter cleaning a pile of books with feathers and squirrel-hair brushes and set out on her own journey of discovery.

First she asked Giles to unlock the strongroom for her and surveyed the shelves with him. Other than a few dead spiders it contained only a pair of rather ugly silver candelabra, which they moved to the butler's silver safe.

'Any ordinary person would store their collections in an orderly manner and would keep small portable items securely in the strongroom, or in locked display cases,' she observed to Giles as she placed the box of intaglios on a shelf.

'Attributing logic to the thought processes of the late Marquis is clearly time wasted,' he replied.

The previous Lord Ravenham was clearly a magpie, she thought, surveying the first cupboard she opened in one of the cluttered and unused reception rooms. It yielded several fossils, some pleasant miniatures, seven books on various subjects which she set aside to take to the library, a pair of old riding boots and a whip.

An acquisitive magpie with, apparently, the attention span of a five-year-old child, she amended.

But if the man had not been logical, then she must be. There was sure to be a plan of the house with the others in the library. She would make a copy and then search room by room in an orderly manner, making sure no possible hiding place was neglected.

Katherine scooped up the armful of books and opened the door. Which way to go? She could retrace her steps back to the hall and from there she knew the way to the library. But was that the quickest route? Another corridor led off to her left and her sense of direction told her it must lead towards the rear left-hand side of the house where the library lay.

She set off, dodging between packing cases and encountering nobody. Clearly, this was not an area that received much attention from the staff, judging by some spectacular cobwebs draping the cornices.

As she thought it, she did encounter someone going about their work. A large tabby cat padded around the corner, tail up. She greeted it, but it gave her the disdainful look that only cats and dowager duchesses can produce and stalked past.

'Go and catch a mouse,' she called after it and received a twitch of the tail in response.

Katherine turned a corner, then another, beginning to lose confidence that she was heading in the right direction. Then she found a staircase leading upwards. It had finely carved balusters and an impressive newel post and was clearly not a service stair, although it hugged the wall and was only wide enough for two people to climb side by side. Perhaps it was a relic from one of the earlier stages of the house.

But what seized Katherine's attention was the group of statues that were crowded into the space beside the first flight and under where the second turned at a half-landing. There seemed to be seven or eight and, although the figures at the front were clearly Roman, there was one at the back that made her catch her breath. Greek, surely? And not a Roman copy.

She put down the books, climbed up a few steps and leant over the handrail to see better. It certainly looked beautiful and behind it was not a stone wall, but a panelled one with doors in it. A cupboard, hidden. Where better to keep something precious? At least, if you were an eccentric who appeared to have forgotten he possessed a strongroom.

The sensible course would be to summon some footmen and have the statues moved out into the corridor. But that would reveal the cupboard and she wanted to look inside it before anyone else did.

Katherine stood in front of the group and decided it would be possible to wriggle her way through to the back, despite them standing in such an untidy muddle, some almost half turned, some facing forward, some back.

Cautiously she began to slide between them, sucking in her breath as she passed a spear point, curving her back to negotiate the bulge of a shield, then sliding past the lifted arm of a nymph ineffectually hiding her modesty with a stole.

Then she was in the small space at the back and could open the cupboard doors. The space inside came only as high as her waist, was perhaps an arm's length deep and its shelf held a mass of heavy, folded fabric. A tapestry, she realised, running her hand over to feel the texture.

'Drat.' Katherine closed the doors, turned to wriggle back to the corridor and found herself trapped like a lobster in a pot.

All the parts of the statues that she had squeezed past were turned towards her: arms, a spear, a trident and a scroll. There was no smooth polished marble surface to slide across, only jabbing projections. She crouched down, thinking to get out on hands and knees, but plinths and sandaled feet, even a leaping dolphin, barred that way.

Could she climb and reached the staircase, haul herself up and over the handrail? Several attempts proved that, no, she could not.

Katherine took a deep breath down to the bottom of her lungs. 'Help!'

Half an hour later, to judge by the distant, faint, chimes of a clock, she had a sore throat and the nasty feeling that she was well and truly stuck. Old tales of young women lost in ancient mansions, trapped in cupboards or chests only to be found as skeletons in fine gowns many years later, came into her mind to haunt her.

'Nonsense,' Katherine said sharply to her own overactive imagination. She would just have to try to push a statue over and she could see just the one, a very inferior Roman figure with the head of a jowly man set on the body of an athletic youth, the kind of thing churned out in their hundreds for men who wanted to show they had a wise old head on a healthy body. If it fell, it was unlikely to hit anything else and should create a space to crawl through.

She didn't like damaging any antiquity, but she was certainly not going to perish for the sake of that one.

Katherine reached through the tangle of limbs, put the one hand that would reach on the torso and pushed.

It did not as much as sway.

Chapter Six

'Help!'

Will stopped in his tracks and listened. Nothing—
clearly his imagination. Then the call came again. But
from where? The ground floor where he was, he decided. It did not sound as though it was echoing down
a stairwell, but there was a maze of corridors at the
rear of the building, inefficiently linking the various
phases of construction, and he had already noticed
how sound was distorted in this house.

'Keep shouting,' he yelled and it came again. A
woman, by the sound of it. A maid fallen down some
back stairs?

'Here!'

It was closer now. He turned a corner and saw in
front of him a huddle of full-sized statues, one of
which appeared to be calling out.

'Where are you?' he shouted.

'Here, behind the statues.'

Not a maid. It was the infuriating Miss Jenson. Not

that he could see more than the top of her head and glimpses of her sensible dark blue morning dress.

'What on earth are you doing?'

'I got in—I can't get out.' At least she did not sound hysterical, although why she thought she was trapped, he was unclear. He was certain he could see a way through.

Will took hold of the nearest statue, a partly draped female nude, and rocked her on her base in an attempt to widen the entrance.

'Careful!' Miss Jenson called. 'That's one of the good ones. If you get some footmen, they can shift them without risk of damage.'

It hardly seemed necessary. She had clearly panicked and, if he was with her to help her out, there would be no problem.

Will took off his coat, breathed in and began to thread his way between the obstacle course of bare buttocks, awkwardly placed elbows, painful spears and jabbing hands.

'No, *no*,' Miss Jenson said. 'Of all the… Oh, why will men *never* listen?'

He had to force his way through the final pair of statues and saw her grab for one as it rocked.

'Do be careful! This is valuable. Genuine Greek.' Miss Jenson looked at him over her shoulder. 'And now we are both stuck,' she announced in a tone of resignation.

'Nonsense. Just follow me out.'

Will turned, not an easy thing in what was now a very small space with an irritated librarian fending him off every time he went too close to her prize statue, like a chaperon with a well-bred virginal debutante to protect.

'All we need to do—' He broke off, faced with a bristling array of limbs and weaponry.

'I told you. We are in a fish trap.'

Will swore under his breath. 'I'll push one over.'

'There is only one that is relatively valueless and that won't take anything with it and I can't even manage to make it rock.' She pointed.

Will stretched out one arm and made contact. 'Why is this one disposable?'

'The bodies—rather unsubtle athletic types—were churned out in their thousands and then portrait heads were put on top. You can see the join.'

'Why? The man is in his sixties, at least.' The head was of a man who was bald and jowly. It looked ludicrous perched on the youthful body.

'"*Mens sana in corpore sano*",' she quoted. 'A healthy mind in a healthy body. Age and wisdom coupled with a fine physique was the ideal for the Romans. Anyway, you have at least three other examples of that about the house.' She patted the shoulder of the youth she was next to. 'While I might consider going hungry for *this* one, I wouldn't miss dinner for *that*.'

'Right.' Will flattened his hand against the statue and pushed. It stayed perfectly still. He shifted position, managed, at the cost of a marble elbow in the stomach, to get his other hand in place and tried again. Nothing.

Well, that was humiliating enough, without a critical female audience.

'Unfortunately, I cannot get close enough to exert sufficient pressure.'

'No,' she said with a sympathy that grated. 'There's never a broom handle when one needs one.'

Will rotated cautiously again. 'What's in that cupboard?'

'Folded tapestries. Useless at the moment, but worth getting out eventually, I suspect. Shall we shout again?'

It was the logical thing to do, but Will disliked the thought of having to be rescued by a party of footmen in his own house. He looked up. 'If I lifted you, could you get to the outside treads of the stairs, do you think?'

'And then walk down to the ground facing inwards and holding on to the handrail?' Miss Jenson tipped back her head and studied the nearest accessible tread, about three feet above the top of Will's head. 'Yes,' she said with a brisk nod.

Will crouched, made a stirrup with his clasped hands and she put one foot in it, holding his shoulders as he rose slowly to his feet. She was a perfectly healthy, well-built young woman and it hurt his fingers. He gritted his teeth.

'I'm the wrong way around,' she said. 'I can't get hold of anything.'

Except my hair and ears, he thought with a wince as she clutched at him for balance.

'I'll put you down.'

That was even harder than lifting her and she slid down his body, landed with a bump and pitched forward on to his chest.

Will, his arms suddenly full of well-nourished young lady, registered warmth, curves and the fleeting pressure of long legs. He took a deep breath. 'I am sorry. Are you hurt, Miss Jenson?'

She laughed, the maddening female, and stepped back. 'Not at all and do call me Katherine, it is ridiculous to be so formal when we are in such a fix. Shall we try it the other way around?'

'If you wish... Katherine.' He bent, she stepped back into his clasped hands and he lifted. This was a little easier because, he guessed, she was steadying herself on the wall. The curve of her hips and bottom passed his face as he resolutely thought of crop yields and cold custard, then he was blinded by the folds of her skirts.

'I can almost reach the step. Can you push me a bit more so I can stand on your shoulders?'

Will set his teeth and pushed and then his face was buried deep in smothering wool, her feet were planted one on each shoulder and the weight on his arms was suddenly relieved. He made a grab for the back of her calves as she swayed, then they were still.

'Oh, for a nice safe library ladder,' the voice over his head said. And then, so quietly he hardly heard it through the muffling cloth, 'And a pair of trousers.'

'What now?' Will asked, turning his head to free his mouth.

'If you can take hold of my ankles and push me up, I can pull until I can swing one foot on to a step.' She sounded breathless.

Ankles? Gentlemen were not even supposed to acknowledge that young ladies had such a thing. On the other hand, this was not the time for such scruples.

Will got a grip on each, trying not to think about the fine bones under the thin knitted cotton. 'Ready?'

'Yes.'

He pushed, shoulders aching, arm muscles protesting, and then she shook her right foot free and the weight miraculously reduced.

'Just keep pushing,' Katherine panted. 'I'm almost…there.' Then, 'Yes! Let go.'

The folds of skirts flapped away and Will looked up, caught a scandalous glimpse of garter, stepped back as far as he could and saw that she had pulled herself up, her body draped over the handrail, her toes on the outside of a step.

'Take care coming down,' he called up. 'Catch your breath first.'

He should have known she would take no notice. Katherine simply rolled over the handrail and landed with a bump on the stairs. 'Ouch.'

After a moment he heard her get up, then she hung over the rail, looking down at him. 'Wait there.' She disappeared and he heard her footsteps vanishing down the corridor.

Wait here? What the devil does she think I'm going to do instead? Levitate?

Will studied the Greek statue Katherine had liked so much in an effort to appear as unruffled as possible before his staff arrived to view him, trapped like a lobster.

Ten, perhaps fifteen minutes had passed. Had she got lost? Then he heard a strange scraping sound that got louder until something began bumping up the stairs.

'Mind your head.' Katherine appeared, pushing a ladder over the handrail.

It was one of the gardeners' fruit-picking ladders, wider at the base than the top, and, when it landed, he saw it was about seven foot tall. Not high enough to reach to the top, but tall enough for him to climb

on to the outside of the steps and roll over the rail as
Katherine had done.

He landed in an undignified sprawl on the uncar-
peted wood, which inflicted several painful bruises,
and she plumped down beside him.

'Phew.' She fanned herself with her hand and grinned.
'I am sorry it wasn't a longer one, but I couldn't manage the biggest I found. I thought you'd prefer it to a
rescue party.'

'How did you manage even that?' He needed to get
some feeling back into his arms before he tried pulling it up.

'Dragged it. They had left it against one of the trees
at the side of the house and I noticed it yesterday.'

Will got up and began to haul the ladder up, an undignified process as he had to lean over the handrail
to reach it. Katherine came to help once he had hoisted
it high enough and they dropped it on the stairs with
a thud and let it slide to the ground.

'Now what shall we do with it?' she asked, walking down and picking up a pile of books.

'I'll carry it around the corner and tell the next
footman I see to return it to the garden,' Will said,
dusting off his hands. 'How it got there will remain
a mystery for ever.'

'Life in an aristocratic household holds excitements
that none of us lesser mortals could dream of,' Kath-

erine remarked as she waited while he propped the ladder up.

Will shot her a look, uncertain whether that was sarcasm or not. That cool, rather judgemental look was back in her eyes, replacing the laughter she had allowed to show as they had sprawled side by side on the stairs.

He gave a mental shrug. It was no concern of his whether an employee liked him or not, provided they did what he paid them for.

'I wonder if it would make life easier if we identified all the large statues that you would like to dispose of,' she remarked as they made their way back to the hallway. 'We could send those off to auction and make some space. I'd suggest we send the poorest specimens to various local auctions where less well-off buyers might take them for their gardens. I cannot imagine Mr Christie's customers would give you much for the one we tried to push over just now. There are auction houses in St Albans and Hertford and Aylesbury, I'm sure.'

'Spread them around a little? Yes, that seems a good idea. When will you do that?'

'We could start this afternoon.'

'We?' They had reached the hall and he stopped. 'Why do you need me?'

Katherine pursed her lips, but not before he caught

a glimpse of a wicked smile. Clearly, she didn't *need* him at all.

'Because it must be your decision on what is sold. It would put me in a very difficult position if I made such decisions without your direct approval.'

When he shrugged and nodded, she asked, 'Do you have any of that pink legal tape?'

'Rolls of the stuff.' Lawyers never travelled without it for tying up documents—the original 'red tape'.

'Then I suggest we walk around and tie some on each of the statues we identify for sale. I was going to see if there is a plan of the house in the library I could copy and use to make certain I checked every room. We can mark that up with the statues for sale as well.'

It appeared that his librarian was going to organise his working day as well as the house and its collections. On the other hand, he was profoundly weary of endless ledgers—his skill was with words, not numbers—and exploring the place was appealing, even if it was in Katherine's rather uncomfortable company.

'Very well. I will collect the tape and meet you in the library.'

'Bring scissors!' she called after him.

Uncomfortable and *managing*.

The library was empty when Katherine returned to it and she sat in her chair and fanned herself with a pamphlet on pig breeding while she recovered from that encounter.

For a moment, as they had collapsed on the stairs, she had almost thought that Lovell had a sense of humour. He certainly was not a man who stood on his dignity, although perhaps he had not had much option under the circumstances.

And, if she was spending a moment being fair to him, he had not attempted to grope her legs. Possibly he recognised that any attempt to do so would have resulted in a sharp kick on the nose, but even so, many men would not have resisted sliding their hands up her calves, or making a veiled but suggestive remark about the view.

But there was no time to sit there marvelling at the fact that the wretched man had one or two redeeming features. Only an inhuman monster or a pantomime villain would have none and she had never thought him that, only ruthless, uncaring and without conscience.

There was a plan of all the floors of the house among the rolls of maps and she spread it out and made a rapid copy of the basic outline of rooms on the ground floor. That would be more than enough to begin with.

Lovell reappeared as she was finishing and she waved the sketch plan. 'Shall we begin in the hall and work around clockwise?'

He shrugged, clearly not caring how they proceeded,

so she led the way to the entrance. 'I think they are all of reasonable quality here. Are there any you don't like?'

'I am supposed to *like* them now?'

'Well, you do have to live with the ones you keep. Surely you wish for your surroundings to be aesthetically pleasing?'

Lovell turned from studying a simpering nymph and shrugged. 'All I require of my surroundings is that they are adequately comfortable, efficient and well organised.'

'No wonder—' She bit off the words *you have no soul*. 'It is no wonder, if you have been working so hard as a lawyer,' she amended. 'Now you can create a pleasing ambiance, somewhere to take pride in, somewhere to relax.'

Lovell snorted, but he turned back to the nymph. 'This can go. I cannot abide smirking females.'

'It is actually quite a good piece, so it can go to Mr Christie.' She dug in the capacious pocket she had sewn in to the seams of all her working dresses and produced a spool of blue tape. 'This is for making book markers. I will use that for the better items. Anything else? No? This room then.'

By six o'clock they had surveyed about half of the statues on the ground floor, identified five to go to the London salerooms and twenty for the provincial ones.

After the first half an hour or so of apparent boredom Lovell had begun to show an interest and to ask questions. Then, by the third room, to express quite decided opinions, often at odds with Katherine.

'That is a much-copied piece, positively clichéd,' she said of a crouching female nude he was studying as the clocks struck six. 'It is well carved, I'll admit.'

'It is charming. Why should I care if there are other versions around? There is only one here. At least, as far as we have found,' he amended, coming close to where she was bending over the figure. 'I like it.'

'In a minute you are going to say, *I don't know anything about art, but I know what I like*,' she said.

'And what is so wrong with that? You are an elitist, Katherine.'

'And you are an aristocrat, Lovell,' she retorted. 'One cannot be any more elitist than that, short of being a member of the royal family.'

'I was not talking about blood lines, but opinions.' He ran one hand over the smooth shoulder of the figure. 'She should have a pool to gaze into, perhaps the one on the South Terrace.'

'It is good marble and would be perfectly safe out there. That is the first time I have heard you express an opinion about how this house should look,' Katherine said.

Lovell straightened up, almost nose to nose with her. 'You really do think me a philistine, don't you?'

'No, I think you are—' she bit off the words just in time '—my employer, who has little time for such considerations.'

They were so close that she had to tip back her head to look into his face.

And I think you are a much better-looking man than I had allowed myself to consider.

Those penetrating blue eyes held intriguing darker flecks, his hair was thick and invited touch and the way he was regarding her held intelligence and humour, both of which were attractive traits in anyone.

This close she was aware of the faint drift of a very discreet cologne, a little peppery; the good smell of freshly ironed linen; the elusive scent of warm, clean male.

Something changed in that deep blue gaze. There was a question there now, one her body had no difficulty interpreting and very much wanted to answer in the affirmative.

Chapter Seven

Katherine ignored the impulse to move closer to Lovell. He was asking her to say *yes* and she had no intention of doing any such thing, much as everything female in her was clamouring to be kissed by that severe mouth with just the hint of a curve in one corner.

William Lovell might be a very attractive man, if one ignored the character of a pit-fighting dog crossed with a snake, but she had no intention of ruining herself and her mission for the sake of a kiss. Or whatever else he had in mind, which, given that his mistress had departed in a temper, doubtless involved his bed.

He had not spoken, so neither did she. Stepping back was all that was required, coupled with a look that even the densest man, which he was most certainly not, could read as a negative.

'I think we have done all we can for today,' Katherine said composedly, ignoring the distracting fluttering sensation in the pit of her stomach. 'As far as I have seen so far there are no large statues upstairs, so a few hours when you can spare the time will deal with the rest. Then the footmen to move and pack them and I will write to the various auction houses and get them on their way. And out from underfoot,' she added as she stubbed her toe on the nymph's base.

'Very well. Tomorrow after luncheon. As you say, let us be done with it.'

Lovell turned on his heel and walked away, leaving her with her hands full of pink and blue tape, a pair of scissors and uncertain just what he meant would be *done with*. A flirtation that had not even begun? At least she need not add a tendency to snatch kisses to his list of sins, which was a relief.

Katherine made her way back to the library to leave the equipment. No forced attentions...yet. It would be as well to be on her guard. This was a virile man who had only recently lost an energetic bed partner and was stuck in the depths of the countryside. A man who was ruthless about getting what he wanted.

But I felt safe with him, that treacherous feminine voice in her head whispered. *I wish he had kissed me. I wish I was a lady...*

What on earth was she doing daydreaming about the man who was the cause of her now being completely ineligible for a respectable marriage?

'Idiot,' Katherine snapped as she opened the library door, making Peter start and drop the book he was dusting.

'Miss Jenson?'

'Not you,' she assured him, picking up one of the books he had been working on. 'You have done a very good job with these, Peter.'

'Thank you, Miss Jenson. I had best go now or Mr Grigson will be chasing me to get ready for dinner service.'

'Yes, of course. Thank you, Peter.'

Katherine sat down and began to tidy her desk without having to think about it. What had she achieved that day? Good progress on the library and the identification of some statues to help reduce the clutter. Both exactly what the Marquis believed he had employed her for.

Two cupboards checked with absolutely no sign of jewellery or related records, let alone the Borgia Ruby itself, and nothing else to take to the strongroom to establish a pattern of using it to lull future suspicions.

And to cap it all she had become far closer, in every sense of the word, to William Lovell, a man she should be keeping at pitchfork-length from her both physically and emotionally.

She had even discovered a few good points to his character and she did not want to do that. She needed a one-dimensional villain, a shadow-play cut-out figure to despise and defeat. Now she had a human being and one she had a suspicion was going to dominate her dreams. And those would not be nightmares.

'Sorry, Papa,' she murmured. 'I will do better from now on.'

* * *

Will took his place at the head of the dining table in no very good mood, not that he allowed it to show. Arnley, his steward, had pointed out to him that it was desirable for the spiritual well-being of his staff if he employed a chaplain.

This, he was told, was especially necessary as one of his ancestors had cleared not only the historic village as part of his landscaping schemes, but had appropriated the parish church as a private chapel, currently unused in the absence of a domestic chaplain. This meant that the staff must walk over a mile to the church in the new village of orderly and picturesque cottages.

When Will had enquired exactly how one went about hiring a chaplain—the local staff registry office, perhaps?—Arnley winced slightly and suggested writing to the bishop.

The steward then enquired whether Miss Jenson would be fulfilling the role of archivist, the previous incumbent having been found cold and still among the dusty boxes and files in the muniments room eighteen months previously.

Will had snapped that he would think about both, then made himself apologise to Arnley for his short temper.

Will supposed that the librarian he would appoint when Katherine Jenson had finished her work and departed could take on the joint role. The library would not need much attention then and the man—it would be a man, *definitely* a man—could concentrate on the archives.

Which led him to think about Katherine—*Miss Jenson*—something he really did not want to do.

She was sitting on his right now, talking across the table to Giles. She was neat as a pin in a simple evening gown and showing not the slightest awareness that a few hours earlier he had been manhandling her over some banisters and trying not to admire her ankles. Or, more recently, that he had very much wanted to kiss her.

And she had known what he had wanted. There had been perfect comprehension in that cool gaze, although he was quite certain she was as respectable and virtuous a young lady as she appeared to be and should have had no idea about such things.

Don't be an idiot and a prig, Will told himself. *Young ladies aren't foolish and unobservant, even if they are brought up to behave as though they haven't a thought in their little feather brains. They know perfectly well why they are told not to be alone with men and if married ladies can feel passion, why can't a single woman, however respectable?*

But it was hard to shake off the accepted belief that ladies felt only pure emotions and accept that Katherine Jenson might desire to kiss him, but at the same time, not like him very much. Or, at all. There were many things to be read in those expressive hazel eyes, but fondness was not one of them when they were looking at him.

It was not until he caught the eye of Mrs Downe and saw her steady, judgemental look that it occurred to him to wonder just why the two women regarded him with such disfavour. A career as a barrister was one that ensured many people disliked him and, in some cases, positively hated him. You could not defeat someone in court in a civil case, or see them found guilty of a crime, and expect them to love you in return.

But these two sparked no recognition at all. Perhaps they simply found something about him not to their liking, which was reasonable enough. He did not set out to be liked and was not at all certain he could charm someone if he tried.

A small devil of mischief prompted him to wonder whether he should attempt just that, make an effort to charm Miss Jenson out of her froideur. He would have to be careful. He did not want to raise expectations in her breast or toy with her affections—that was the work of a rake and a scoundrel. No, just see whether he could coax a smile at best, a reduction in the dislike at worst.

Best to begin with the chaperon. Will smiled at Mrs Downe, enquired whether she was finding her stay at Ravenham Hall comfortable and how she was filling her time.

'Most comfortable, thank you. I find that walking, sketching and reading pass the hours unexceptionally. The countryside is delightful hereabouts and I shall presume on your kindness in letting me drive out in the gig again very soon.'

It was all said pleasantly, with a smile. But barristers have to learn to be actors in order to win over juries and present their cases with confidence, however much they might be out of sympathy with their client or bored with a routine case.

Mrs Downe was acting a part, that of complaisant companion, he was certain of it, but that might simply be because she was here out of duty and would have much preferred to be in London.

As for Katherine, she remained a mystery. She was clearly exactly what she said she was—a perfectly competent librarian. She was hard-working and she had the knack of training at least one of his footmen.

She also appeared to be very knowledgeable about Classical sculpture—she had not been acting there, he was certain. There had been a focus, an intelligence, that was far from the glib utterances of someone playing a part.

And yet, something was awry. A mystery, Miss Jenson. But then, Will enjoyed mysteries.

* * *

Katherine looked up from her timbale of salmon to find that Lovell was smiling. At her, or about her? she wondered. If one did not know that he was a ruthless, manipulative hunter without a conscience or scruples, one would think him a handsome, likeable man. A desirable one, too. Unfortunately, that impression showed no signs of diminishing.

She turned her head and asked Giles a question about the history of the house, hoping to find the reason for the staircase where the statues had been stored. He admitted he did not know any details and the conversation became three-sided, drawing in Elspeth who said she was certain that the central block was Tudor in origin.

'1493,' Lovell said, making them all jump. 'So just into the reign of Henry VII. Extended under Charles I, one wing demolished as a result of a siege during the Civil War, extensively remodelled under Anne and the version you see now dates from the reign of George III.'

'You take an interest in architecture?' Katherine asked, surprised.

'Not at all. I found the only book in my bedchamber was a history of the house written by the late archivist. He probably died of boredom with his own company, if the prose is anything to judge by. I couldn't sleep the other night, so I read that.'

Why couldn't you sleep? Katherine wondered.

If that was habitual, then she must take care if she wanted to do any exploring by night.

The men had excused themselves from the after-dinner tea tray, so Elspeth had it carried up to their sitting room.

'What on earth were you doing all afternoon with statues and the Marquis?' she asked, dropping a slice of lemon into her cup. 'I thought you were devoting the time to searching for the…object.'

'I was. I just became, er, distracted. And getting rid of some of those statues will make it easier to move about the house.'

'But to spend so much time in Lovell's company,' Elspeth persisted. 'Surely that is the last thing you wanted to do?'

'It was. Is. But I am getting to know him better and knowing one's enemy is always a good thing, don't you think? And I am lulling him.'

'That man does not need *lulling*,' Elspeth said grimly. 'He needs shutting in the cellar while we search this place from top to bottom. He is suspicious of something, I'm certain. Why, he even tried charm on me at dinner.'

He tried out-and-out seduction on me, with those blue eyes and that wicked mouth.

She had thought at the time that it was as simple as

a man feeling carnal desire, but now she wondered. Was he suspicious of them? Of her? What lengths might Will Lovell go to if he was distrustful of her?

'I would not like to attempt to subdue him and lock him in the cellar,' Katherine said with an attempt at humour. 'He is hardly the stooped and weedy lawyer one expects. But it will not come to that. I will carry on searching and doing my level best to lull any suspicions he might have.

'But what can he be dubious about? My references were impeccable and genuine, he can see I know what I am about and he has never encountered me before. In court I was always veiled. I do not take after Papa in looks, so, even if he recalls him—which I doubt— I would not stir any memories. I am quite safe.'

My secret might be, my mind might be, but my foolish emotions, they are not at all safe.

The next morning Katherine attacked the library with determination, keeping Peter and another footman and two maids busy cleaning, clearing and dusting.

The collection was beginning to take on form now, with very little religion, but a substantial amount on art and antiquities, languages, the Classical writers, history, travels and memoirs. There was not much law, but then, why would the late Marquis need books on the subject when he had a tame lawyer on call?

The work absorbed her, as it always did, and Peter made her jump when he came and said, 'Luncheon is served, Miss Jenson.'

'Thank you. Can you be spared to carry on with cleaning the books this afternoon?'

'Until four, Miss.'

She thanked him and went in search of Elspeth, whom she found in the small dining room with Giles Wilmott.

'Is Lord Ravenham not joining us?' she asked him when she had helped herself to a slice of cold chicken pie and some salad from the sideboard.

'He has ridden into St Albans,' the secretary said. 'I have no idea how long he might be away. Did you need to speak to him, Miss Jenson?'

'No, just idle curiosity,' she said with a smile.

Inside she was delighted. Lovell's disturbing presence was out of the house which meant she could rummage to her heart's content all afternoon.

With her sketch plan of the ground floor, she began in the room where she had left off, opening every cupboard and drawer, removing a few books and stacking them to be taken to the library and placing anything easily portable of any value on a table.

It was important to be as open as possible, to make a point of displaying everything. She was in a position of trust and had no intention of betraying that, other than with the one exception. And it was all too easy to raise suspicions, handling small valuables when one was all alone.

The haul in that small room was not encouraging. There were no records about purchases or lists of items and the only jewellery was a bracelet made up of Roman cameos, a set of Whitby jet mourning jewellery and a pearl necklace. They looked more like family pieces that had been there for years, rather than recent acquisitions.

Katherine numbered the room on the plan, made a list of what she had found in her notebook and carried the jewellery in search of Mr Arnley, the steward, to have them locked away in the strongroom.

When she went back to collect her notebook she paused just inside the door and studied the panelled walls. Was it possible there might be a concealed cupboard? It was worth checking, although the panelling was fairly plain, with none of the carved ornamentation one read about in Gothic novels, where a careless twist of a boss would send the heroine tumbling into a skeleton-hung passageway or the lair of the arch villain.

She began by walking around, tapping each section of panels from floor level to as high as she could reach. At every point there was the dull sound of solid wall behind the grey-painted wood.

One wall, then the second, passing the fireplace and

on to the third. Her shoulder was getting stiff from constant raising, stretching, then lowering. Katherine sighed and leaned against the next section, flexing her arm.

'What the devil are you doing, Miss Jenson?'

Lovell's voice made her start and she came upright, twisting to see him standing in the doorway.

'Searching for hidden compartments, of course,' she said. There was no other remotely believable explanation she could think of.

'Really?' He raised one dark brow incredulously.

'Yes, really.' She half turned away, tripped over her own foot and hit the wall, putting out one hand to steady herself. It slid down the panelling and something gave way under the pressure.

Katherine jumped back and found Lovell by her side. 'There. You see?'

'I do see.' He smelt of fresh air and leather and, not unpleasantly, of horse, and sounded exceedingly dry. 'And I see that you, Miss Jenson, are the most accident-prone female I have ever encountered. You fall off ladders, you find yourself trapped behind statues and now you throw yourself through walls.'

'I have not thrown myself through,' she pointed out. 'I am this side of the wall, with you.'

'Yes.' He did not sound as though that was necessarily a desirable outcome. 'I suppose we had better see what you have found.'

They reached the black space together, shoulder to shoulder, and bumped heads when they both stooped to look inside.

'My wall, Miss Jenson. My secret cupboard.'

Chapter Eight

Katherine stepped back and did her best to control her impatience. Lovell appeared to be doing something inside the panelling, then an entire section swung inwards, like a door.

'How wonderful, I've always wanted to find a secret passage.'

'It is probably a priest hole,' he said, his shoulders still blocking her view. 'We must be within the original Tudor building.'

'I'll fetch a lantern.'

'Whatever for?' Lovell turned back, dusting his hands together.

'To explore, of course.' Katherine stopped halfway to the door. 'Surely you want to see what's in there, where it goes, what it contains?'

'It is absolutely no place for a lady to be scrambling about in. Ask Wilmott to join me and bring two lanterns.'

'Yes, my lord, whatever you say, my lord,' Katherine muttered to herself as she ran along the corridor towards the study. 'And just you try to keep me out of there.'

Giles looked up when she burst into the study. 'Is something wrong?'

'I have found a secret room and Lord Ravenham wants you to come and explore it with him and bring lanterns,' she panted.

'A secret room?' Giles suddenly looked about fourteen. 'There are lanterns in the hall,' he added, jumping to his feet and striding off, Katherine on his heels. He snatched up two and lit them both from the fire that was kept burning all day long in the draughty entrance. 'Where?'

'The little room at the end of that passageway.' Katherine pointed, waited until he was out of sight, then lit another lantern and followed. When she reached the doorway, she stopped outside and listened.

'I should go first, my lord.'

'Very noble, Wilmott, but I doubt there is anything more perilous down there than some spiders and a rat or two.'

Their voices faded and Katherine looked in to see the light of their lanterns dwindling away. This was certainly more than a simple chamber if there was a passage. She tiptoed across the room and stepped in through the panelling, telling herself that spiders and rats were more scared of her than she was of them and that there were two large men between her and the skeletons or whatever else this secret way held.

The walls were brick and narrow, twisting sharply in a series of dogleg turns, making it difficult to keep a sense of direction. The top was low, brushing her hair unless she ducked her head—the men must be bent over uncomfortably.

Then the voices in front of her were suddenly closer and she could see the light from their lanterns clearly. They must have stopped, so she did, too.

'Very well,' she heard Giles say and before she realised it, he was around the corner and right in front of her.

'Shh,' she whispered.

He grinned. 'We've found a door,' he murmured back. 'I'm going to locate it outside.'

It was a wriggle to pass each other but, being the gentleman that he was, Giles turned to face the wall, and so did she and they squeezed past without too much embarrassment, at least on Katherine's part.

She could lurk where she was or she could go and look at this door. Katherine decided that she might as well risk Lovell's wrath and brazen it out. Lantern high, she went around the corner.

'That was fast, Wilmott.' Then Lovell turned and saw her. 'What do you think you are doing, Miss Jenson?' Obviously tired of stooping, he had crouched down on his heels and was leaning back against the wall. He made no effort to rise.

Your valet is going to have something to say about the state of your coat, she thought, deciding she would not mention the large cobweb draped across one shoulder.

'I found this, so I think it only fair that I explore it, too.' Katherine held up her light and saw the passage ended in a door, so dark that she could not make out what it was made of until she reached out and tapped it. Solid oak, by the feel of it.

'Is it locked?'

The lamplight shining from beneath made Lovell's face look devilish, a mask of dark shadows and flickering flame. If she had seen it without knowing he was there, she would have screamed the place down, Katherine admitted to herself.

'Yes, Miss Jenson. That is why I am sitting here in such comfort.'

She took a deep breath and ignored the sarcasm. 'This cannot be a priest hole.'

Lovell looked around, then up to the brickwork curving over their heads. 'I agree. It was built as part of the house, not carved out afterwards, and that means it is too early for there to be any need to be hiding priests of any denomination, Protestant or Catholic.'

'Mr Wilmott is taking a long time.'

'Have you seen the state of the garden on this side of the house? He will probably need the gardeners armed with billhooks and saws to get through the tangle.'

'At least he knows roughly where it is,' Katherine pointed out. 'He needs to locate the window of the room, then go around the corner. The walls must be very thick.'

'When this was built it was in the early years of the first Tudor king. The Battle of Bosworth was still fresh in the memory, I imagine. This would have been a defensive manor house—it certainly had a moat once, long since filled in—and I think this must have been a sally port, an escape route for the defenders to get out at the back if they were attacked.'

'The late Marquis would have found this fascinating.'

Lovell grunted. 'I doubt it, at least in his last years. He coveted objects, not history.'

She had been wondering how to lead round to discussing his cousin, now he had handed her the opportunity.

'Was he always so...obsessive? I had assumed he was a connoisseur, that his collections would be beautifully curated and well displayed.'

Silence. Clearly, she had presumed too far. Then Lovell sighed. 'He was, when I first knew him. There are three other houses—the town house, a hunting lodge in the Shires and a very pleasant estate near

Bath. They are all well furnished and appropriately decorated.

'But he began to change about eight years ago. He stopped visiting the other houses, he started buying wildly—horses and objects—and he retreated here. I hadn't realised quite how bad it had become, because I never got beyond the most public rooms and the study.'

It seemed the near darkness had made him feel able to confide, so Katherine ventured, 'He had many horses?'

'Almost forty. I have sent all but a few to Tattersall's for sale. Not that he rode or drove all those, of course—he collected fine bloodstock to gloat over, it seems. That is what killed him. His heir, the only first cousin he had, apparently twitted him about a pair of match bays he had bought at great expense.

'Randolph flew into a passion and challenged James to a race. He hadn't driven for months, perhaps years. The bays were so fresh the grooms tried to stop him, but he flew into a rage with them, laying about them with a whip, they told me. He lost control, careered into James's rig and they were both killed.'

'Forgive me, but was he, perhaps, no longer in his right mind?'

'A polite way of putting it, yes. He had become like an old dragon, hoarding objects and animals like fabled gold, creating a great pile of it that he guarded jealously.'

'He was not always like that?'

'No, not when I first knew him. Randolph had been indulged since birth, the longed-for son after his parents' years of childless marriage. He was self-centred to the extreme and with no consideration for others, but he was rational.

'He believed I had the mindset for the law and decided I was likely to be of use to him if I had the proper training. He paid for my education, made certain I had the right contacts at the Inns of Court, saw me trained to be a lawyer.'

'You didn't resent it?'

'I am the elder son of a younger son of a younger son. My destiny was to manage a small estate, hardly more than a farm. Randolph gave me an education, access to the wider world, a career that interested me, enough money to ensure my younger brother has all he needs to make our family estate prosper. I could put up with his demands, his…eccentricities—I owed him my loyalty.'

Katherine waited, but that seemed to be all he was prepared to say. It was more than she had hoped for and enough to reassure her that the Borgia Ruby must be in the house somewhere. And it gave her an insight into why Lovell had fought so fiercely for his cousin and employer, even though he clearly hadn't felt any affection for the man. It still didn't excuse—

Thud.

She jumped as Lovell rose to his feet in one smooth movement and pounded on the door with his clenched fist.

'No way of unlocking it from this side.' Giles's voice penetrated faintly. 'I'll come back.'

Lovell stooped to pick up his lantern. 'After you, Miss Jenson. I suppose it is too much to hope that you will not now go and fight your way through the undergrowth to view the door from the other side?'

Katherine stepped out into the room, blew out the candle in her lamp and shook out her skirts. 'My lord, it is your house. If you tell me that you do not wish me to satisfy my antiquarian curiosity then, of course, I will obey you.'

'You amaze me.' Lovell emerged, too, rolling his shoulders as he straightened up. 'I would have thought that nothing would stand in the way of your curiosity, Miss Jenson. Of course you may go and look, but do not expect to bring suit against me if you sprain an ankle or fall into some unfilled section of moat. And what, might I ask, is amusing you now?'

'You have cobwebs in your hair.'

With a muttered curse he went to look in the over-mantel mirror.

'I do have a comb.' Katherine dug in her pocket and came up with the small one that she always carried to repair the effects of dusty shelves on her appearance.

'No, let me,' she added as he reached for it. 'They are all over, especially at the back.'

To his own surprise Will stood still and let the managing female comb his hair. It was that, he reasoned, or risk going out with cobwebs on the back of his head.

It had nothing to do with the fact that she put one hand on his shoulder to steady herself as she reached up, her breath tickling over the nape of his neck. And, ridiculously, it amused him to be ordered about by the woman, a novelty, given that he was used to barking orders and having them obeyed.

Or perhaps he was just lacking in female company and ought to give more thought to wooing a wife. There was the succession to think about now, the title, the entails.

'I'm sorry. Was that a knot?'

'What?' He stared at Miss Jenson as she stood, comb in hand.

'You frowned so fiercely that I thought I must have pulled a tangle.'

'No. I was considering something that fills me with a singular lack of enthusiasm. Come then, if you really want to plough though bogs and brambles.'

'I will just go and change my shoes. I can make my own way.'

She vanished through the door in a flurry of skirts

before he could call after her that she, too, had her back hair covered in cobwebs.

She found him and Giles and two gardeners standing in front of the tangle of briars that had once been a rose garden. Miss Jenson was dressed in a drab coat and a pair of half-boots that could only be described as *stout*. She had more concern for practicality than appearances, he noted, then saw with a smile that she had combed her hair and all her cobwebs had vanished.

'That was a singularly foolish place to choose for a rose garden,' she observed, pulling her left foot out of the mud with a squelch.

'That it be, Miss,' Tompkins, the head gardener, said, nodding sagely. 'The old moat be under there and it's fed by springs. You can drain it all you like, fill it in like they did, but you can't make it dry. They don't mind a heavy soil, they favour a clay, do roses, but waterlogged is another matter. In fact...'

He rambled on as Will tried to remember how many gardeners he had. Just the two, he rather feared, because he had to get this house looking respectable if he was going to bring a bride to it. A garden, not a wilderness, was essential, any lady would expect it.

'Miss Jenson!'

'Yes?' She was already well into the narrow pathway Wilmott and the two men had managed to cut through to the wall.

'What do you think you are doing?'

'Looking at the door, of course.' She didn't add, *You idiot*, but he could almost hear the words hanging in mid-air.

Will refrained from rolling his eyes: one did not criticise one member of staff in front of others. 'Come along, Wilmott. You wait here, Tompkins and—'

'Smith, my lord.'

He fought his way along the narrow path, cursing the mud sucking at his boots, until he was at the door where Miss Jenson was bending down to peer at the lock.

'We need a key,' she announced. 'Or can you pick locks, my lord?'

'Why should we want to open it? This is more secure left as it is.'

'I suppose so.' She sounded disappointed as she looked around. 'It is very well disguised, isn't it? Set back in the angle of that buttress. I think it would be quite hard to see when the moat was full.'

'If they kept a small boat in the tunnel, then anyone wanting to escape the house could open the door, launch the boat and row across,' Wilmott said, arriving behind Will.

'All very interesting,' Will lied. 'I'll have this undergrowth cleared and drains dug,' he added, looking at his secretary's feet which appeared to be sinking into the mire. 'It must increase the damp in the—'

With a strange sucking rumble the ground opened up around Wilmott and he vanished into the hole with a shout of alarm.

Will grabbed for him, was too late and found himself tipping forward, only to be hauled back by a pair of determined hands on his coat tails.

'Wilmott!'

'Here, sir.' He sounded unhurt, at least, although he was not in sight. 'The springs that fed the moat must have been working away and undermined the fill. There's quite a cavern down here.'

'Stay still. Don't risk moving about. We'll get ropes and a ladder down to you.'

'Right you are, sir. Very interesting, this. I can see the stone walls of the foundations.'

'Never mind the damn architecture! Tompkins, Smith—ladders, planks ropes, more men, on the double.'

He looked across the hole. A good eight feet, too far to jump with no run-up. They were stuck on this side, although at least they had firm stonework to stand on. 'You still all right, Wilmott?'

'Yes, sir.' His secretary sounded less confident now. 'I think this could have gone at any time, all the way along. Bits keep dropping off, I can hear them hitting the water.'

Will listened to faint splashes. Worrying. If more fell, Giles could be buried. Or if water gushed through, he might be swept away. He made his voice as indifferent as possible. 'Well, stand under the opening, then.'

There was a faint laugh from below and he settled his shoulders back against the door. Miss Jenson sat on the step at his feet.

'What was I saying about you being accident-prone?' he asked.

'I am not down that hole and I wasn't anywhere near him when he fell,' she protested.

'You create an aura of chaos.'

'I do not! I create order out of chaos, or haven't you seen your library recently?'

'True.' It was he who seemed to be plunged into chaos by her, in ways he couldn't quite pin down. 'What is your given name?'

'Katherine. I did tell you, I am certain.'

'Probably.' And probably he had been too busy grappling with the fact that he'd been demented enough to employ a female librarian and antiquarian to recall it.

'Well, Katherine, what do you make of this situation?'

'That if we had a key, we could get off this ledge.'

A snort of laughter escaped hm. 'Do you always say what you mean?'

'No, very frequently I have to bite my tongue,' the infuriating female said from the level of his knees.

There was another loud splash from the hole.

'Mr Wilmott? Giles, are you still safe?'

She sounded very concerned about him, Will thought, then mentally kicked himself. Of course she was concerned, anyone would be. He wasn't becoming jealous of his own secretary, was he?

'Sinking a bit,' the voice from the hole confessed, sounding rather more anxious.

'Hold on, we'll soon have you out. I had best lie flat and reach down to him,' he added to Katherine and began to shrug out of his coat.

Katherine stood up. 'Then I will hold on to your ankles and then Giles can catch hold of your hands. It had better be you, your arms are longer,' she pointed out, unanswerably. 'But hurry up.'

And, curse her, she was right. Not about who would have to do the lying down—there was no way he would allow a woman to do that—but that something must be done now.

Goodness knew where the gardeners had got to. Will crouched down, testing the ground in front of the step, then spread out his coat and stretched himself full-length on top. As he began to work closer to the hole, hands caught hold of his ankles. He levered himself over the edge and let his arms hang down at full stretch.

'Thank you,' Wilmott said fervently from below and he felt hands fasten around his wrists. 'I'm up to mid-calf, but I think I've stopped sinking now you are taking my weight.'

'Excellent,' Will said, wondering just how heavy the man was. His secretary was not fat, but he was tall and it all seemed to be bone made of lead. 'I was just thinking how difficult this was going to be to explain to the coroner. Accidental drowning in a non-existent moat, perhaps.'

That made Giles laugh, which was not helpful. Will felt himself move a little and dug his toes in. The grip on his ankles tightened.

'I can't get a good hold through the leather,' Katherine complained. 'And you are sliding.'

'I had noticed that.'

'Dig your toes in some more while I try something else.'

The hands on his ankles vanished and the next thing he knew a weight descended on his backside.

'There. I'm sitting on you now. That should do it.'

Will realised suddenly that he was grateful for the burning ache in his shoulders, a powerful distraction from the fact that Katherine Jenson's admirably neat posterior was pressed to his rump.

Chapter Nine

'Did you say something? Are you all right, Lovell?'

'Umph.'

Fair enough, she thought. She was sitting very firmly on his backside. *His very admirable backside...*

A lump of earth fell off the edge of the hole and Giles gave a startled yelp.

Where were those gardeners?

They appeared even as she thought it, accompanied by two grooms, carrying three ladders and two planks between them. They laid the ladders across the hole on either side of Lovell, then laid planks on top of the rungs, before the smallest groom edged out with the third ladder.

There was a splash and a squelch as it was dropped into the hole and then Giles's head appeared.

The groom seized him by the collar and helped him out to sprawl on the far side. 'Best crawl away, sir,' the man advised and the secretary, black with mud, found the energy to drag himself clear.

He rolled over and sat up. 'Go and help His Lordship!'

'Gerroff me.'

It was a growl and Katherine shifted back to Lovell's thighs, then his knees and finally to the doorstep, grabbing his ankles again as he scrabbled backwards, sending clods of earth into the hole.

'Stay there.' He gestured at the two men who were beginning to edge out across the planks. 'Move the ladders together.'

The skinny groom wriggled across and pulled up the ladder in the hole and was dragged back by his feet, then the others shifted the makeshift bridge until the ladders touched.

Lovell stood up, his face and body thick with mud. 'Well, Katherine? We can wait for a locksmith or brave the gaping cavern.'

It was beginning to look exceedingly cavernous now and the way across seemed rickety, to put it mildly, but she was not going to sit shivering on the doorstep for however long it took to find a locksmith and get that door to yield.

'The cavern, of course.' She took a step forward towards the plank and was swept off her feet, up into his arms, and Lovell was running, striding across the gap, planks clattering, and on to firm ground.

He skidded to a halt, chest heaving.

Around them the men were talking excitedly, there

was the sound of the ladders and planks being hauled back. Katherine was aware of it vaguely, a background buzz to the sound of Lovell's breathing, the sensation of being held, the strangely not unpleasant smell of hot man and mud.

'You can put me down now,' she said.

He did not reply, simply walked off, around the side of the house, up the steps to the main door which, as it was ajar, he opened by the simple expedient of kicking it and into the hall.

This time she could hear the babble of voices clearly and one cutting right through them.

'My lord, is Miss Jenson injured?'

Katherine lifted her head from where it was resting very comfortably against Lovell's sodden shirt front. 'I am perfectly all right, thank you, Elspeth.' She tried wriggling. 'You can *put me down* now, my lord.'

'What, and make this floor even muddier? Grigson, a great deal of hot water is going to be required for Miss Jenson, myself and Mr Wilmott, who will be along shortly.'

And then the wretched man marched past the gaping servants and carried her up the stairs, into her bedchamber, through into the dressing room and deposited her, in a state somewhere between hysteria, fury and excitement, in the empty bath.

He stepped back and assessed the object she was sitting in. 'Am I mistaken, or is this a sarcophagus?'

'Yes. Roman,' Katherine said faintly. 'It isn't very practical because the marble doesn't hold the heat.' She rallied slightly, but found standing up was beyond her. 'What do you think you were doing, carrying me?'

'I thought that bridge wouldn't stand up to two of us going across, so speed and one pair of feet seemed sensible.' He stretched and began to roll his shoulders.

'I can understand that, but then to carry me inside— you must have strained your arms holding Giles for so long like that.'

He shrugged. Or perhaps it was simply another exercise. She averted her gaze from the disconcerting sight of muscles moving under the wet fabric.

'I am hardly a featherweight.'

'I had already discovered that, remember? You stood on me to get away from those statues and then you so obligingly anchored me down.'

You are supposed to disagree with me!

'In fact, I am clearly feeding my staff too well. Wilmott is deceptively hefty.'

Katherine took a grip on her temper and ignored the other sensations that were disturbing her internally. 'He is a very well-built gentleman. Well, thank you very much. I can manage now.'

Lovell looked down with what she had become to think of as his lawyer look: unreadable but penetrating.

Katherine thought he was about to speak, then Jeannie came in, Elspeth on her heels.

'Miss Katherine!'

'Lord Ravenham, you are in a *lady's dressing room*.'

He turned to Elspeth with a smile. 'So I am. Fortunately the lady is fully clothed. I will see you at dinner, Mrs Downe, Miss Jenson.'

'What on *earth* is going on?' Elspeth demanded as the outer door closed behind him.

'We have a moat again,' Katherine said, beginning to struggle with the water-swollen fastenings of her gown. Not that it was fit to be called a gown any longer. 'Jeannie, you might as well cut this off me. I think it is beyond saving.'

She began trying to explain everything to Elspeth. 'I found a secret passageway and we explored it and it came to a door. So we all went around to locate it from the outside. Giles Wilmott fell in to the remains of the old moat and Lord Ravenham and I were trapped against the house wall. He had to hold on to Giles's hands to stop him sinking any deeper in the mud and I had to hold on to him to stop him falling in after Giles.'

'A moat?' Elspeth ran to the window and looked out. 'I don't see it.'

'It was filled in ages ago, apparently. Springs have been scouring it out over the years, I assume. I do hope

Lovell thinks to check the plans to find out the extent of it before half the house falls down.'

It was incredible. She sounded quite calm and rational and inside she was in chaos.

'There's hot water coming,' Jeannie said. 'Lots of it. Thank goodness we can drain this thing, because we are going to need to fill it at least twice.'

Whoever had conceived the idea of making a marble sarcophagus into a bath had at least considered the practicalities. It was raised on blocks and there was a drain hole in the bottom with a pipe that vanished into the wall.

Katherine stood passively while they stripped off her clothes and, with the plug out, poured water over her until the worst of the mud had gone. Then she replaced the plug, sat down and wallowed in clean hot water while Jeannie took away her clothes, holding them at arm's length.

'I shall go and have a look at this moat for myself,' Elspeth declared. 'At a safe distance.'

Alone at last, Katherine tried to get her emotions in some kind of order. The day so far had revealed Lord Ravenham to be arrogant, authoritarian and quite without consideration. No new insights there.

But he had rescued Giles without hesitation and had kept his temper, despite having his arms half pulled from their sockets, finding himself face down in mud, being sat on by his librarian—female—and ruining a very good pair of boots. That all had to go on the plus side of his account, however reluctant she was to see it growing.

Where to put the fact that she had found herself alarmingly aroused by him, she had no idea. All that male physicality, the way he had lifted her, the sensation of being in his arms... None of that should go to his account in either column—positive or negative. It was all down to her inexplicable reaction to the man.

The next morning Will spread out the three house plans that he had found in the library, holding the corners down with the little weights Katherine had shown him.

Infuriating woman, but efficient, even if that efficiency involved sitting on his rump to stop him falling into the moat that he hadn't known he owned. Add immodest to infuriating and quick-thinking to efficient.

He growled under his breath as stretching to unroll the paper made his abused arm and shoulder muscles complain. A hot bath and a night's sleep had helped, but even so, they ached.

His stomach growled in company and he would go and have his breakfast soon, but he had wanted to look at these plans before the library was full of maids, footmen and a certain librarian. If nothing else, he needed to be certain the house wasn't going to collapse into the other three arms of the hidden moat.

'Oh, good, you have found plans that show the moat,' a voice said behind him, making him let go of one corner.

'I will call you Kat,' Will said, reaching out to flatten the roll again without looking around. 'You creep around like one.'

'Ladies walk quietly and with decorum,' she said piously, ignoring his shortening of her name. 'What date are they?'

'These are dated seventeen-five and show the house before and after the major works at that time. Here is the moat.' He pointed to the plan on the next table. 'That is the present house, drawn up in eighteen hundred.'

Kat moved to stand beside him, bringing a faint, distracting, hint of jasmine scent with her, and studied the oldest plan. 'The moat enclosed a large area and the new house was built well within it.'

Will pointed to the top of the left-hand arm. 'The springs feeding it come in there and were managed by a sluice gate here. 'He indicated markings at the bottom of that arm. 'The other three sections were filled by that one source. The water overflowed into a stream that led down to the lake.'

He moved to the plan showing the Queen Anne house. 'As far as I can make out, they channelled the spring water through some kind of pipes down to the sluice and out. I think these symbols show that they blocked up each arm of the moat and then filled the whole thing in, assuming that the water would be safely channelled away through the new drains.'

Kat moved to stand between the two tables, looking from one to the other. 'The present house is definitely safely inside the hidden moat, except perhaps the orangery over here.' She tapped the small extension on the far side from the door to the secret passage.

'I agree. It does not appear that we are about to plunge into the abyss,' Will agreed. 'The pipes they used to contain the spring water must have burst or rotted and the fill has been gradually washed away into the lake which is probably silted up with it, if we could only hack our way through to inspect it.

'The mass of tangled roots must have been all that was holding up the earth. No wonder Wilmott went through it. I'll have to get new pipes laid.'

'Why not have the moat excavated on that side, repair the sluice, make certain the blocking to the other arms of the moat is sound and then have a water feature? It wouldn't make much more work than digging down and laying pipes,' Kat pointed out. 'You could build a little jetty where the sally port is and the ladies of the house would be able to drift about in boats on hot summer days. Charming.'

'Which ladies?' he enquired, lifting the weights and letting the plans roll up with a snap, resisting the urge to say that he had employed her to organise his library, not landscape his grounds and certainly not drift about in boats.

'You will be marrying soon, I imagine,' Kat said, collecting the maps up and tying the tape around each. 'Title, entails, heirs.'

He had been mentally filing that thought under 'To Be Attended To Later' in his list of things to be done and had no intention of contemplating it now.

'Improving the grounds to appeal to a wife will have to take second place to clearing the inside of this house. No lady is going to want to be faced with this as her country seat.'

'There are always the town house and the others you mentioned.' Kat bent to slide the plans back on their shelf. 'But I suppose, if one marries a marquis, one wants the principal seat to be in order for entertaining and flaunting and so forth.'

'Flaunting?' Will raised one eyebrow in the manner which always used to reduce an unsatisfactory witness to stammering incoherence.

'If one has become a marchioness then I imagine one would want to flaunt the fact. Discreetly and in the best possible taste, of course,' she added in a tone that hinted at suppressed amusement.

Will considered the suggestion that someone would consider marrying him a matter to be flaunted, then reminded himself that he was no longer simply a lawyer. The cachet of being a marquis would trump every fault from doddering old age, through poor personal hygiene to an obsession with pig breeding in the eyes of ambitious parents and his personal attributes would have nothing to do with it.

'Have you eaten breakfast yet?' he asked to change the subject. 'Or, like me, did you first want to be certain the house was not going to collapse around our ears?'

'Exactly that,' Kat agreed, joining him as he walked towards the door.

'And how to you expect to fill your day, now that you are reassured on that point?'

'In the library this morning, then completing our survey of the statues, if you can spare the time. Thank you,' she said as he opened the door for her. 'I have written to the various auction houses and expect a reply very soon.'

'I will certainly join you, provided you can assure me my life is safe on this occasion, Kat.'

'Your life?' She looked up at him and he seemed to see both amusement and alarm in her expression. A strange combination.

'To date you have flattened me by falling from the library steps, you have trapped me behind statues and compelled me to climb staircases from the outside, you have lured me through secret tunnels and you have almost precipitated me into the abyss.' He followed her in to the empty breakfast room.

'The library steps incident was the result of a fault in the equipment of this establishment,' Kat retorted as she sat down. 'I warned you not to come into that group of statues. *You* insisted on going into the passageway and I prevented you from falling into that hole. Would you care for coffee?'

'Thank you, Kat. You have an answer for everything.'

'I hope so, at least, for those things which fall within my sphere of knowledge.' She passed him the coffee cup. 'I do not recall giving you permission to shorten my given name, Lovell.'

'It suits you,' Will said, earning himself a look from narrowed eyes. 'Can I fetch you anything from the sideboard?'

'I doubt I should be flattered,' she said tartly. 'A little bacon, thank you.'

She sat there neat as a pin, dressed plainly in her simple cotton working gown, her soft brown hair firmly trapped in a snood of knotted black ribbon, and answered him back as composedly as another man would have done. She countered his accusations, she flattened his teasing, she remained perfectly polite—and positively exuded femininity all the while.

Will, forking bacon on to one plate for her and eggs, sausage and bacon on to another for himself, confessed he was baffled by her.

Kat was pleasant and yet he could not shake off the nagging suspicion that she disliked him.

It was not the caution and mistrust that any single lady might feel being alone with a man, he was sure of that. She had shown not the slightest concern about being in that tunnel with him, or in any of the rooms. When that inexplicable urge to kiss her had come over him she had understood perfectly well and had shown no uneasiness in wordlessly rebuffing him.

And it was not as though he necessarily expected to be liked. He was demanding, authoritative and determined, he knew that, and people could take him as they found him. So why was this young woman making him even think about the matter?

It was because she *was* a cat, he told himself, buttering toast. They were quite capable of unsettling anyone, just by sitting around and staring.

He should avoid her as much as possible…yet he found her company stimulating in much the same way as he enjoyed the clash with a good opponent in court. It made his brain work harder, his blood flow faster. Very strange.

Chapter Ten

Katherine ate luncheon alone with Elspeth. Lovell and Giles had apparently taken theirs in the study.

'They've got all kinds of ledgers out, Miss Jenson,' Arnold, one of the footmen, explained as he brought in a jug of lemonade. 'Something about crop yields, I think. His Lordship sounded a bit...testy-like and Mr Wilmott looked fit to tear his hair out, if you'll pardon the expression.'

'Lovell is going to have to employ a new estate manager by the sound of it,' Elspeth observed when they were alone again.

'I expect he wants to understand the problems before he hands them over to someone else,' Katherine said. 'I know I would. If things are in a mess, he will not want to start a new man off like that.'

'How is your own work progressing?' Elspeth asked.

'Very well in the library. Peter the footman is proving an excellent assistant. I really must encourage

Lovell to find him better employment—he is wasted as it is.

'I hope to identify more statues that we can send for sale this afternoon, which will be a start on setting the house to rights, but it sounds as though Lovell may not be able to join me for a while yet. How do you intend to spend the afternoon?'

'Catching up with my correspondence, which has been sadly neglected while I have been spending so much time out of doors sketching.'

'Well, do not be tempted around to the west side of the house or you'll risk plunging through, like poor Giles did.'

'How is the *other matter* progressing?' Elspeth said, keeping her voice low.

'Hardly at all, but now I think I am lulling Lovell into not noticing where I go or what I do, so soon I will be able to explore where I want.'

Elspeth looked up from her bread and butter with a frown. 'I think you need to be very careful with the Marquis. He is formidable, for all that he is being very pleasant to us.'

'I can be formidable, too,' Katherine said darkly. 'And I am not a woman to be intimidated.'

Katherine was able to finish inspecting all the large statues by herself within an hour and went back to her room feeling decidedly weak at the knees with excitement. Where was Lovell? Surely crop yields couldn't take much longer?

She made her way downstairs after washing her hands, tidying her hair and removing the large apron she wore when she was working. Possibly she looked cool, calm and collected, but inside she was bubbling with excitement.

As she passed the study door it opened and Lovell strode out, Giles behind him. The secretary rolled his eyes at her, looking like a man very much in need of a tankard of strong ale.

'Ah, Kat. Have you been waiting on me?'

'I do have the remainder of the statues for you to consider and I think—' She broke off at the sound of someone knocking at the front door.

Arnold, the footman, trotted past and they heard his voice. 'I will ascertain whether His Lordship is at home.'

'Now what?' Lovell muttered as Arnold reappeared, bearing calling cards on a silver salver.

'That was Lady Bradley's footman, my lord. Her Ladyship and her three daughters are in their carriage outside, enquiring whether you are receiving.'

'No.'

'Excuse me, Lovell, but you are going to have to start receiving neighbours very soon,' Katherine said. Her news could wait, she told herself. Its subject had for several thousand years, after all.

'The drawing room is in a perfectly acceptable state and you do look as though you would be better for a cup of tea.'

'Where is Mrs Downe?'

'In our sitting room, I believe.'

'In that case you and she will join me, if you please. And you, too, Wilmott—I can see you trying to slide off. If you think I am going to be trapped alone drinking tea and making banal conversation with four ladies, you are much mistaken. Some dilution is needed.'

It would be amusing to witness Lovell having to be civil to a matron and her three daughters, all no doubt exceedingly interested in the arrival of a titled, young and single gentleman of high rank.

'I will go and fetch Mrs Downe,' Katherine offered, managing, somehow, to keep a straight face. Revenge came in many forms, it seemed.

'Very well. Arnold, invite the ladies in to the drawing room and order tea.'

'I will just go and make sure I'm respectable,' Giles said with a meaningful cough.

'What? Hell, I suppose I had better do so, too.' Lovell stalked off and Giles and Katherine exchanged grins before both hurrying for the stairs.

Katherine and Elspeth entered the drawing room first and both curtsied to the group of fashionably dressed ladies waiting there.

'Good afternoon, Lady Bradley,' Elspeth said, looking every inch the senior clergyman's wife that she had been. 'This is Miss Jenson, His Lordship's librarian, and I am Mrs Downe, her companion. We are sorry to have kept you waiting. Lord Ravenham will be down shortly and refreshments are on their way.'

Lady Bradley, a handsome matron of, Katherine estimated, forty-three or four, bowed in return, managing not to look too surprised at Katherine's role. 'Good afternoon. These are my daughters Claire, Millicent and Penelope Bradley.'

The three young ladies curtsied, at which point Lovell and Giles came in, the introductions were performed all over again and everyone sat down. The young ladies, seated in a demure row on the sofa, kept their eyes modestly lowered while their mother, Lovell and Elspeth went through the ritual of small talk.

'My late cousin was not someone much given to socialising, I believe,' Lovell said after the weather, the pleasantness of the drive from Westhaye Manor and Lord Bradley's intention to call very shortly had all been disposed of.

'We certainly found that to be the case,' Lady Bradley said. 'I understand the late Marquis was much involved in scholarship and was somewhat of a recluse. I do not recall him ever holding any social events of any kind at the Hall. Even the village Midsummer festivities were no longer held here, as they have been for many years. A sad disappointment to the neighbourhood.'

The hint that Lovell should remedy this lack immediately hung unspoken in the air.

'My cousin was a great collector, which means that most of the rooms here—including the ballroom—bear a close resemblance to a warehouse,' Lovell said. 'I regret to say that it will be some time before I am able to offer any hospitality beyond morning calls.'

Katherine noticed with amusement that he avoided any mention of the fête, let alone a commitment to hold it next year.

'There is no ballroom?' Miss Bradley asked plaintively with what, Katherine guessed, was intended to be a melting look at Lovell. 'Oh. We were *so* much hoping you would be holding a ball, my lord.'

'Not for some time. I am sorry to disappoint you.'

Oh, no, you are not, Katherine thought, amused. *You are delighted to have such a good excuse not to entertain.*

'Wilmott and I are much involved in restoring the estate and Miss Jenson, although an indefatigable worker, is still imposing order on the library.'

'A lady librarian,' Miss Bradley remarked. 'How very unusual.' She seemed undecided over whether to be shocked or intrigued by this phenomenon.

Giles, who had been silent after the greetings, suddenly said, 'Miss Jenson is also a learned antiquary.'

'Good heavens,' Lady Bradley said faintly. 'Whatever do your parents have to say about that?'

'My father, who educated me, is dead. My mother completely approves.'

'My dear late husband, who was Dean of Westchester Cathedral, always said that we ladies should use what talents we have been blessed with,' Elspeth remarked with the air of one quoting sacred writ.

Katherine bit the inside of her cheek to stop herself laughing. Dean Downe had been a clergyman who firmly believed in exercising his own talents for good living and would have been completely incapable of believing a female had any intellect at all.

She suspected that Elspeth was twisting a remark of his about housekeeping or sewing. Managing the Reverend Algernon Downe had required considerable skill and tact and it must have helped that he had clearly never realised just how intelligent his wife was.

The other ladies looked suitably impressed. They clearly thought it strange, but faced with a clergyman's widow as chaperon, Katherine's accent and simple, but good, clothes, even the most suspicious mind could hardly put a scandalous interpretation on her presence in the household.

'I do hope you will be able to call, Mrs Downe,' Lady Bradley said graciously, accepting a second cup of tea and launching into a description of all the good works and charitable causes in the area that she was certain a clergyman's widow would wish to be involved with.

Whether it was deliberate or not, this forced Lovell and Giles to converse with the young ladies and all three proved that they had learned their lessons in innocuous chit-chat and modest flirtation perfectly.

If it were not for Will and his late cousin, I would have been a young lady like that, flirting in an unexceptional manner with eligible gentlemen, looking forward to marriage. A family...

Lovell's face was a mask of polite interest, but Katherine knew him well enough now to tell that he was seething with impatience. There were several of what she understood card players called 'tells': he fiddled with his cuff, tapped one finger on his knee and his smile became harder and more fixed.

Should she rescue him? She supposed it was only charitable and Giles was looking positively cross-eyed with the banalities he was forced to utter whenever Lovell fell silent.

'Would you care for another cup of tea, Lady Bradley?' she enquired sweetly. 'I can ring for more hot water.'

'Goodness, is that the time? How it does fly in congenial company.' She rose to her feet. 'Come, girls. Delighted to have met you, Lord Ravenham, Mrs Downe. And Miss, er... Mr...'

Lovell showed them out himself. It was not so much

a courteous gesture, Katherine thought, as a fervent
desire to make sure they really were off the premises.

He came back and collapsed into his chair. 'Why on
earth did people think it is a good idea to raise young
ladies to pretend to be lacking in any intelligence at
all? Goodness knows what those three are like behind
the curls and simpering. One would assume they had
feathers for brains.'

'I believe many gentlemen feel threatened by female
intelligence and so it is thought best not to challenge
them with any evidence of it,' Katherine said.

'Something went wrong with your upbringing in
that case,' Lovell remarked.

Did she detect a shadow of a smile? Katherine pretended to ignore the comment. 'You will have to brace
yourself for more of the same as soon as Lady Bradley has boasted all around the district that she was
the first to call.'

'In which case I expect all of you to rally around in
support, regardless of what you are doing at the time.'
He got to his feet. 'Which reminds me, I promised to
inspect statues with you, Kat.'

Katherine saw Elspeth's eyebrows rise at the short-
ened name, but she said nothing.

'Yes, it should not take long. I have been around
them already and noted some.' She followed him out
and along the corridor to the next group, suppressing

her excitement over her find. Let him judge for himself when he saw it.

'This and this are poor Roman work,' she said as they reached the first two. 'This, I am sure, is a modern copy and—'

'Thank you, Kat.' Lovell put one hand on the shoulder of a Roman matron who looked stiffly out at the world from under a tightly curled mound of hair.

'What for? This is what you employ me for.' He was very close, but not precisely looming.

'For rescuing me just now. That was not agreed when I took you on.'

'I was rescuing all of us,' she said. 'Besides, I thought you were about to explode like a keg of gunpowder.'

'Did you? I was certainly seething with impatience, but I had not thought I was so easy to read.'

'I have begun to know you, my lord. I am sure that acting in court taught you a lot about control, but some things betray you.' She tapped her finger on the statue's other shoulder in imitation of his gesture.

'Acting in court? It is not a stage.'

'But surely it is? You cannot truly be feeling indignation on your client's behalf about every petty matter, nor feel outrage about every alleged fault, let alone hide your feelings about every defendant who is dragged before you under a mask of disapproval and disbelief about each one of them. Or can you?'

'My feelings in a case are neither here nor there.

It is a lawyer's role to present his client's side of the matter in the strongest possible form.'

'Even when you do not believe in it? What if you are certain your client was a murderer? Or a thief?'

'I rarely take—*took*—criminal cases.' There was a flush of colour up over his cheekbones now.

Irritation or embarrassment?

'No, I suppose your late cousin's endless civil litigation kept you well employed.'

And I am going the right way to getting myself dismissed, she realised with a shock.

Something had released this hostility and she had an uneasy feeling that it was Lovell's closeness, the warmth that had been in his voice when he had thanked her.

'I apologise,' she said hastily. 'I knew someone who was badly...bullied in a court case. Very unfairly. I still feel annoyed about it on their behalf.'

'Passionate, I would have said.' Lovell's hand slid across the back of the statue and caught hers. 'Now who is showing their agitation?'

His grasp was warm and compelling, but not so fierce that she could not have slipped her own fingers free. Skin to skin she could feel his pulse, strong and perfectly steady whereas hers was all over the place.

I want...want you to kiss me.

For a hideous moment she thought she had said it out loud, then realised he would hardly be standing there, unmoving, if she had. Either he would have turned on his heel in disgust or...

'What do you feel about this statue?' she asked, moving her hand down the arm as though testing the quality of the surface. His fingers slid away and Katherine found she could breathe again.

'She looks as though a puppy has done something regrettable on the best Axminster carpet,' Lovell said. 'Or whatever the Roman equivalent was. I can happily part with her.'

He sounded perfectly calm and not at all like a man in the grip of an urge to do something unseemly with his librarian, so it was clearly her own imagination.

And as for her reaction, that surge of desire, that was inexplicable. She hated the man. She wanted to show him up for the liar, cheat and the bully that he was, she wanted him to apologise, grovel. Not kiss her.

'What about these?' Her voice sounded too high-pitched, but Lovell did not seem to notice.

Soon he would see the thing that had taken her breath away and she hoped, very much, that he would feel as she did about it, although why that should be important, she could not have said.

'Those can go,' he said, frowning at a group of very dull senatorial types. 'But this...'

He moved slowly towards the pale figure of the youth, carved in yellow marble. The figure stood tall and straight, the folds of his robe falling in precise folds to his sandaled feet. His gaze was fixed somewhere over their heads, one hand was lifted as though holding something and Katherine felt the same awe she had experienced when she first saw it.

'It is Greek and early, I am certain,' she said, not trying to hide her excitement now. 'It is something very special and I think you should ask an expert to assess it, perhaps one of the scholars at the British Museum. If I am right, then it is precious.'

'It is incredible.' He sounded almost awe-struck. 'Stylised and yet so real it seems to breathe. Who was he?'

'A charioteer, I think. He was holding the reins, perhaps at the start of the race.'

'Wonderful.' Lovell prowled around the figure. 'Powerful. Where are we going to put it?'

We?

'You want to keep it?'

'Of course. I'd happily throw out everything else I have found in this house to keep this.'

Will watched Kat as she backed away from the statue, head cocked to one side, considering. He had the clear impression that his enthusiasm had made her very happy, as though she was responsible for conjuring up the charioteer.

But no, he realised as she stopped and frowned in

thought. *She is simply happy that someone understands and shares her enthusiasm.*

'I know,' she said suddenly. 'The perfect place. Come on!' She caught his wrist and ran and Will let himself be towed along, fascinated to see what Kat had thought of, disarmed by the way that she had so far forgotten herself in her excitement as to take hold of him.

She skidded to a halt in the hallway and gestured at the far wall opposite the front door. 'That niche. We paint it a darker colour—blue, perhaps? The statue would look superb standing there. The guardian spirit of the house.'

'You are a romantic, Kat,' Will said, making no effort to free his wrist. He rather thought she was unaware she was gripping it.

'Of course.' She looked amused by his surprise. 'You would have to have a heart of stone to study the objects and the stories from the past and not find romance in them.'

She tugged again, impatient to inspect the niche, and he followed her. A few minutes ago he had wanted to kiss her. Now he knew that he would like to sweep her up in his arms and carry her to his bed while this glow of excitement was on her.

Will made himself study the alcove. It was semi-circular in plan, cut back into the wall and with a domed top. It was clearly meant for a full-sized statue and the charioteer would stand there comfortably, safe from knocks.

'A dark blue, definitely. What do you think?' she demanded.

'Evoking the seas of his homeland?' Will suggested.

She was making him as romantic as she was. Perfectly ridiculous. He was the least romantic person he could think of. Lawyers had no business languishing over rugged landscapes or tales of chivalry or storm-tossed oceans.

'Oh, yes.'

She spun around and instinctively he gathered her in to him by the hand she held and suddenly there she was, warm and happy and bubbling with enthusiasm, almost pressed to his chest, laughing up at him.

'I want to kiss you,' he said harshly, knowing he was warning himself as much as her.

Chapter Eleven

The laughter drained away from Kat's face, leaving not the rejection Will expected, but a warmth and a curiosity.

'Yes,' she said and went up on tiptoe to touch her lips to his.

The kiss was sweet, fleeting, almost innocent. She dropped his hand and stepped back immediately, leaving him on fire with desire, wildly out of all proportion to the cause.

'Goodness,' Kat said. There was colour in her cheeks and her eyes were wide, but she seemed considerably more composed than he felt. 'Goodness,' she repeated. 'Well, there's a warning about getting overexcited about romantic things! And it isn't even as though he's a statue of Eros.'

'I must beg your pardon,' Will said, holding her gaze. *Please do not look down...* 'That was unconscionable. Be assured such a thing will never happen again.'

He turned sharply on his heel before she had the opportunity to notice just how aroused that had made him and strode off to the study. By the mercy of whichever guardian spirit looked after marquises who had temporarily taken leave of their senses, there were no servants in sight.

As he thought it, Arnley came around the corner. Will halted and the steward stopped, too, awaiting his pleasure.

'The hall is to be redecorated immediately. Have someone discuss colours with Miss Jenson.'

'Miss Jenson, my lord?'

'Yes. I intend placing a statue in the niche there and she knows what will best set it off.'

'I understand, my lord. I will see to that at once.' He bowed and hurried off, leaving Will to reach the study with a sense of relief. Sanctuary.

'Sir?' Wilmott put down his pen and stood up.

Will waved him back to his seat and sat down himself. At least the shock of almost running into Arnley had subdued the evidence of his arousal.

His secretary gestured to a pile of papers in front of him. 'I was just summarising the decisions you reached this morning, sir, and making a list of actions, but is there is anything else you prefer me to be doing?'

'No. Carry on. I have some things to think about.'

Like what the devil had possessed him to find Kat

Jenson so damnably tempting. She could not be further from the kind of woman who normally took his fancy. In fact, if one were to consider what was the exact opposite of Delphine de Frayne, Kat was the image you would come up with.

Pleasant enough to look at but, compared to the face of a wicked angel, masses of jet-black hair, flashing eyes and a lavish figure, there was no competition from regular features, smooth brown hair, calm hazel eyes and a neat figure.

A passionate temperament would surely trump calm good sense, and a virgin with a fine mind could, surely, never hope to compete with the sensual skills that Delphine possessed.

But Kat was not competing, was she? That kiss was the product of high spirits and curiosity. She was no wanton. A quick pressure of her lips and she had gone.

Now, he assumed, she would analyse the experience, probably catalogue it under 'What on earth is all the fuss about?' and pretend it had never happened when they next met.

Will shifted uncomfortably on his chair. Was that what he should do, too? Ignore it?

A respectable young lady would expect a declaration after a kiss from a gentleman, however fleeting. Was a librarian a respectable young lady? Kat was certainly respectable, young and a lady, even if of apparently modest standing.

He supposed her parents were country squires or something similar. Go back a generation or so and you would probably find connections to titles and great names, just as you could with his bloodline.

But… He could still swear that she did not like him, that she disapproved of him in some way. He had caught her sometimes watching him with a cool appraisal that sent a shiver down his spine. Was that the calculation of a husband-hunter? Was that what she was after—a title?

If so, she was going about it in a very strange way.

'Sir?'

'What?'

Wilmott was looking at him strangely. 'You sighed, sir. Heavily.'

'Heavy thoughts.'

'If it is any help, I have drafted an advertisement for a wood reeve.' His secretary passed a sheet of paper across the desk. 'I can send that off today, if it acceptable.'

'Yes, excellent. When you have done that, please consult with Miss Jenson about moving as many of the large items of statuary and the crates into the ballroom as possible. Then Mrs Goodman can set to work on having everywhere else thoroughly cleaned. If she requires more maids, or to employ women from the village for the rough work, then tell her she has *carte blanche* to hire however many she thinks necessary.'

'Yes, sir.' Wilmott looked somewhat startled, as well he might, Will conceded. They had been working through estate matters thoroughly, at a steady pace and not considering the house at all, now that Kat was employed.

'I want the place in a tolerable state by early summer next year,' he said, with the distinct feeling that he had just jumped off the edge of a cliff. 'I intend staying in London for the coming Season and finding myself a wife.'

'The London house is in a reasonable condition, sir?' Giles asked.

'Yes. It will simply require a thorough early spring clean,' Will said vaguely. He had committed himself now, he had said it out loud. He was in search of a wife and he intended doing so by means of the Marriage Mart that was the Season's focus.

'I have no reason to be secretive about this. Warn the staff that there will be a need to prepare the London house during February.'

Wilmott was already making notes. Given the way that news spread about a large household, his plans would be common knowledge by dinner time and Kat would be warned that she should harbour no expectations. Not, of course, that she had any, but it was best to be on the safe side.

Strangely this did not make him feel any more settled, but that was probably the prospect of the bear pit that was the Season, something he had only touched the very fringes of before. But he knew enough to be aware that he would be prey, that he might as well have a target painted on his back labelled *Very Eligible Nobleman.* Ambitious mamas would be circling like sharks that had smelt the blood in the water.

'Right. What is next?' He sat up straight, pulled his chair up to the desk and pushed all thought of marriage, women and hazel-eyed librarians to the back of his mind.

That had been... Extraordinary. Extraordinary that Lovell had wanted to kiss her. Extraordinary that she had let him, or, rather, that she had kissed him. And completely extraordinary that such a fleeting brush of the lips should make her feel so very peculiar.

Katherine sat down on one of the hard shield-back hall chairs to get her breath back. Something inside her seemed to fizz with excitement, she felt decidedly warm and, incredibly, she could still taste him on her lips.

It was probably also extraordinary that Lovell had immediately apologised and left her. One heard so many stories about predatory employers taking advantage of defenceless females. Governesses and maidservants seemed particularly vulnerable to such attentions.

But Lovell *hadn't* taken advantage. Yet more confirmation that this man was not the ogre she had thought him to be, he was something much more complex.

And as for her own behaviour... Well, she would not think about that now. Probably it was the result of high spirits after finding that wonderful statue. She would feel quite calm in a minute.

'Ah, Miss Jenson. I was hoping to find you.' It was Mr Arnley, the steward.

Katherine stood up, fixed what she could only hope was a vaguely intelligent expression on her face and smiled. 'Yes, Mr Arnley. How may I help?'

He launched into an explanation about painting the hall and Katherine nodded and promised to see the painter the next day. 'And are you the correct person to ask about crating statues that Lord Ravenham intends to send to various auction houses, Mr Arnley?'

He was, so now she could add discussions with the estate carpenter to her list of things to do tomorrow. At least paint and sawdust should keep her mind off other, completely inappropriate, things.

She parted from the steward, went to check on the library and glanced at the clock. Incredibly she still had two hours in hand before she needed to change for dinner. Time to begin checking the room next to the one with the door to the secret passage, perhaps.

She left the door wide open, set her notebook and pencil on the small table it contained and looked around, wondering what purpose it had served. A small parlour for the ladies, perhaps. There would have been a good view of the grounds in the days when they were properly cultivated.

As it was, it housed four tea chests, what looked like a canvas-wrapped painting, a large chest of drawers, several upright chairs and a fire screen on a pole. She would start with the chest of drawers.

Katherine lifted the clock, to the table, making a note in her book.

French ormolu clock. Mid-eighteenth century. Out of fashion and not a well-known maker.

Then she began lifting out the drawers, one at a time, and stacked them on the floor, allowing her to shift the carcase away from the wall. Nothing hidden behind it, nothing under it.

Now she could tackle the drawers, one by one. Katherine replaced the clock on the top of the chest and carried the lowest drawer to the table.

She was halfway through the third drawer when she felt the warning tingle that she was being observed and glanced up.

Lovell was in the doorway, leaning against one jamb, arms folded, watching her.

She put down the box she was examining and stood up, but he waved her back to her chair.

'You left the door wide open, there must be a draught.'

That was certainly a more prosaic opening than *And just why did you kiss me?* she supposed.

'Yes, but I am going through rooms that contain all kinds of objects, many of them small and valuable. That could lay me open to the suspicion that some might find their way into a pocket, so the more open I am, the better I feel about it.'

She saw Lovell glance at her notebook where she listed everything she had found, drawer by drawer.

'I select my staff with care and I choose to trust them,' he said.

Katherine opened the box she had been looking in, lifted out a ring and handed it to him. 'A nice, if small, diamond. So easily hidden. Very tempting.'

'My assessment of your character, Kat, is that not only are you too honest to pocket as much as a seed pearl, but that you what makes you honest is not fear of being caught committing a capital crime, but your own self-esteem and sense of what is right.' He handed back the ring with barely a glance at it.

She could only stare at him, surprised. It was true, when she did find the Borgia Ruby—and she would—then she would not simply take it. That would be wrong—some money had been paid for it, even though in the course of a fraud, and Lovell had some stake in it until she had returned that.

He had not known what his cousin had done, she was certain of that now. If he could assess her char-

acter, then she thought she was beginning to understand his. But she could not forgive him for the way
he had fought that case. Never.

'Thank you,' she managed to say. 'Even so, the
sooner the small portable items of value are in the
strongroom, the better. This is a large house and, if
we had an intruder, we might not realise it.'

We? This is not your house, she reminded herself
sharply.

'So, you are moving these.' He poked one long finger into the tray of snuffboxes, two necklaces, a few
rings and a miniature in a jewelled frame, stirring
them about. 'What else?'

'Books go back to the library. Furniture, paintings
and clocks stay where they are. I am no expert on any
of those, so it is a matter of your choice when we, I
mean, *you*, come to arrange the rooms.'

Why was she beginning to feel so possessive about
this house? To cover up her slip she chattered on. 'I
know people who can give you reliable estimates on
anything you do not care for. Reliable, that is, if they
realise you are not about to sell to them directly and
instead employ them on a fee.'

Lovell smiled, the twist of his lips cynical.

Such nice firm lips...

'Are you telling me that not all experts can be
trusted?'

'If they are also dealing then, naturally, they will

be looking to make the best profit for themselves. But they would expect you to compare estimates. I would not recommend anyone to you who I would not be prepared to trust personally. Not all dealers are criminals, no matter what the late Marquis thought.'

His gaze sharpened and she swallowed hard. Had she given herself away, revealed resentment?

'It is a small world, word gets around,' she explained. 'Your cousin had a reputation for prosecuting anyone he thought had done him down.'

'He was a vindictive man.' Lovell shrugged. 'Carry on, then, Kat. I have ordered that all the packing cases and all the remaining statuary are to be moved into the ballroom. That should make things easier.'

There was a tap on the door frame and they both looked around to find Giles Wilmott holding a letter. He had an expression on his face of mingled amusement and alarm.

'My lord, the bishop is sending you a chaplain. He should arrive tomorrow. The Reverend Quintus Gresham.'

'Good G——, that is, how the blazes did he know I wanted one?' Lovell frowned. 'I am not even certain I *do* want one.'

'In that case, I beg your pardon, sir. I fear I have exceeded my authority, but I assumed after your conversation with Mr Arnley on the subject...'

'Very well. I suppose he was right. It is a long walk

for the staff to get to church and next year the household will have expanded.'

Will it? Yes, of course, Katherine realised. Once the house was habitable again, Lovell would want to entertain. His new wife certainly would and that meant more servants, from scullery maids to ladies' maids to grooms.

The pang of something perilously like jealousy surprised her. Of course, she was growing to know the house and its contents, but she had not expected to feel such a sense of ownership. The library, of course, was becoming exactly as she had hoped and it would be painful if someone changed that—not that she would be here to see it—and she most definitely felt possessive about the charioteer statue.

'Kat?'

'I am so sorry, I was wool-gathering.'

'Will you and Mrs Downe be available to greet our new chaplain tomorrow?'

'I will, certainly, and I am sure, even if Elspeth has any plans, she would be happy to change them. But will you not be interviewing him first?'

Lovell grimaced. 'If the bishop has sent him, then I suppose he will be suitable for the position. I have no idea how to interview a chaplain. I shall offer him a month's trial—he may take a dislike to us, after all.'

Us. He meant the household and himself in particular. But the word had given Katherine another uncomfortable little jolt.

She was becoming very attached to this place and she would be sorry to leave, she realised. It was almost as though her mission to find the ruby, and to expose the lies about her father, was something apart from the day-to-day life she lived at Ravenham Hall. And that was a very unsettling thought.

Chapter Twelve

'The Reverend Gresham, my lord,' Grigson announced.

They were all gathered in the drawing room drinking coffee. Elspeth had taken it on herself to order it every day and then to extract Lovell and Giles from the study and Katherine from the library for, as she put it, 'a conversable twenty minutes to refresh us from our labours'.

Her own labours were the result of volunteering to survey all the hangings, curtains and upholstery in the house with Mrs Goodman and to decide what needed cleaning—all of it—what required repair—much of it—and what was beyond help.

As they all put down their coffee cups and prepared to greet the new arrival Katherine wondered enviously how Elspeth managed to stay so pin-neat and free from dust. At least she herself had washed her hands, tidied her hair and taken off her apron before taking coffee, so she was not in too much of a mess to greet a clergyman.

They all stood as he came in and Lovell went forward to shake his hand. Beside her Katherine heard Elspeth's sharp intake of breath and closed her own mouth with a snap.

Oh. My. Goodness.

The bishop must have sent them the most beautiful clergyman at his disposal. Blond hair, blue eyes, straight nose, strong chin topped a slim six foot of youthful manhood.

Katherine blinked, fastened a smile of welcome on her face and waited to be introduced.

'Mrs Downe, Miss Jenson, Wilmott, this is Mr Quintus Gresham. Gresham, Mrs Downe's husband was the late Dean Downe of Westchester cathedral. She is companion to Miss Jenson here, our librarian. Giles Wilmott, my secretary.'

Everyone shook hands, Elspeth rang for more refreshments and they sat.

Mr Gresham was about twenty-six or seven, Katherine thought. His manner was modest and his accent well bred. Presumably, with the name of Quintus, he was the fifth son of a gentry family with elder brothers taking the roles of the heir, the spare and the Army and Naval officers.

She often wondered how the careers of younger sons were decided. Did they have any choice in the matter? Perhaps they all sat down together and decided who would look best in scarlet and rode well, who didn't get seasick and who had an aptitude for study. Or, more likely, it depended on what influence their father had, and with whom, at the point they were of an age to leave home.

Was having the looks that would excite someone creating a stained-glass window of angels actually an advantage for a young clergyman? Probably not.

After twenty minutes of polite conversation about the bishop's health, his journey and his interest in a county he had never visited before, Mr Gresham finished his coffee and Giles offered to take him to his suite and help him settle in.

When the door closed behind them Elspeth fanned herself with her hand. 'My dear, what an extraordinarily good-looking young man!'

'Incredibly so,' Katherine agreed. 'I was thinking he could model as an angel for a stained-glass artist.'

Lovell cleared his throat pointedly.

'Well, he is handsome,' she said. 'Poor man.'

'Poor man? Even I can tell that he is likely to excite the interest of every female for miles around, including you ladies. I saw your faces when he walked in.' Despite his joking tone, Katherine suspected Lovell was not that amused by their reaction.

'Exactly my point. Just think how difficult that must be for a parish priest. He would be hunted by every hopeful spinster and would have to take particular pains never to arouse gossip or speculation. On the other hand, many matrons would be very glad to secure him as a husband for their daughter. That may well be why the bishop has sent him here, to a household.'

'And how am I expected to protect him from over-amorous housemaids?'

'It is not the same situation at all,' Katherine snapped, suddenly discovering she was finding this no more amusing than Lovell was. 'In a well-regulated household the female staff are safe from unwanted male attention and the same should be true in reverse. The balance of power is quite different between a domestic chaplain and one of the staff and a parish clergyman who might find himself compromised in any number of ways.'

'And this is a well-regulated household, is it?'

'You have an excellent housekeeper, butler and steward, my lord. It would be better if there was a lady of the house, of course.' She put a slight emphasis on *lady* and saw his eyes narrow.

Yes, my lord, I am *suggesting that having your mistress in the house was not fair on the staff.*

'That will have to wait until after the Season, when I intended to remedy that lack,' Lovell said. He spoke so politely that it was clear he was nettled.

'Then, providing Mr Gresham is of upright character, which one sincerely hopes he is, given the bishop's recommendation, there should be nothing to worry about,' she retorted, just as politely. 'Now I must get back to work.'

It was always satisfying to get the last word, so why was she feeling so unsettled? Safe in the library again, Katherine tied her apron strings, sat down at her desk and stared unseeing at a pile of harmless local histories that Peter had dusted and placed ready for her attention.

The honest answer was that it had been a shock to hear Lovell announcing his intention to seek a bride. It should have been no surprise—of course he was and they had spoken of it only the other day. So why...

Because I want him.

The words popped in to her mind with a suddenness that startled her.

Well, of course you do, she argued back. *You are female, possessed of good eyesight and he is an attractive specimen of the opposite sex. You kissed him, didn't you?*

It isn't that, came the insidious little whisper. *You are jealous that he wants to marry another woman.*

No! Stop it. Remember who he is, what he did. Remember why you are here. Remember why you are no longer able to marry any gentleman of good standing, let alone a marquis.

A marquis? What is the matter with me?

She felt herself go hot and then cold.

'Is something wrong, Miss Jenson? Those books are the ones you wanted me to work on, aren't they?'

Peter, brush in one hand, was regarding her with some anxiety.

'Oh. Yes. Absolutely correct, thank you, Peter. I was just thinking of something rather...rather unpleasant. I had no intention of glaring at you.'

He returned her smile. 'Shall I do the rest of the shelf?'

'Yes, please.'

And I will apply myself to my work and to avenging Papa.

And what was all that about? Will wondered, staring at Kat's retreating back.

Her shoulders were back, her head up and she was positively radiating irritation.

Was it because he had teased her and Mrs Downe about admiring Gresham's looks? Whatever it was, the conversation had moved rapidly to what felt remarkably like a lecture on the management of his household. Had that been a covert reproof for having Delphine in the house? He rather thought it had been.

Kat was creating an excellent library for him out of chaos and her work with the statues had not only revealed some fine pieces and the magnificent charioteer, but had already begun the work on clearing the house. But she was a disturbing presence to have around, not least because he found her mysteriously alluring. She was not the type of woman who normally attracted him, not at all. But she was the first female he had found himself living with in a domestic setting since he had left home. He was coming to know her as a person—at least, as far as she allowed him.

Perhaps the attraction was because of the slight edge of hostility that he sensed from her. Was that simply a challenge to his masculinity adding a perverse erotic frisson? And why, bizarrely, had he felt disappointed when she had virtually ordered him to marry for the sake of the household?

Surely, he wasn't such a coxcomb that he expected her to want to take that position herself? That he hoped she wanted him for more than a fleeting, experimental, kiss?

He was a marquis, Will reminded himself, still finding the concept faintly incredible. Marquises married the daughters of aristocrats, not librarians, and Kat knew that perfectly well.

And he had more immediate worries—like what, exactly, was he supposed to do with a chaplain?

Kat solved that problem for him at luncheon by asking Gresham straight out what a domestic chaplain in a great house did.

He had regarded her solemnly. 'I have to confess I asked my lord bishop precisely that question when he spoke to me about this position. I understand that I will be ministering to the spiritual needs of the household and holding a service, or services, as Lord Ravenham requires, on Sundays. I can also hold morning and evening prayers for the household, if that is you wish, my lord.' He directed a slight bow in Will's direction.

'If baptisms, weddings, the churching of women and funerals are required, naturally I will perform those,' he added. 'Then there is the welfare of the tenants, to whatever extent you require me to be involved, my lord.'

'Call me Lovell, or sir,' Will said. 'I do not know to what extent the tenants will wish to attend the chapel here as opposed to the village church and I assume that you will need to form some kind of working relationship with the Vicar there, Mr James.

'As for services, Matins on Sunday will suffice, I think.'

Across the table from him Mrs Downe cleared her throat. 'And daily morning prayers, do you not think, Lovell? Until the ballroom is cleared, and while the staff is relatively small, the drawing room, perhaps, will be large enough.'

'And grace before meals, of course,' Kat added with a sweet smile that was clearly intended to tease him.

'As you say, ladies.' Will smiled back. 'However, I suspect that you may find work needs to be done on the chapel before it is fit for services, Gresham. It was the parish church—fortunately a very small one—and in recent years the late Marquis did not use it, except, perhaps for storage.'

'You have not seen inside, my...sir?' Gresham looked a little daunted as it began to dawn on him that his employer was probably not a deeply devout man.

'I have not. But I am sure Miss Jenson will enjoy exploring it with you. She is a notable antiquarian and excellent in organisation.'

He had said it to tease, expecting that Kat would demur, make an excuse that she was too busy. Surely she didn't want to spend time poking about a dirty church with a clergyman?

She smiled at him. 'You are too kind, Lovell. I would be delighted to explore the chapel with you, Mr Gresham.' The chaplain received a far warmer smile.

Apparently Kat would welcome being given leave to spend hours with the handsome chaplain. He hardly thought that spiders and leaking roofs were the attraction.

'Shall we go and look now, Mr Gresham?' Katherine suggested as they rose from the table. 'If there is work to be done, then the sooner it is begun, the better. I expect it will be locked. Do you have a key, Lovell?'

'I have no idea. I suggest you ask Arnley. My steward,' he explained to the chaplain.

Mr Arnley had produced a heavy iron key on request and Katherine led Mr Gresham across the gravel carriage sweep, down the overgrown path through the shrubbery and up to the wall of the little graveyard.

'This could do with the attentions of the gardeners,' she said. 'But you can say that about the entire gardens and I should warn you about walking around close to the wing of the house where they are clearing the undergrowth—the ground is unstable there.

'The late Marquis was, to put it politely, eccentric. To be more accurate, he was an obsessed collector who was losing his grasp on reality and who neglected everything else except the objects of his desire.'

'I see,' he said, clearly not doing so in the slightest. 'Allow me.' He took the key from her and, by dint of using both hands, managed to turn it in the lock. 'Oil is required, I think.'

The door opened with a screech of rusty hinges that would have not been out of place in a Gothic novel and Gresham stood aside to allow Katherine to enter first.

It was a dubious privilege, she thought, lifting her skirts clear of dust and the evidence of both bats and pigeons.

'At least it has not been used as a storehouse,' she observed. 'I can see nothing that a thorough cleaning will not remedy. It is rather charming.'

'I agree,' Gresham said, earning her approval.

'Modest and simple. The glass all appears to be intact and I can see no trace of leaks in the roof.'

'Oh, look.' Katherine stopped by a table tomb topped with the effigies of a knight in armour, his lady at his side. 'How lovely. They are holding hands and look at his lion and her lapdog at their feet. I can't see an inscription, but it looks fourteenth century to me. I wonder who they are.'

'Perhaps Lord Ravenham's archivist can tell you.' Gresham prodded a kneeler with the toe of his shoe. 'Mice, I fear.'

'There is no archivist yet, although I rather suspect that I will be given the task as soon as the library is in order.'

The chaplain was clearly consumed with curiosity about her employment and, contrarily, Katherine felt no compulsion to explain herself. He was simply going to have to accept that a lady might have respectable employment outside the schoolroom.

'Is there any church plate, do you know?' Gresham opened a door. 'This looks like the vestry, but I can see no lockable cupboard to store it.'

'It is probably in the house, although, when you come to look around, you will see that it might be a while before we find it.'

'I have my travelling communion set,' he said, shaking out a ragged surplice with a grimace of distaste. 'That will suffice for the moment.'

'Shall we go back and find Mrs Goodman, the housekeeper, and see what she can do about finding some women from the village to clean inside? You cannot hold services as it is now.'

They walked back through the shrubbery. 'Where were you before you came here?' Katherine asked. 'A parish?'

'No, I was only ordained a month ago. I was expecting to be sent somewhere as a curate, so this was a surprise,' he admitted.

'Do you mind?' she asked bluntly. 'Would you have preferred a parish?'

'I am happy to serve wherever I may be of use,' he said, sounding, to Katherine's ears, rather stilted.

'May I be impertinent and ask whether a great house, and estate, of this size is something you are accustomed to?' Katherine risked a quick sideways glance and saw he was biting his lip.

'No. Our family is gentry, I suppose. My father has a small estate in Wiltshire. But the bishop is his cousin, so I owe this preferment to him.'

'This is an unusual household,' she said. 'You may already know that the Marquis has only recently inherited from a second cousin who was, as I said, eccentric. Things are at sixes and sevens and you will find us very informal. Lord Ravenham is unmarried, so there will be much to do connected with the welfare of the tenants, I am certain, even if the household is rather small at present.'

'Thank you. That is reassuring,' he said with the first unforced smile Katherine had seen. 'I am anxious to be able to contribute, but I am aware that I am not experienced.'

'I am glad to be of help,' she said, smiling back as they entered the hall.

It had not taken Kat and his new chaplain long to become friends, Will thought, emerging from the study in time to see them coming in through the front door, smiling at each other.

'Oh, Lovell.' Kat turned the smile on him. Was it his imagination that it was several degrees cooler?

'We were just on our way to see Mrs Goodman about getting the chapel cleaned. It will take quite a few women, and men with ladders as well, but the building seems sound. You don't happen to know where the communion silver and the altar candlesticks are, do you?'

'I suspect the candlesticks may be the large brass pair in my bedchamber. I'll ask Petrie to bring them down. My valet,' he added to Gresham, who was looking somewhat subdued. The effect of being organised by Kat, no doubt.

'I hadn't realised you had one,' she said brightly.

'Although, of course, you must do. He is somewhat reclusive, is he not?'

'He is used to a lawyer's chambers and wigs and gowns and had been looking forward to my spending a great deal on fashionable clothes and residing in considerable splendour. This does not come up to his expectations. He tends to lurk and has embarked on a campaign to eradicate the clothes moth as an outlet for his ill humour.'

Gresham was looking blank and Kat patted his arm. 'I told you,' she said, 'this is an unusual household. Shall we find Mrs Goodman?'

She glanced back as they passed Will and he could have sworn that one eyelid dropped in a wink, then they had gone and he could hear her voice fading as they reached the baize-covered door to the servants' stair.

'Sir?' Wilmott said from inside the study. 'I have found those rent books for the missing years that we needed.'

'Excellent.' He turned back to his desk. 'It appears that my new chaplain is seized with nerves at the strangeness of us and my librarian has decided to mother him.'

Wilmott, head bent over a dusty ledger, snorted. 'If she is feeling motherly, then at least she's not going to fall in love with him, then.'

'Don't be ridiculous,' Will snapped.

Chapter Thirteen

To Katherine's relief morning prayers went well the next day. The staff seemed to appreciate it, Lovell clearly approved of the brevity of the service and Mr Gresham did not make the mistake of prosing on, but introduced himself and then led the household in the Lord's Prayer and read a blessing.

At breakfast he asked whether Lovell had any particular tasks for him. 'I had thought of speaking to the indoors staff individually this morning, if that is acceptable. Just a quick word so I can learn names and encourage them to come to me if they think I can help. This afternoon, I wondered if I should begin visiting the tenants, but I do not know how many there are and how long it might take me to call on them all.

'I did not presume to bring a horse,' he added with the air of a man willing to tramp for miles if that was what it took.

'Take any mount from the stables that you think will suit, except for the big grey,' Lovell said.

'Or I could drive you in the gig,' Katherine offered. 'You will need a map, a notebook and your travelling communion set in case anyone is sick or infirm.'

Lovell's brows drew together and she added, 'I have been inside for days and I declare I am feeling quite frowsty. I would appreciate the fresh air and change of scene, if I may have a half-day off.'

'I have a list of the tenant families,' Giles said. 'I can plot them on a sketch map for you if that would help.'

'Then that appears to be your day organised, Gresham,' Lovell said.

Katherine wondered just what was putting him so out of temper—behind the smile there was coldness in the blue eyes.

Well, if she was in disgrace for taking a few hours after luncheon to help the chaplain and to, hopefully, bring some comfort to the tenants, then so be it.

'The tracks seem to be in very poor condition, dear,' Elspeth warned. 'The main carriage drive is not so bad, but I confess I did not have the resolution to try any of those through the park when I have driven out.'

'I am sure neither of us has any intention of proceeding at anything but a walk, believe me,' Katherine said with a laugh. 'After luncheon then, Mr Gresham?'

It was a relief to escape from Lovell's brooding presence. Katherine glanced back as she reached the door and found that he was watching her, his expression cool. She shivered. Was he suspicious of her? Surely he could not have discovered her true identity?

'This should be the correct way,' Gresham said, Giles's sketch map unfolded on his knee. He sounded doubtful as they began to follow the track, Katherine guiding the pony around ruts and hollows.

'Elspeth was not exaggerating about these tracks,' Katherine said. 'I am not at all surprised by how neglected this is,' she said. 'You recall I told you how eccentric the late Marquis was. He neglected everything, it seems.'

'I took the liberty of exploring the house a little, in between speaking to the staff,' Gresham said. 'It will take a great deal of effort to restore it to the state one would expect of a nobleman's dwelling.'

'I know,' Katherine said, with some feeling. 'But the people matter more than the mansion and I suspect that in the absence of a caring lord, let alone a lady of the house, their interests will have been sadly neglected.'

'I will do my best, Miss Jenson,' Gresham said stoutly.

She glanced across and saw he was looking determined, the travelling communion set held firmly on his knee, the map balanced on top of it. This was his first experience of ministering to a flock, of course. He must be nervous.

'My goodness, look at these potholes! If anyone is in need of labouring employment, then mending these tracks will be a good start.'

'I will make a note of it,' he said, wriggling on the seat in an effort to get his notebook out of his pocket one-handed while steadying the box and map with the other.

Katherine leant to one side to give him more room while she guided the pony on to the grass to get around yet another deep rut.

They were just back on the track again when a deer erupted from the bushes almost under the pony's nose. It threw up its head in panic and began to back rapidly.

Katherine was momentarily blinded by the map flapping up in her face, then the gig lurched abruptly, a sharp object jabbed her in the ribs and she felt herself falling. She hit the ground with a thump that almost knocked the wind out of her, had a moment to be grateful for the thick grass, and then something hit her head from above and the world became black.

Will walked along the terrace at the back of the house, picking his way over uneven slabs and tufts of grass and weeds.

More gardeners needed.

More of everything needed and, in his case, more patience and less suspicion, he acknowledged ruefully.

As a lawyer he was trained to be suspicious, to be

constantly looking out for lies and evasions, to expect hidden motives and to think the worst of people.

Now this household, the estate and the tenants were in his care and his responsibility was to trust and nurture them. If he couldn't begin by trusting his chaplain, let alone his hard-working and intelligent librarian, there wasn't much hope for him.

The statue of the crouching nymph that he had ordered to be brought outside and set by the little pool at the end of the terrace was in place and he went to look at it.

Not close enough to the edge, he decided, bending to push it nearer so she could look down into the murky green water. He could see his reflection behind her, dark and blurred as he grunted with effort and finally managed to get the statue into a better position.

Will straightened up, stretched to ease his back and suddenly laughed at himself for his sour mood. It was ridiculous to be brooding because the handsome Mr Gresham appeared to have made friends with Kat. Surely friends were all they were.

It was excellent that someone was making an inexperienced young man feel at home, excellent that Kat had someone else to talk to instead of him, prowling irritably about the place.

All that was wrong with him was insufficient exercise and an excess of accounts. He would take his hunter Ajax out for a gallop, get some fresh air and see if he could find a few tenants. It would not be right for his chaplain to know them better than he did. Besides, Kat might need some help—he had no idea how well either of them could drive.

Half an hour later Will turned the big grey stallion off the carriage drive and down the first turning he came to, keeping the impatient horse to a steady trot. This was no track for speed. He added road mending to his mental list of things to be done and noticed the fresh marks of carriage wheels crushing the grass to the side of the worst potholes. Kat and Gresham must have come this way, too.

The track curved, then rose and, as Ajax crested the slight rise, Will could see several hundred yards of track in front of him. Halfway along was the gig, stationary, and a man was standing by it. There was no sign of Kat.

She could have stopped and descended for any number of reasons—the pony had gone lame, she had seen an interesting flower, the track was too damaged to continue. Even as those explanations flashed through his mind, he knew something was wrong. Careless of ruts or holes, Will sent the horse down the track at a gallop.

By the time he reached the gig and flung himself out of the saddle Gresham was on his knees next to Kat's sprawled body. Beside her head silver vessels glinted incongruously in the grass. There was no blood, he saw with relief.

'What the hell happened?' He pushed Gresham aside and knelt, wrenching off one glove to search for a pulse at Kat's throat. Beneath his fingers he felt it beating strongly under her jaw. Alive, then.

'A deer frightened the pony, it backed into the hole and the gig lurched. Miss Jenson lost her balance and I lost my grip on the wooden case holding the communion vessels. She landed on the soft grass, but the case struck her head.' The chaplain sounded anxious, but he was reporting rationally.

Will judged the distance between the gig's seat and the ground, felt the turf. The distance was not great, the uncut grass was soft enough and without stones. It seemed unlikely that Kat would have suffered more than bruises from the fall. It was the blow to the head they must worry about.

'Can you drive?'

'Yes, my... Lovell.'

'Then turn the gig. I'll lift her.'

A gig had no space for anyone but the driver and passenger and there was nowhere to lay Kat flat. Gresham led the pony around on the grass, rather than try to turn on the track, which showed sense, Will thought through his anxiety, then he climbed up and tied the reins around the whip in its holder.

'If you pass her up, sir, I can hold her while you climb in.'

Lifting a completely limp young woman was not the easiest thing, even for a fit man. A twinge reminded Will that he had been heaving lumps of marble about recently, but he rose steadily to his feet and got Kat on to Gresham's knees.

Will tied Ajax to the gig then, at an agitated word from the chaplain, picked up the chalice and paten, stowed them in the box and jammed them between the young man's feet.

Kat stirred slightly when he took her back in his arms, but was silent again as he arranged her safely, her head on his shoulder, his arms tight around her.

It was extraordinary the wave of protectiveness that swept over him. Presumably, he rationalised while bracing himself to hold her steady and trying not to shout at Gresham to whip up the pony, this was the effect of being the Marquis and responsible for a large number of people in his employ.

'Kat?' he murmured as she stirred. 'Keep still, you have had a bang on the head, but we are almost home now.'

Home? He had never thought of Ravenham Hall like that before, only as a huge liability that he had inherited. Now he realised that it *was* home and that Kat was part of it, presumably because she had been there almost as long as he had.

'Take us around to the stable yard, there's level access into the house from there,' he ordered Gresham, pleased at how steady the young cleric was.

It took only a moment after they entered the yard for the grooms to realise that something was wrong and four of them clustered around as Gresham climbed down and went to the pony's head.

'Fetch a hurdle and something clean to put over it,' Will ordered and two of them ran off, returning minutes later with one covered in grain sacks.

They laid it on the ground, then came and stood two on each side of Will so he could hand his burden down to them. They were strong, fit, young men and they managed easily, placing Kat gently on the sacks.

As Will jumped down Gresham led the pony to the wall, tied it up and then ran for the house.

Mrs Goodman and Mrs Downe were waiting for them as they negotiated the kitchen door.

'My room, I think, my lord,' the housekeeper said. 'Then we don't have to manage the stairs until Miss Jenson is feeling a little better. I have sent Arnold for the surgeon, Mr Henderson. He's good on a horse is young Arnold, he'll be as quick as may be.'

'Just lay her on top of the bed, my lord,' Mrs Downe said, preceding them into the housekeeper's parlour and through to the bedchamber.

Will lifted Kat from the hurdle and carried her to the narrow bed with its patchwork quilt.

'Now, what happened, exactly?' she asked as he stepped to one side.

'She fell from the gig over rough ground. I do not think that was serious or caused any damage—she landed on soft grass. But the travelling communion set fell out after her and struck her on the head.'

'Tsk. Not wearing a bonnet, I suppose,' Mrs Downe said as Will smoothed back the tumbled hair over Kat's forehead.

'Her bonnet came off and blew away as she fell,' Gresham said from the doorway.

'There's a lump at the back, but no bleeding,' Will said, his fingers exploring gently. 'It seems as though the box hit her with a side, not an edge or a corner.

'Thank Heavens for that,' Gresham said.

Will thought, but managed not to say, that Heaven should not have been allowing anyone to be struck with such a container.

He slipped his hand out from under Kat's head and she opened her eyes, clear hazel staring bemusedly back into his.

'Ouch,' she said faintly. 'Where am I and what happened?'

Will bent closer and was relieved to see that her pupils both seemed to be normal. The danger with head injuries was the damage inside the skull, he knew that. But at least she was rational. Bleeding from the ears and nose—that was another danger sign, he recalled and peered closely at all three.

'And what on earth are you doing?' Kate demanded querulously. 'My head aches.'

'You fell out of the gig and were hit on the head by the box containing the communion set.'

'Goodness,' she said faintly. 'How bizarre.'

'You are now on Mrs Goodman's bed and I am just checking there is no bleeding.'

'My lord, if you were to perhaps move...'

Will straightened up abruptly. 'Yes, of course, Mrs Downe. We will send the surgeon down as soon as he arrives and if there is anything you need, you only have to ask.'

She would be perfectly all right, he told himself as he left the room, pushing Gresham in front of him. 'Out. She does not need either of us, I am glad to say, in your case.'

The back of the younger man's neck and his ears turned red. 'You refer to the last rites, my lord? Yes, we must indeed be thankful that it was not more serious. But I blame myself.'

'Really?' Will caught up with him as they emerged into the hallway. 'And why is that?'

'I should have been driving. Or perhaps I could have caught her.'

'If Miss Jenson wanted to drive, it would take a stronger man than you to stop her, Gresham.' The chaplain still looked wretched so Will added, 'If you had caught at her you might well have pulled her under the wheel. As it was, she fell on the grass clear of that danger.'

What was the matter with him? He was becoming soft, trying to soothe an anxious young man and worrying himself over a slightly dented librarian.

Over a young woman who was his responsibility. A hard-working, intelligent, spirited young woman who was somehow—and probably without the slightest intention of doing so—reconciling him to this monstrous house and the weight of duties that went with it.

Grigson hurried past him to answer the knocking on the front door and a tall, ugly man stalked in, shedding coat and hat into the butler's arms as he came.

'Henderson,' he said tersely. 'Where is my patient?'

'Ravenham,' Will snapped back, secretly amused by the surgeon's no-nonsense approach. 'She is downstairs, conscious, making sense, but complaining of a headache, which is unsurprising as she was hit on the head.'

'By what?' Henderson demanded.

'The box of a portable communion set.'

Silence. Then the surgeon glanced at Gresham in his sombre black with the white clerical bands at his neck and remarked, 'I would suggest you employ a chaplain with a less militant approach to the spread of the faith, my lord. I have always found that simple persuasion is the best method of conveying information.'

'It was an accident. This way.' Suppressing a smile, Will turned towards the back stairs. 'Down there. You'll find Mrs Goodman, my housekeeper, in charge.'

He dismissed Gresham to do whatever chaplains did—write a sermon, perhaps?—and went to scan the post that Giles, who had ridden into St Albans, had left on his desk in the study.

He had left the door open and, less than twenty minutes later, emerged at the sound of footsteps striding down the hall.

Henderson stopped when he saw him. 'Nothing broken, no signs of concussion. I have given her something for the headache and told her to rest. An intelligent young woman, she'll know if she needs to see me again. Good day to you.'

'And good day to you,' Will replied as the surgeon let himself out, banging the front door closed behind him.

Not a man with a soothing bedside manner, but he had more confidence in the surgeon than all the smooth-talking doctors he had encountered. They, of course, despised surgeons as mere technicians because they worked with their hands, despite the fact that, with their practical approach, they saved more lives than the medics.

The house would certainly be calmer with Kat confined to her bed, he thought, going back to the letter from Truefit, the chief clerk at his legal chambers. Will was a sleeping partner now, leaving his two barrister colleagues to run the firm, and Truefit wanted to know what to do with the paperwork relating to the Ravenham estate and his late cousin's cases. Did His Lordship wish it to be stored at the chambers or sent to him, and if so, to where?

'Send everything relating to the Ravenham estate and to my late cousin's affairs here to the Hall,' Will wrote. Then as an afterthought added, 'Is there an opening for an intelligent young man? I have an under-footman who shows promise.'

He answered a few minor points the clerk had raised and was sealing the letter when he heard the door to the service stairs open. It would be Mrs Goodman coming to report on Kat, no doubt, he thought, going out to meet her.

Instead of the housekeeper, the figure doggedly making its way towards the foot of the main stairs was Kat. She was sporting a rakish bandage around her head, her hair was in a long plait and she was wearing a brown wool robe that barely skimmed her ankle bones. Her feet were bare.

'What in Hades do you think you are doing?' he demanded.

'Don't shout,' she said, glaring at him. 'My head hurts. I am going to bed.'

'You *were* in bed and told to stay there. And of course your head hurts. If you will go throwing yourself out of moving vehicles, you should expect it to.'

'*My* bed. The rest of your observations are inaccurate and unfair,' Kat said with dignity. This was somewhat undermined by her appearance and the fact that she was steadying herself on the wall, then on the console table as she shuffled past it.

'How the devil did you persuade Mrs Goodman to let you out?' Will demanded, advancing on her.

She was pale, there were scratches on her check from the dried grasses she had landed on and, from her expression, every step jarred her aching head.

Something inside Will shifted, painfully.

'I didn't tell her. She left me to sleep. I can't take her bed, poor woman—she was intending to sleep on the sofa in her sitting room.'

He could stand there, argue with her, tell her that the housekeeper could have the pick of any empty bedchamber in the house. Instead, he took two strides, picked her up and carried her to the stairs. He was coming to know the feel of her in his arms. To like it.

Kat gave a gasp of alarm, then held on tight, and whatever it was inside him twisted again.

Chapter Fourteen

Infuriating man. Domineering creature.

Katherine wanted to protest, to kick, to demand he put her down, yet, somehow, she did none of those things, but tightened her arms around Lovell's neck, let her aching head rest on his shoulder and closed her eyes.

It was because she was feeling so sore and shaken from the fall, of course. It was nothing to do with the fact that being carried up a sweeping staircase again by a large, strong man who smelt of leather and citrus and male skin was breathtaking and she did not want it to stop.

Lovell shouldered open a door, walked across a room, through another door and Katherine found herself being deposited firmly on the side of her bed.

'Get in and stay there,' he snapped, jolting her into reality again.

Standing in front of her was not the dashing hero of a Minerva Press novel who had just come to the rescue of the heroine, but an irritable, overbearing lawyer-turned-marquis who was every bit as disagreeable as she had always thought him.

The thought crept into her mind that climbing the backstairs had almost exhausted her and that she would probably have had to manage the main staircase on hands and knees if he hadn't found her, but Katherine was in no mood to be reasonable about this.

This man was the enemy, the man who had destroyed her father and, foolishly, she had let herself become friendly with him, attracted to him. Somehow she had managed to separate William Lovell, King's Counsel, from Will Lovell, the Marquis of Ravenham, and that was a betrayal of her parents. And it was all her own fault.

'Go away,' she said.

'Get into bed.' He rested his balled fists on each hip and looked at her through narrowed eyes.

'I will. Now *go away.*'

She closed her eyes.

Go away because I want to have a good weep, you horrible man. My head hurts, I have been an idiot and I still haven't found either the ruby or the evidence of your lies. I have let myself enjoy being here, my work here. You.

Lovell shifted, turning away. There was the soft tread of retreating footsteps on carpet. The sound stopped.

'Kat, are you crying?'

'No!' She opened her eyes and, through a blur, saw him in the doorway staring at her.

'Yes, you are.' He sounded exasperated, angry even. Now he would go away because men could not cope with tears.

'You infuriating female.' He strode back, sat down beside her, thrust a large handkerchief into her hand and gathered her efficiently against his shoulder. 'Use that. Don't make my shoulder wet.'

'I'm not infuriating, you are,' she managed to say through a layer of linen, her cheek pressed against superfine coating.

Lovell snorted. 'I'm an idiot.'

'Yes,' she muttered.

Hate you.

But despite his words, his tone, he was holding her gently and rubbing her back with his free hand, his palm making warm circles though Mrs Goodman's sensible dressing gown.

She must be strong. She must rest and then get back to work. She *would* find the ruby and the evidence that would clear her father. And she would not allow herself to fall in… To *like* William Lovell.

Katherine wriggled free, blew her nose loudly and inelegantly and said, 'Thank you. I will go to bed now. Perhaps you would be good enough to let Mrs Goodman and Mrs Downe know where I am.'

Lovell released her with unflattering speed and walked away. 'I will.' She thought she heard him mutter, 'I should lock the door. She needs a keeper.' Then, even more to himself, 'Bloody fool.'

Katherine spent the next day in bed, her headache diminishing as the bruises from the fall flowered into purple glory.

Elspeth lectured her on imprudence in between dosing her with bitter willow-bark tea and dabbing the bruises with arnica. She reported that Ravenham was out of temper, Mr Gresham appeared to have pulled himself together and had gone out visiting tenants all by himself and Mrs Goodman had hired five women and two men from the village and set them to cleaning the chapel.

'It is beginning to look rather fine now that the men have gone up ladders to clean the windows and have dusted the ceiling and beams. They even found some charming medieval floor tiles in what must have been the Lady Chapel. I have begun making altar cloths from linen and some brocade curtains. The kneelers are in a deplorable state. Mice, no doubt. Perhaps the kitchen cat...'

Katherine let it all wash over her as she lay there, turning over and over in her mind what she would do when she found the evidence that Lovell had fabricated the charges of dealing with the French enemy against her father.

The first thing would be to send it somewhere safe where he couldn't find it. But then... Her father had not been charged with any crime, so appealing to the Lord Chancellor to have a conviction overturned was irrelevant. It had been a civil case and it was Papa's reputation that had been destroyed.

There were newspapers that were radical in sympathy and might well take up the case provided they were confident they had proof—standing up to a marquis was not for a faint-hearted editor who feared charges of libel. Several editors had ended up in the stocks for that.

Or she could confront Lovell. Threaten him with exposure and demand that he make a public retraction of his 'evidence' against her father. That might be the better course—then she had the newspapers to fall back on if he refused.

It would mean standing up to him, of course, and she quailed inwardly at the thought. But, she told herself, she would draw on her anger and that would give her strength.

And, in the meantime, she must constantly remind herself just who she was dealing with and not allow herself to drift into a kind of friendship with her employer. Or allow herself to look at him as an attractive man, one she wanted in the most basic of ways.

* * *

For the next week Will felt as though he was living in the midst of a hurricane, which was decidedly strange, as the household was beginning to run like clockwork around him.

Men arrived to remove the crated statues destined for the salerooms, gardeners cleared and repaired the terraces to the extent that many of the less valuable statues could be moved outside, rooms opened up.

His chaplain, his secretary and his steward seemed intent on bombarding him with decisions to be made until he snapped and ordered them to talk to each other.

Gresham could liaise with Arnley and Mrs Goodman over what the tenants needed in terms of repairs and assistance, he declared. Wilmott could talk to everyone and draft advertisements for whatever positions were still to be filled. Mrs Downe—who he really must speak to about recompensing her for her efforts—and Mrs Goodman could supervise the cleaning and reordering of the various rooms and deal with the textiles.

And somewhere in the centre of this whirlwind was Kat and it felt as though she was the axis on which everything spun, leaving him like some cog that somehow did not mesh with the machinery. Yet he still gave the orders, the staff still deferred to him and he hardly saw Kat except at meals and morning prayers.

Was she avoiding him? She professed that she was quite recovered, had no headache and needed to work.

Finally, he took himself off to ride alone through the parkland, letting Ajax have his head, trusting the horse's intelligence and sure-footed stride to keep them out of trouble.

When he set off he told himself he would look for the second lake that showed on the estate plans, somewhere off towards the low hill crowned by a building with a hole in its roof. Then he promptly forgot about it in thoughts of Kat. When Ajax skidded to a halt with a snort, his front hooves sunk into a muddy bog, Will almost went over his head.

He had found the lake or, more accurately, its ghost, a small pond in the middle of a reed bed. Will surveyed it with a sigh. More expense to get this clear.

Turning Ajax, who was mincing disdainfully through the mud like a society lady suddenly finding herself in a puddle, he looked back the way he had come and saw where a stream must run from this bog towards the house. It would join up with the lake that the moat drained into and would make a handsome feature through this valley.

Add landscape gardener to the list.

But the work would create a great deal of employment for the local men and that was important. He must remember to think like a landowner, someone with responsibilities to the community, and not like a lawyer with one hand tight on the purse strings.

Will guided Ajax around the edge of the reed bed, making for the folly. At least, he assumed it was intended as a *faux* ruined temple and wasn't simply a copy of one that had been allowed to tumble into disrepair by neglect.

The latter, he discovered as he reached it and swung down from the saddle, leaving Ajax to crop the grass that grew long and lush around it.

It was a little circular building with an arcade of Classical columns surrounding a central drum-shaped room, clearly copied from etchings of Roman temples. The double doors creaked open when he pushed at them and pigeons flapped up in a panic as he found himself standing in the rubble where part of the domed roof had fallen in.

It was a mess now, but it would be a delightful spot with a view down the valley over the lake if both it and the watercourse were restored. And, he realised, it was another location where the statues, of which he still seemed to have an unnecessary number, could be placed.

Which brought him back to thinking about Kat. Will sat on the low platform that supported the ring of columns and stared out towards the chimneys of the Hall that could just be seen above the trees.

He had kissed her once. A mistake that had haunted

him ever since, with guilt for taking advantage of someone in his household and a nagging desire to do it again. And again. And more.

Perhaps she had sensed that when he had carried her upstairs and that was why she was avoiding him now. He did not think he had let his feelings show, but Kat, even through a headache, was probably sensitive to atmosphere. She might be a virgin, but she was not naive.

She had accused him of having to be an actor as a lawyer. Perhaps that was true. Whether it was or not, he had to act now as though he was completely indifferent to her as a woman. In a few months she would be out of his life, because he could not imagine that his new marchioness, whoever she might be, would be accepting of a female librarian with the same status in the household as his secretary or chaplain.

The mental image of this unknown lady was vague in his mind, her face hazy, although for some reason she had brown hair. She would be organised, efficient, raised to manage the demands of an aristocratic household and the social life that went with her rank.

Will realised that up to that point he had been thinking about this theoretical wife in much the same way he would have done about a court case that was still some way in the future. He had been making preliminary lists of actions to carry out, research to be done.

This unknown young woman who would take his

name, bear his children, was a cipher, an object to be obtained, and he suddenly felt ashamed of that. And then irritated with himself.

What was he supposed to do? As plain William Lovell, barrister, he had been free to choose a wife, follow his inclinations and fancy, although she would be intelligent, from much the same background as he was himself, able to entertain and to support a man rising in his career.

Now he was constrained by rank and duty. He could curse his cousins for their recklessness, leaving him shackled to the title and all that went with it.

He got to his feet, grinning ruefully at his own thoughts. There would be few other men who would be so ungrateful as to resent a high title, estate, wealth— if there was any of it left in the coffers by the time he had beaten his inheritance into shape.

Having to restrict his choice of bride to a small circle of eligible ladies was a small price to pay for all that, surely?

From her sitting room window Kat watched the rider on the grey horse cantering back towards the house. She had come upstairs to wash her hands and tidy her hair before luncheon and had been feeling decidedly pleased with herself.

The library was now in a state where all that was needed was for Lovell to decide what he wanted to keep and what was to be disposed of. There was space for anything else that was found scattered around the house and her draft catalogue was complete. Now she was free to search all day, every day, until she found the ruby and the documents that related to it.

Now, the sight of Lovell upset her equilibrium, as it did every time she encountered him. It was as though she was a piece of paper that had been torn neatly down the middle. On each side was a picture of Katherine Jones, alias Jenson, but one of those Katherines wanted to expose William Lovell for what he had done to her family. The other Katherine simply wanted him.

She had been avoiding him because of this, she was well aware. That must stop, because she did not want him to suspect that anything was wrong, that she was anything but what she should be—a hard-working expert set on ordering the chaotic collections he had inherited.

Katherine willed the corners of her mouth to turn up in a faint smile and opened the sitting room door.

The small dining room was empty when she reached it, but Elspeth joined her after a few minutes, followed by Mr Gresham and Giles Wilmott. They were deep in a discussion of the restoration of the chapel when Lovell came in, seeming to bring with him a breath of fresh air and the scent of the outdoors, despite the fact that he had changed from breeches and riding boots to pantaloons and Hessians and had donned a different coat.

When he had helped himself from the sideboard and taken his seat, Katherine said brightly,' I saw you riding back just now. What a very fine horse that is.'

He seemed slightly taken aback at her smile, but answered readily enough. 'Ajax? Yes, a fortunate purchase. A grateful client was selling him and gave me first refusal.'

'Were you exploring the estate or visiting tenants?' she asked.

'I had not intended to do more than take a ride at random, but I have discovered an upper lake and what might be a rather charming building—an eyecatcher. Or it will be charming, when it has been repaired. There are holes in the roof and it needs cleaning.'

'A sham castle, perhaps?' Elspeth asked. 'Or a hermit's cave?'

'No, this is a little circular temple with a view down the valley towards the lower lake. It would make an excellent summer house for picnics when I begin to entertain. I thought it might be a suitable location for some of the superabundance of statuary.'

'What a good idea and, as it is not a hermitage, you are saved the expense of employing a hermit to live in it,' Katherine said with a perfectly straight face.

'Do people really go to those lengths?' he asked,

knife poised over some cold salmon. 'I had assumed it was a joke.'

'Oh, no, there are at least three that I know of. Pa— Er…someone I was acquainted with in the antiquities trade was employed to find suitable pieces of ruined churches—small windows and so forth—for one and, when he arrived to supervise their setting, he found there was already a hermit in residence and he knew of two others.'

Goodness, she had almost blurted out *Papa* just then. And then it would be no great feat to discover which landowners had real hermits in their employ and the names of the advisors on the design of their dwellings.

But there is no reason for Lovell to do that. Not unless he is suspicious of me, Katherine reassured herself.

'Thinking about follies and restoring silted-up lakes—I assume it is silted? Yes, of course, it would be—must be a great change for you, Lovell. You will miss the cut and thrust of the courtroom, I imagine' she said, anxious to steer him away from her slip of the tongue.

'Yes,' he agreed, apparently not offended by the personal question. 'I enjoyed the research before the case came to court and the interest of the adversarial contest. One has to think on one's feet, literally, and there is little of that here.'

'You clients will be sad to lose you,' Elspeth said, unwittingly helping Katherine, who was wondering how to probe further.

'My partners continue the practice,' Lovell said. 'I shall retain an interest, but no longer be actively involved. Which reminds me, I must find a secure room to house the files of cases relating to the estate. I have just instructed the clerk to send them here.'

Katherine suppressed her smile of delight and covered her smile by taking a mouthful of lemonade. That would save her having to search for any documents that the late Marquis kept here, or, at least, made finding them less urgent, because, surely, what she would need to confront Lovell with his libel of her father would be with the legal documents. The old Marquis would have kept the real receipt, she reminded herself ,and she still needed to find that.

'I believe you have a proper muniments room,' she said. 'There will be many old documents, files of papers and so forth, that are no longer in use. It will all be stored together and would be the perfect place for your legal records.'

'I believe it has been locked up ever since the previous archivist died there,' Giles said.

They all stared at him and he hastened to add, 'He isn't in there! He was buried, of course.'

'Do show me later, if you would,' Katherine said. 'It would be best to check that it is as fireproof as possible. It needs to be secure, but accessible, with all the essential records kept together, so that if there is a fire, they can be removed quickly to safety.'

'It is in the basement,' Giles said. 'Just before the strongroom.'

'That is excellent. If I find anything that I think should be in there I can take it directly.'

He blinked at her eagerness and Katherine realised she might have let her delight in what everyone else would think a very dull and mundane subject show.

'Please pass the butter,' she said hastily.

Chapter Fifteen

After luncheon Katherine inspected the room Giles had described and agreed it was ideal, although much in need of tidying and dusting. But there was a table and some spare shelves and two keys.

Giles gave her one. 'You might as well keep this as you will be the person putting most items in there, I imagine,' he remarked, putting the other back on his key ring along with the one for the strongroom.

Katherine had made a point of not asking for one for that because she wanted to establish a clear pattern of seeking out valuables and then bringing them to be secured. Building up a trust that, she was very well aware, she intended to betray.

But it is justified, she told herself as she marked off yet another downstairs room on her plan of the house and carried a small trove of valuables along to Giles.

'Some silver, but not the chapel silver, I'm afraid,' she said. 'And these are some rather nice Italian micromosaics. I've found a folder of family genealogies. That can go in the muniments room.'

'What progress are you making?' The deep voice from right behind her had Katherine spinning around. She lost her balance and had to be caught by Lovell.

'Goodness, you made me jump!'

His hands were still resting on her arms just above the elbows where he had steadied her, not holding, merely making her feel as though they were resting against bare skin.

'Progress? Let me show you my plan.' That gave her an excuse to move away slightly and unfold it on the desk. 'You see? I have ticked off each room I have searched and made a note of what items of furniture remain and what I think the original purpose of the room was.'

'Excellent progress,' Lovell said. 'But you haven't found what you are searching for yet, have you?'

Whatever was the matter with Kat? She was staring at him as though he had grown another head.

'What? I—'

Damnation, I have alarmed her again by grabbing hold of her.

She out up a hand as though to brush back a lose strand of hair and Will was momentarily distracted by the way the light brought out hidden golden highlights.

He moved back a couple of steps. 'The chapel silver,' he explained. 'There ought to be a chalice and a paten and a jug at the very least, surely? You mentioned it the other day. And the candlesticks, of course. I must bring down the ones from my bedchamber and you can see if they are suitable.'

'Oh, of course. I am sorry, I was confused because I am attempting to find everything portable of value. The candlesticks would be brass, I believe, if they date back to before your cousin's time so, if the ones from your chamber are large, then they may well be from the church.'

Kat seemed to be talking almost at random and he wondered if she was still suffering the after-effects of the blow to her head.

'You should get outside,' he said abruptly. 'Out in the fresh air.' He saw her cast a glance out of the window and added, 'Not now, it is becoming overcast. But tomorrow, if the weather is fine. Do you ride as well as drive?'

'Why, yes, although it has been some time.'

'Then we will ride out tomorrow and I will show you the little eyecatcher temple. There is a very steady mare in the stables. It looks as though it would be a positive armchair ride, so you need have no anxieties about another fall.'

'Ah, I see what it is,' Kate remarked in a rallying tone, seeming to recover from her moment of imbalance. 'Not so much a holiday for me but work to be done assessing your folly.'

Will winced inwardly. It was not a building that was his folly, he was well aware. It was becoming too attached to his librarian for propriety. Or wisdom.

'But of course,' he said, echoing her tone. 'I will be a positive tyrant until we get more of those confounded statues out of the house.'

'Very well, provided you really can find me a ride that is prepared to tolerate a sack of potatoes on its back.'

'Having had you sitting on me when poor Wilmott was being swallowed by the moat, I am sure the cob will be able to cope.'

Now I have made her blush. I used to have a sure touch with women. What has changed?

'After breakfast then, Kat?'

'Very well. After breakfast tomorrow.' She glanced at the old-fashioned German clock on the wall. 'Now I have just time to finish the next room this afternoon. It is more of a closet than anything and shouldn't take me long.'

She smiled at them both and left the room, once more neat, composed and industrious.

Will realised he was still staring at the closed door when Wilmott cleared his throat.

'Sir?'

'Yes? Sorry, I was brooding on the pair of brass

candlesticks in my bedchamber.' His secretary was looking blank. 'From the chapel.'

'Oh, yes, sir. I believe Miss Jenson is quite correct and most churches had brass. It isn't something one notices, but I seem to recall...'

Will stopped listening, thinking instead of what he would take with them to the folly. A sketchbook, perhaps, so he could draft out some thought about landscaping the lakes from the viewpoint of the temple. A rug to sit on, some refreshments. It would not do to have Kat getting overtired.

'I'll just go down to the stables,' he said, cutting across whatever Wilmott was saying. Something about drains? 'I want to make certain that mare is as reliable as it looks.'

Her riding habit was at least three years' out of date and possibly had moth holes, Katherine thought as she made her way to her next room. But that hardly mattered. This would be a ride over rough parkland on an old cob, not Rotten Row at the fashionable hour, and the last thing she wanted to do was look dashing or attractive.

The door, when she reached it, opened on to a windowless space and it was hard to see what its original function might have been. Now it was a store cupboard for items that looked more suited to below stairs.

Katherine began to carry out brooms, buckets, long poles with feathers on the end which must be cobweb dusters, a box of clean rags that someone had thriftily hoarded for cleaning and which seemed to have been home to several generations of mice, and several useful small stepladders. Of course, staff not wanting to carry cleaning equipment up and down stairs might well have found this hidey-hole, confident that the old Marquis wouldn't care.

She could have done with those stepladders when she and Lovell were trapped behind the statues, she thought, carrying the last one out.

That just left a very dusty Buhl cabinet. A rub with one of the rags showed fine inlaid woods and brass and it certainly did not deserve to be hidden away there.

The curved double doors at the front opened with a reluctant creak to reveal six shelves stuffed with small boxes.

Jewellery boxes. Katherine's heart seemed to jolt inside her. Had she found the dragon's hoard of gems?

It was hard to resist simply sweeping everything off the shelves and opening each one, scrabbling through until she found the ruby, but caution stopped her. Everything must seem open and above board—she must hide the thing in plain sight.

What she needed was to carry all the boxes through to a table in one of the rooms she had already searched, lay them all out and list them. Then everything could be taken to the strongroom and she would make a great deal of the discovery—of everything except the Borgia Ruby which would never reach the strongroom.

If it was there…

The disappointing thing was that there appeared to be no paperwork with the boxes. Somehow, she was going to have to get into the files that Lovell's clerk was sending from London. But that could wait. She needed a large tray, or a box—

A cry of pain and the crash of falling objects made her leap to her feet and run to the door to find George the footman entangled in the buckets and brooms she had taken out.

'Are you hurt?' She helped him to his feet. 'I am so sorry, I should have realised that anyone coming around the corner would fall over these things.'

'I'm quite all right, Miss. I wasn't looking where I was going.' He dusted down his livery and peered at what surrounded him. 'Where did these come from?'

'Out of this little room. When you are recovered, George, please will you see they are taken below stairs and added to the cleaning equipment there?'

'Of course, Miss.'

'What the blazes?' It was Lovell, Giles at his heels. 'I heard what sounded like someone dropping several suits of armour from a great height.'

George scooped up an armful of brooms and hurried off, leaving Katherine to face the men over a fallen stepladder and half a dozen rather dented buckets.

'I have discovered a large number of jewellery boxes,' she announced. 'And I would welcome some assistance in carrying them to a room with a table.'

'Buckets,' Lovell said, picking two up and handing them to her. 'You fill them, we will carry them.'

Breathe. In plain sight, she told herself, taking them and turning back to the cabinet. *Show no interest, make this seem ordinary.*

'Thank you. The second room along to the right has a table that would be suitable.' Katherine made herself start filling the pails without studying the boxes and handed out the first two as the dressing gong rang.

'If we can clear them before we go to change for dinner, then I can lock the door,' she said brightly, taking the next bucket from Giles. The timing was perfect, both men in too much of a hurry to be tempted to open the boxes or take much interest in them.

'This is rather a nice cabinet,' she added as a further distraction. 'Buhl, of high quality. Shall I have it moved to the drawing room? It would look rather well in there once it has been polished.'

Lovell, taking the final bucket from her, nodded as he passed it to Giles. 'Certainly.' He regarded her quizzically. 'I have to tell you, Kat, that you have a smudge on the end of your nose and your skirts look as though you have been using them as dusters.'

When she gave her nose a swipe with one hand and shook out her skirts with the other, he added, 'Run and change for dinner. We will lock these away for you.'

There was no way to protest that she wanted to do it without appearing suspicious. 'Thank you,' she said with a smile and turned away, then added over her shoulder, 'Just leave them as they are—the buckets were quite dry and the boxes will come to no harm.'

Dinner was purgatory. Katherine itched to go and examine the jewellery boxes, search through them for the Borgia Ruby—there had been at least a dozen cases that would have fitted it—but instead found herself making polite conversation about the desirability of whitewashing the interior of the chapel and whether Mr Gresham should use his travelling communion set in the chapel in the hope that the original pieces would be found in the house or whether a new set should be ordered.

'You could write to the Goldsmiths' Company in London to ask for a recommendation,' Katherine suggested to Lovell. 'They must have members who specialise in church silver. Or I can make enquiries among my contacts and see if there is an old set on the market, if you prefer.'

'Neither,' he said decisively. 'I know exactly what

would happen—the moment I have committed to considerable expense, the originals will turn up in this madman's attic of a house.'

'Very true, my lord. I agree that all efforts should be made to find the original vessels and my small set is quite adequate for now,' Gresham said earnestly. 'I am happy to say that, thanks to the efforts of Mrs Goodman and her workers in cleaning and the repair work that has been carried out, I can hold our first service this coming Sunday. I must also thank Mrs Downe for creating a most handsome altar cloth. I believe the chapel will present a very decent appearance.'

Katherine tried to reply appropriately and join in with the conversation as it turned to the chaplain's visits to the tenants and the good news that he had found no cases of severe want.

'What a relief,' she said vaguely, her mind on the ruby. She could not go and search through the jewellery boxes that evening. She had never worked after dinner before now and doing so now would only draw attention to her. She could ask for the room key and then search late at night, she supposed, but that would be impossible to explain if anyone found her. Lovell had said he was a light sleeper, she reminded herself.

It would have to be in the morning, a rapid search and then when she had located it, she could go to the library and be observed placidly cataloguing books.

* * *

'I went to the stables to look over that mare I had mentioned as a nice quiet ride for you, Kat,' Will said as the soup plates were removed and the fish course brought in.

She stared at him blankly and it seemed for a moment that she was a hundred miles away and wondering who on earth he was.

'For our expedition to the temple folly after breakfast,' he said patiently and saw her gaze sharpen and focus.

'Oh, yes, of course. Forgive me, I was—'

'Miles away?' he suggested.

'No, not at all. I was quite definitely *here,* but I was making mental lists of things to be done tomorrow and had quite forgotten the temple,' she said, smiling.

Something in the very brightness of Kat's tone did not ring true and Will glanced at her sharply. For a second as their eyes met, hers widened, then the shutters seemed to come down and Kat was once again the perfect young lady with a demure smile and, apparently, not a thought in her head beyond small talk.

Will found himself strangely affected and it took him a moment to work out why. Desire was there, of course, that flash of unwilling attraction that he felt whenever he was close to her. And the answering spark that made him think that it was mutual, however careful she was not to show it.

But the strange sense he had that Kat disliked him, despite that attraction—that had gone and what he had seen in her eyes just then had been impatience, quickly veiled.

Not impatience to be in his arms, that was for sure, he thought. He watched her shift her position as though to make herself more comfortable on the rather hard dining chair and in the process moving so that she was angled away from him. Their eyes would not meet now if they both glanced up at the same time. Was that deliberate?

The others at the table were engrossed in a vehement discussion about some aspect of parish relief, from what he could make out. That was what happened when one put a clergyman, a clergyman's widow and a man responsible for keeping an eye on his employer's expenditure together, he supposed.

'But you must agree, Giles, that it is the responsibility of landowners to support the needy in the communities on their estates,' Mrs Downe was saying.

'Yes, but all those in prosperous situations in each parish should also have an obligation—'

Abruptly Will turned away again. Nobody was going to go hungry in any parish or estate where he had a responsibility and that was enough for him.

He looked at Kat's profile. She was carefully probing her fish for bones, her profile giving nothing away.

On impulse he said, 'Why do you dislike me, Kat?'

She dropped her knife on to the plate with a clatter and made a business of picking it up again.

'Dislike you? What an extraordinary question, Lovell!' She put down her knife and fork as though giving up on the fish. 'What have I ever said to give you that impression?'

'Nothing,' he admitted.

It isn't what you say.

'Well then. My goodness, but this fish is difficult. Tasty, but as bony as a kipper. I declare it has defeated me.'

Will tried it and found himself unable to speak through a mouthful of bones. Once he had dealt with them it occurred to him that not only had Kat not answered his question, she had not refuted the statement either.

Miss Jenson's thought processes were proving as obscure as the waters in what remained of his lakes was muddy.

Chapter Sixteen

It was a long night and, when Katherine could snatch at sleep, the dreams crowded in on her.

Why do you dislike me, Kat? Lovell asked himself, looking at her out of a strange fog, the Borgia Ruby pinned to his coat over where his heart would be, the stone seeming to pulse like blood. Then, as she reached for the stone, he had faded back into the mist and there was just his voice echoing faintly. *Why... why...why...*

Katherine came down heavy-eyed to breakfast early the next morning in her old riding habit and ate a hasty meal with Elspeth for the look of it, almost quivering with impatience. She would forget the dreams, forget Lovell. Only one thing mattered.

'I will just run along to see Giles for a moment,' she said. 'If Lovell comes, tell him I assume it is at nine o'clock that he wants to ride out and I will meet him at the front of the house then. There are one or two things I want to check up on first.'

She found Giles standing in the study sorting through the post which had just arrived.

'Good morning. Could you let me have the key to the room we locked those jewellery boxes away in last night? Only, I woke in the night with a positive conviction that, although the buckets were dry, there might have been rough surfaces which would damage the boxes, and that would be such a pity.'

She smiled at him, positively radiating fussy female anxiety, and Giles dug the key out of his pocket.

'Yes, of course. Keep it.' He handed it to her, his attention already back on the opened letter in his other hand. 'What the devil is this about, do you think? It appears to have been written by a drunken spider during a thunderstorm.'

'Try it the other way up,' Katherine suggested, already halfway to the door, pursued by Giles's snort of exasperation.

Her hand shook as she turned the key in the room where the men had stored the jewellery cases, half afraid it had all been a dream and she hadn't found them after all. But there they were, a prosaic row of four domestic buckets, incongruously brim-full of small cases and boxes. There was fine Morocco leather in a rainbow of colours, shagreen, plain polished wood, metal...

Katherine tipped the nearest bucket out on the table, rapidly pushing the contents around to sort them. Small ring boxes here; the thin, flat ones that would hold necklaces there; larger ones for parures of jewels… Nothing was the right size for the Borgia Ruby.

If she could only recall the box when Papa had brought it home… But she had been too excited to look at the jewel itself and she had hardly registered the case it came in.

Another heap, then another. One bucket left. She emptied that, pushing aside the precious contents with a haste that she would never normally have shown.

And suddenly, there it was. A scuffed, dark blue leather case, large enough to fill the palm of her hand, domed to a height of about two and a half inches and secured with an elaborate, and clearly very old, catch.

She scrabbled at it, broke a fingernail and made herself stop. The box was an historic artefact, too, original, part of the provenance of the jewel, and she was in danger of damaging it.

Katherine took a deep breath, put the box down carefully and waited for her hands to become steady. She reached for it again.

'There you are, Kat.'

It was impossible that her heart could have leapt up and lodged in her throat, but something seemed to have done so. With an effort that made her dizzy, Katherine reached out and lifted two other boxes of much the same domed shape and placed them next to the ruby's box. Then she turned.

'I could not resist gloating over such a hoard,' she said with a light laugh—a triumph considering that she seemed to have no air in her lungs. 'And I had a foolish fear—you know the way worries strike you at three in the morning?—that the buckets might be rough inside and would have damaged the cases. But all is well. Is it time for our ride?'

Lovell barely glanced at the table. He certainly did not seem greedy for gemstones.

Winning, control, that is what matters to him, Katherine reminded herself. *Not so very different from his cousin, only with Lovell all is rational, sane and orderly.*

'Yes, the horses are ready, if you are.'

'Oh, I expect I can drag myself away,' Katherine said, following him out and locking the door behind her. When Lovell strode off in front of her, she slid the key down inside her habit shirt, snug under the edge of her stays. She had the ruby now, that was all that mattered. That and finding the documents relating to it.

There was something different about Kat that morning, Will thought, as they trotted away from the house and turned on to the track that led to the folly.

There was an excitement about her that he could sense fizzing under her usual calm demeanour. It was not anything she said—she had not spoken since thanking him for boosting her into the saddle—nor even something in her expression. Her face showed nothing except mild pleasure at being out in the open air.

He was becoming sensitive to her mood, he realised, and the thought made him uneasy. He was already finding her too attractive for comfort, or propriety, and he did not want to consider what this awareness indicated about his feelings for Kat.

For Miss Jenson. For my librarian. For my employee.

'Is your mount to your liking?' he asked abruptly, more for something to break the silence than for any concern that she was having difficulties. The mare was moving easily and he could see Kat's confidence in her relaxed hand on the reins and her gaze, sweeping over the view and not tensely focused on the path ahead.

'She is delightful and a very easy ride. Is she one of your cousin's horses that you retained when you inherited?'

'Yes, I thought she would be suitable for my—for any lady visitors.'

He almost said, *my wife,* because that had been in the back of his mind when he had made the selection of which animals to keep. He could have achieved a good price for her, but the mare's breeding and manners made her an ideal mount for a lady of status. A marchioness.

Or for the contrary female at his side. She might be out of practice, as she had said, but Kat had a natural grace in the saddle and a firm but gentle hand on the reins.

'Look, there is the folly ahead now.' He pointed to where it was just visible and Kat brought the mare in close alongside Ajax who sidled a little, showing off to the mare, Will supposed.

'Steady,' he said to the horse. 'She's not interested in you, you fool.'

He might do well to apply his own words to himself, he thought, as Kat gave a little snort of amusement. The mare ignored Ajax with as much uninterest as her rider habitually showed the stallion's master.

'Will you breed from her?' she asked. 'These two would make a fine pair.'

'I had not given it any thought,' he said shortly, shifting slightly in the saddle and trying to think of some remark that would get them off the subject of mating.

'Did you say there is a lake here?' Kat asked, to his relief. She shaded her eyes, peering ahead at the long grass and scrubby bushes that lay between them and the temple on its little hill.

'It was a lake, but it is about as impressive as a village duckpond at the moment. I almost rode straight into the marsh surrounding it. In fact… Yes, here is where I had to turn.'

Kat followed him as Ajax, still with the air of a cat who had been dropped in a muddy puddle, picked his way through the boggy ground to the foot of the hill.

'It is going to be an incredible amount of work to clear this,' she observed when she could ride alongside him again. 'But I imagine the employment will be very much welcomed in the village and all around and the effect of two lakes between here and the hall will be magnificent.'

'It would put your little boating pond in the old moat in the shade,' he said, straight-faced but intending to tease.

'That will be *romantic*,' Kat retorted.

'*I* am *not* romantic.'

Again, that slight, barely ladylike, snort of amusement which he was finding perversely endearing.

'I know,' she said. 'You are a lawyer to the bone.'

'And lawyers are never romantic?' Will demanded. What was the matter with him? Were they flirting?

'Oh, I suppose there are some,' she said airily. 'Noble, idealistic types who set out to defend the innocent and right wrongs. I imagine you would have to be a romantic to try to do that, given the way that our legal system works.'

'Here is the folly,' Will snapped quite unnecessarily as they had arrived in front of it.

'Now this is delightful.' Kat kicked her foot out of the stirrup and slid to the ground without waiting for him to dismount and help her. She had tossed the reins over a bush and was running up the steps on to the circular platform ringing the temple before he had reached the ground.

He was not going to chase after her, damn it. Will took the mare's reins and led both horses into the shady spot he had found before, loosened their girths and tied them so they could crop the lush grass.

When he returned there was no sign of Kat, but the doors stood open. He found her inside gazing around.

'The roof is the priority,' she said without turning as his boots crunched over the broken plaster on the floor. 'Once that is fixed all it will need is cleaning and a coat of limewash.'

'White?'

'No, more a stone colour, as it was originally.'

Yes, ma'am. Your orders have been noted, ma'am.

'What is this door?'

'I have no idea.' To be honest he hadn't noticed it before.

Kat had already opened it and disappeared inside. 'Oh, how ingenious,' she called. 'There's a little scullery on one side and a privy on the other. This place was clearly designed as a summer house for picnics. Come and see.'

Will pretended he hadn't heard and went out again.

His interest in inspecting sculleries, let alone privies, was limited and he had no intention of finding himself in a confined space with Kat.

She found him again after a few minutes, still bouncing with enthusiasm. 'This is perfect. We can have statues all around this plinth looking out between the pillars. That should take care of virtually everything left in the house and will finish this to perfection.'

'I had thought a mown area in front.' He gestured down to the gentle slope that ran from the steps for perhaps ten feet before it became steeper and plunged down towards the bog. *Lake*, he reminded himself.

'And some seats to go around up here against the wall.' Kat gestured vaguely behind herself. 'They will need to be curved, but quite simple in style, I think. Nothing beyond the abilities of the estate carpenters. The interior needs some furniture too. Day beds, perhaps, and a dining table and chairs.'

Will's imagination leapt at the thought of day beds, of making love in this secluded place with the doors thrown open to the sunlight. Or by moonlight. There might be nightingales…

'I shall assess the best position for the mown area,' he announced and, before his brain supplied pictures to go with the imaginings, jumped down to ground level and strode off to where he had left the horses.

He came back with the saddlebags he had ordered

to be packed with food and drink and the large blanket that had been rolled up and strapped behind.

When she saw what he was doing Kat ran down the steps and helped him spread it out. She sat down in the middle, jumped up and moved it a foot to the right. 'That's perfect now. Perhaps a little terrace could be cut here. Just look at the view.'

Will sat, too, carefully keeping to the far end of the blanket. He pulled one of the saddlebags towards him and took out the sketch pad and pencil it contained, sitting with one knee up as a makeshift easel.

He was going to need someone with expertise in moving earth and directing rivers, he thought, drawing as best he could the lie of the land and then cross-hatching where he imagined the restored lake would go.

What would happen to all the mud dredged from the marshy areas and how long before the scars of the work healed? What would this bride he was planning to bring home next year make of a landscape that looked as though a major battle had been fought over it?

But then, the daughter of an aristocratic house would understand about the need to improve the estate, create a fine park and grounds. Many of the famous grand landscaped parks still had not matured into the form their designers had projected decades ago. Aristocrats built and planted for their heirs, he reminded himself.

Which brought him back to the reason for marrying—practical considerations. It was hardly as though he was planning on making a love match and needed a romantic hideaway to bring his bride to.

As he thought it Kat said, 'Why did you ask me that last night?'

'What?' He dropped his pencil and scrabbled for it in a tangle of blanket fringe and dry grass.

'You asked me why I disliked you. What have I ever said that made you think such a thing?'

'You never have—unless it was to show your mistrust of lawyers generally. No, it is the way you look at me sometimes,' he admitted, carefully not glancing at her as he spoke. 'Obviously it was my imagination,' he lied, convinced it was no such thing.

'I can be judgemental,' Kat admitted. 'Perhaps it shows in my expression. You have many admirable qualities, Lovell.'

'I do?' Surprised, he turned to look at her and saw amusement and, under that, a steady, unsettling, watchfulness.

'You have intelligence, a willingness to work hard, occasional humour. You treat your staff well, you take your responsibilities seriously.'

'I thank you for such a glowing report,' he said, torn between being flattered and nettled. 'And what is there in the balance in my disfavour?'

'You are a lawyer,' she said simply, her gaze steady

on the long view down the valley. 'And like all lawyers, you persecuted those less strong, simply at the
whim of your employer.'

'We are back to my regrettable lack of romance, I
assume.'

'You cannot help it, I expect,' she said in a kindly
tone. 'It must be like having red hair, or blue eyes.'

As he opened his mouth to retort she flopped back
on the blanket, staring upwards.

'Look how lovely the sky is this morning. What
kind of clouds are those?'

'I have no idea.' To his surprise Will found he was
lying down, too, the sketch pad at his side, the pages
ruffling in the light, warm breeze. 'You will have to
ask a librarian, if you can find one, and they will look
it up. Surely there is a book on the subject.'

She gave a little gasp of laughter and suddenly he
found his irritation ebb away. It *was* a beautiful morning, the sky was blue with those strange little white
clouds, looking as though cherubs were blowing puffs
from celestial pipes. This place belonged to him and,
just now, he was lying on a blanket in the open air
with bird song all around and an attractive—if con-
fusing—woman next to him.

Something touched his hand and Will realised that
he had reached out, and so had Kat, at the same moment. Their fingers brushed, curled together, clung.

He turned his head slowly and found that she was

looking at him, those hazel eyes a deep and rather lovely green that seemed to catch both sunshine and shadows and trap them there in fathomless depths.

'Those are not the eyes of a woman who dislikes me,' he said.

'No,' she agreed after a moment, her voice a little strained. 'But they may be the eyes of one who is having very dangerous thoughts.'

Already his body was heavy with need, tight with the effort to control it. Will rolled on to his side, facing her. 'Irresistible thoughts?'

'I hope not,' Kat said seriously but, as she spoke, she curled over towards him, her free hand reaching to touch his cheek. 'But we could find out?' she added, frowning, as though confused by her own words.

Will caught her in his arms, rolled so that he was above her, his weight on his elbows, his body cradled between her thighs, his legs tangled in the folds of her habit.

A foolish garment for seduction, he thought, then told himself that he was not in the business of seducing virgins and, surely, Kat was one—and what the devil was he doing now in that case?

Satisfying my curiosity, a wicked little voice in his head said, nudging aside his conscience.

And satisfying hers as well, it seemed. Kat's mouth opened, warm and generous under his, and she wrapped her arms around his shoulders, her fingers exploring the nape of his neck in a way that had him exerting every ounce of self-control in an effort not to rip at the fastenings of her jacket.

Will thrust with his tongue and, after a tiny start of surprise, she answered him, hers tangling and challenging in return, bold and brave and, he realised as he sank into the glorious warm femininity of her— innocent.

Yes, she knew what this was about, but it was new to her and he should stop now.

Now, he reminded himself, perhaps a minute later as his hand found her right breast and she sighed into his mouth. *Now, while you still can.*

Will rolled away and lay panting, half on, half off the blanket.

'That,' he said when he recovered his breath, 'was a very bad idea.'

Chapter Seventeen

Don't stop. Please don't stop.

Katherine sat up and her head spun. She drew up her knees and rested her forehead on them, arms clamped around, as though she could disappear into a tight bundle, somehow safely containing all her tumbling emotions.

I am in love with him.

'That was a very bad idea,' Lovell said, his voice harsh.

Katherine lifted her head, but found she could not look at him. 'Certainly, it was,' she managed to say after a moment.

Was falling in love ever a good idea? This, most definitely, was a disaster.

'I apologise,' he added. It sounded as though he meant it, as though he was regretting those few frantic minutes very much.

'There is no need. It was…mutual.'

There was a kestrel hovering over the marsh below,

focused on something far beneath it. Something small and quivering and fearful, no doubt.

Like my heart.

'You are an innocent. I do not seduce innocents.'

That shook her out of her frozen state and she turned to stare at him 'I am not an innocent. I knew perfectly well what we were doing.'

'In theory, no doubt.' He was lying at the far edge of the blanket now, eyes closed, mouth hard. 'You are a virgin.' It was almost an accusation.

'Yes.'

'And in my employment. My responsibility.'

The kestrel stooped like a bullet and vanished into the tall grasses. Something had probably just died.

Katherine kept her lips tight closed. Anything she said might betray her and she had already betrayed herself, and her father, by falling in love with this man.

Lovell was still speaking and she made herself listen. 'My honour demands that I protect you, not ravish you.'

At which point, mercifully, Katherine lost her temper, although with whom, she could not have said.

'That is, of course, excellent. As long as *your* honour is satisfied, nothing else matters,' she snapped.

He sat up abruptly and they glared at each other.

She swallowed hard, fighting back all the words that were clamouring to be said. Instead she remarked politely, 'Your neckcloth is under your right ear.'

'You have two buttons undone,' he countered, equally helpfully.

Who smiled first, Katherine was never certain. Perhaps it was simultaneous. And then they were laughing.

'We are two healthy adults who, apparently, find each other attractive,' she said when she had recovered herself a little. 'It was not wise to test our willpower like that. Thank you for ending it.'

Lovell ran one hand over his face as though to scrub away his feelings of guilt. 'You are generous. I deserve a slapped face at the very least.'

I love you. No amount of slapping is going to make that right, ever again.

After a moment, Katherine shrugged. 'As I said, we are adults.'

She shuddered to think of the consequences if they had made love. What if Lovell had decided he was honour-bound to offer to marry her? Or he thought that as she was so loose in her morals she should become his mistress? Katherine had no idea which was a worse prospect—to find herself in a marriage brought about solely because of 'duty' or for the man she loved to so misunderstand her as to offer a *carte blanche*.

But now she was in love with her enemy, the man who had ruined her father, the man she had vowed to revenge herself on.

What was the right thing to do? She knew now that

he could be trusted not to take advantage of a woman foolish enough to offer herself to him. Should she tell him about the ruby, have faith that he would accept her father's innocence, his cousin's lies and the part he himself had played in her father's disgrace? Or was she asking too much, blinded by her own feelings for the man?

She must be cautious, she decided. These feelings were too new, too untried. Unreliable. She must secure the ruby, find the papers, be able to prove without doubt to Lovell that she was telling the truth.

'I have a simple picnic in these saddlebags.'

'Perhaps not,' she said, regretful. 'We should go back now, Lovell.'

'Call me Will.'

Katherine got to her feet, careful of the trailing skirts of her habit. 'That would lead to suspicions that our relationship is something it is not.'

He seemed taken aback, as though he had not considered them as part of the household, but as some separate entity. 'You are right. That was thoughtless. You have blurred my mind, but that is my fault, not yours.'

'Perhaps you should recall your mistress,' she suggested, taking one end of the blanket to help him fold and roll it.

'Delphine?' Lovell stopped, the fabric half gathered in his hands, and stared at her. 'You know, I had completely forgotten her.'

'Now that is a difficult feat, I should imagine,' Katherine said drily, collecting up his sketchbook and pencil.

Will grimaced. 'She was exceedingly hard work.'

Will. I wish I could use his name. I like its simplicity.

'But it had its compensations?' she asked, aware how shocking the question was.

'It did,' he admitted. 'But I find I have lost my appetite for over-rich fare. It was like dining at the Regent's dinner table for every meal. But I should not be making such thoroughly improper observations to a lady.'

'Amusing, if improper,' Katherine said, stuffing the sketchbook into the saddlebag and handing it to him.

The horses seemed glad to see them, bored, perhaps by being left so long. The big stallion snorted, stamped one hoof and then butted Lovell with his nose.

'Ajax is impatient,' he observed, tightening the girth, then moving to Katherine's mare to do the same. 'He fancies your mount, but she is not receptive.'

That is not his rider's problem, Katherine thought. *Lovell—Will—finds himself with a female who is all too receptive and he has to exercise self-restraint for both of them.*

She put her booted foot in his cupped hands and was tossed up into the saddle.

'Are you eating properly, Kat?' he demanded as she gathered up the reins and found the stirrup.

'Yes, of course. Why?'

I have not yet reached the stage of pining away for love of you. That may yet come.

'You seem lighter than when I lifted you out of our prison of statues,' Lovell said as he swung up into the saddle.

Katherine averted her eyes from the long, muscled legs. 'There is all the difference between briefly tossing me up to a saddle and having to hold me up for minutes at a time while I trample all over your head and shoulders.'

He gave a snort of amusement. 'Of all the things that I imagined myself doing when I inherited this title, tossing librarians over banisters was not one of them.'

As they rode down the hill in silence Katherine added another good quality to her mental assessment of Lovell's character. Surely virtually any aristocrat in the land who had found himself trapped in such a way would have lost his temper and shouted for help, not scrambled to freedom in a thoroughly undignified and practical manner and then been able to joke about it days later.

The scales she was using to weigh his character were tilting more and more in his favour. Only the lead weight of his treatment of her father kept the balance on the opposite side.

Her father, and who else had he ruined on behalf of

his cousin, the man with the power, the man with the money? The man Lovell himself admitted was not a sane and reasonable person and yet whose orders he had followed, whose interests he had defended.

As soon as they had squelched through the marshy borders of the lake she touched her heel to the mare's side and let her run.

Behind her she heard Lovell curse. Ajax, seeing the object of his desire racing ahead, must have wanted to chase and she suspected that Lovell was in no mood to give him his head. If the master could not satisfy his desires, then he was not going to allow his mount to do so.

Although there the comparison ended. The bay mare was in no mood for the stallion's attentions and, Katherine suspected, any attempts on his part would be met with teeth and hooves. But Lovell had received no assistance from her to control the situation.

She let the mare gallop as far as the carriage drive, then trotted around to the stables where grooms came running to help her down.

'His Lordship is right behind me,' she said over her shoulder as she gathered up her long skirts and strode towards the side door into the house. The ruby was calling to her now, the desire to finally hold it in her hands almost overriding her confusion of feelings about Lovell.

Jeannie was in the dressing room when she reached

her room and tutted as she helped Katherine out of the habit. 'Did you fall off, Miss Katherine? There's dry grass all over the back of this.'

'No, I sat down to admire the view from a hilltop and the grass is untended and rough. Just my plain working dress, please, Jeannie.'

She washed her hands, bundled her hair into a net and made herself walk downstairs calmly.

As she passed the study door, she could hear three male voices and slowed for a moment. It was Giles Wilmott and Mr Arnley the steward reporting progress to Will.

Lovell, you idiot, she chided herself.

'...on the moat. The underbrush is being dragged away and burned, the material they are digging out will be spread on the fields on the upper ground. It is very thin chalk there and that rich silt will benefit the crops considerably...'

Katherine hurried past, the door key tight in her hand, dodging around the dust cloths and trestles that the decorators had set up as they began painting the hallway. She paused for a moment to touch the statue of the charioteer, shrouded in dust cloths.

You know about luck—wish me luck.

At last.

The boxes were just as she had left them and she reached instinctively to close the door. But, no, that would not do. She had always made a point of working in an open room and must do so now. With her back to the opening, she sat and pulled the box towards her.

The antique clasp was complex and stiff and cost her another broken nail before she could release it. The lid with its faded impressed gold ornament opened stiffly and she held her breath.

The interior lined in faded velvet was empty.

Ridiculously, Katherine shook it, as though the jewel might be somehow hiding, but not so much as a gold link fell out. It was definitely the correct box, its interior carefully moulded to hold each element of the ornate piece in place.

With great care she placed it back on the table, then burst into tears. The storm lasted only a moment, then she wiped her eyes, blew her nose and forced herself to think.

The late Marquis would not have sold the ruby without its box—he would know as well as she did the importance of keeping the two things together—so the jewel was still somewhere in the house, perhaps with the papers that related to its acquisition. *To its theft.*

Panicking and flapping about searching everywhere would do no good. It was known she had discovered the collection of jewellery boxes, so she must sort through them, list the contents and take them to the strongroom. Anything else would be highly suspicious.

* * *

Katherine returned to the task after luncheon and, having checked all the boxes that might just have held the Borgia Ruby, had the idea of asking the chaplain to help her as she listed the contents.

'I have noted twenty rings, five sets of necklaces and earrings and two pairs of bracelets so far,' Mr Gresham said after an hour. 'What on earth did a bachelor want with these? Surely, they are not all family pieces?'

'They are a magpie's hoard,' she said. 'He collected for the sake of collecting, of owning. It seems he did not even wish to display what he had acquired— merely to know that he had all this was enough until he had the urge to buy something else.'

'Poor soul,' the chaplain said compassionately. 'An empty life, indeed.'

'Indeed,' Katherine echoed. However, though her feelings about Lovell were shifting and becoming more nuanced, she could not find one ounce of sympathy or forgiveness for his late cousin. And Will Lovell had aided him in all his bullying, spiteful prosecutions.

The two of them carried the first stack of boxes to the strongroom, set out on trays instead of bundled into the buckets, and Giles opened the heavy door for them.

'Did you find anything of interest?' he asked as they

were arranging the final items on the shelves along with Katherine's inventory.

'They all need assessing by a good jeweller—Rundle, Bridge and Rundle, the royal jewellers, for example,' she said. 'I suspect some pieces are very good. If Lovell wants to pay for clearing and landscaping his lakes, then he need look no further than what we have just brought in.'

'A string of pearls for a string of lakes?' It was Lovell, materialising silently behind her.

Katherine fumbled with the last box that she was straightening on the shelf before she turned to him.

'Some of these were empty,' she said, gesturing to the ones she had put at the end. 'Have you any idea what your cousin might have done with the contents? I am rather concerned to think of valuable pieces unprotected by their cases.'

'Well, he didn't lavish them on opera dancers or courtesans,' Lovell said.

Giles cleared his throat. 'Er, he was not interested?'

Katherine knew what he was implying. She'd had an uncle who, her mother had explained, was not 'the marrying kind'.

'No idea,' Lovell said wryly. 'But I suspect that most women aren't prepared to sit around being items in a collection to be gloated over and ignored as human beings. Especially those who were lovely enough to attract his collector's eye. They would have far better prospects with gentlemen of equal wealth who would give them a much better time.'

Mr Gresham cleared his throat and shifted, clearly uncomfortable at the turn the conversation was taking.

Katherine caught Lovell's gaze and saw he was thinking exactly what she was—thank goodness the young cleric had not encountered Delphine de Frayne. She bit her lip to stop the laughter that was bubbling up at the mental image that evoked and Lovell turned away, coughing.

'Come and see the hall, Kat,' he said and strode away without waiting for an answer.

She ran after him and found him around the corner, leaning against the wall and laughing.

'Whatever would Delphine have made of him, do you think?' he managed to choke out after a moment.

'Breakfast,' Katherine said crisply. 'And probably dinner, too. She would have made a dead set at him, just because she could, or because she wanted to make you jealous,' Katherine speculated. 'He is very good looking, after all.'

'He is that attractive?'

'Goodness, yes. An archangel just waiting for a wicked woman to push him over the edge into darkness. I expect that is why the bishop sent him to us—he would be stalked unmercifully in a parish, poor thing.'

I said, sent him to us, *not* to you, she thought, wondering if Lovell had noticed her slip, but, if he had, he made no comment.

'And he is a very nice man. I like him very much,' she added.

'Just as long as he doesn't send us any more handsome clerics in need of sanctuary. One is more than enough,' Will said with no humour in his voice.

'Now, come and see what you think of the new paint,' he demanded and the coldness had gone as though it had never been. 'They have just cleared the ladders away.'

He caught her hand and pulled her towards the front of the house and Katherine made no effort to free herself. His hand was strong and warm, with rider's callouses rough against her softer skin. She could feel his pulse against hers and a wave of longing swept over her. It was all she could do to let her hand lie passive in his and not to twine her fingers into his.

'Close your eyes,' Lovell said as they neared the archway into the hall.

Blind, she allowed herself to be led to where she guessed the front door was, then he turned, so their back was to it.

'Now you can look, Kat.'

Katherine blinked. It was so much lighter, the dingy old walls painted a light creamy buff, although she hardly noticed that because facing them from his niche, pale and timeless against the blue of the Aegean Sea, stood the charioteer.

'Oh. Oh, *Will.*'

'Thank you for finding him, Kat. I could so easily have called in some dealer who would have taken all of those statues and never told me what a wonder I had.'

'He would have taken your nymph as well,' she said, teasing a little, because she was embarrassed by the emotion she was feeling.

'You are unkind to mock my nymph. She looks very well by her little pool on the terrace.'

'I imagine she has great appeal to gentlemen.' The crouching figure possessed a very pert backside and an expression which showed she was well aware of the fact.

'She is very lovely, but she is only stone and has no heart. I prefer flesh-and-blood beauty, Kat.'

And that puts me in my place, she thought, catching a glimpse of herself in the mirror that hung facing the foot of the stairs. *A very ordinary young woman. Perfectly acceptable looks, perfectly common or garden colouring and features. Well past the age of being eligible for anything much except genteel employment. Very firmly on the shelf. Just because a handsome aristocrat who is missing his mistress decides to kiss you, almost makes love to you, that is nothing to be proud of. There is no foundation to build castles in the air upon.*

'A penny for them.'

'What?' She almost jumped. Lovell was still holding her hand.

'A penny for your thoughts.'

'Nothing. I mean, all I was thinking was that this light buff colour would be perfect for the interior of the temple folly. And you are holding my hand.' She gave it a little tug.

'So I am,' he said, continuing to do so. 'I had no desire to put you to the blush, Kat.'

'You have not,' she protested.

'Then why are you that charming shade of pink?' He lifted their joined hands, kissed the tips of her fingers where they emerged from his hold and then released her.

'Because you are flirting with me,' she said hotly, turned on her heel and fled.

Faintly, from behind her, she heard Lovell's, 'Damnation', but she did not stop until she reached the safety of the library.

Inside all was blessed calm: a housemaid polishing the atlas stands, Peter the footman sitting in front of a pile of dusty almanacs, soft brush in hand, and one of the estate carpenter's assistants measuring a broken cupboard door.

This was her world: books, ideas held between their covers, emotions described, but safely contained—and no perilously attractive marquises in sight.

Chapter Eighteen

'**D**amnation.' Of all the idiotic things to do, to kiss Kat's hand like that when only hours earlier things had almost gone so disastrously wrong between them that he might have ended the day discussing the arrangements for a wedding with his chaplain.

She wouldn't expect it and he had not the slightest suspicion now that Katherine Jenson was out to entrap him. Oh, no, she had no need to—he was proving quite careless enough without any assistance from her.

'My lord? Is the new paintwork not to your liking?'

Will turned to find Arnley regarding him anxiously. 'I think it is excellent work,' he said. 'I was merely remembering something. Nothing to do with redecoration at all.'

'Are there any other rooms I can have the men work on, my lord?'

Will almost said that he had made no decision, then thought of the library. It would please Kat to have that decorated, surely? Suddenly it felt important to hold out some kind of olive branch.

'Yes. Ask Miss Jenson what she wishes to be done in the library.'

'Certainly, my lord.'

Will watched his steward bustle off towards the library, thinking vaguely that the man walked like a partridge, head forward, backside sticking out. The comparison made him smile.

'Good news, sir?' It was Wilmott, the inevitable papers clutched in one hand.

'Just a foolish thought about game birds. What have you there to plague me with?'

'A response from the landscape gardener that I approached—the one that Lord Larchfield recommended. If you recall, I wrote to His Lordship on your behalf, having read his article in the *Gentleman's Magazine* about the work he had done at his Shropshire estate.'

'And what does he say?'

'That he will be arriving as soon as possible with his assistant and will draw up proposals and costings for you.'

'The man's eager,' Will said, suspicious.

'He writes that the prospect of improving the estate of so notable a personage would be an honour. He professes himself greatly stimulated by the grounds that, from what I described, offer such scope for radical transformation.'

'Hmm. The problem is, I have no idea what work of this kind should cost. He could lead me by the nose.'

'Ah.' Wilmott was looking decidedly smug. 'I have taken the precaution of making enquiries about works carried out at a number of estates by a variety of landscapers and have a very fair idea of what is entailed.'

When Will raised an eyebrow he added, 'We secretaries do our best to help each other out—where it can be done without compromising the private affairs of our employers, naturally.'

'Excellent work, Wilmott. Now, write to the three most prestigious London jewellers and tell them each to send someone to assess the jewellery Miss Jenson has located. I want it valued and I want to know what they will offer for it.'

'You intend to sell it all, sir?'

'No, but there is a great deal I will not wish to keep. I can see no point in hoarding antiquated pieces no future marchioness will wish to wear. Although I suppose somewhere in all this chaos there are papers relating to which items are entailed, so nothing can be sold until those have been identified.'

It was about time he started thinking about this theoretical marchioness who would be wearing the family gems, instead of worrying about his librarian and his decidedly inconvenient attraction to her.

Redecorating the library should please Kat. Will caught himself up. His future *wife* would probably not care if he had the library painted purple and green. What she—his *wife*—would want would be a delightful bedchamber, a boudoir and the public rooms done out in the very latest fashion.

Which probably meant being formal and uncomfortable, not a place where a man could fall into a sagging, but comfortable, armchair after a ride without having to change out of breeches and boots. That was what he had now, a pleasantly informal retreat where his household gathered around in the evening before dinner with embroidery, books and the chess board.

Mrs Downe and Mrs Goodman between them had transformed the drawing room, the smaller parlours and the dining room into calming places to be, even though the furniture was old fashioned, the fabrics faded and the scheme of decoration left much to be desired.

Comfortable and homely. He would just have to make the most of that while he had it. Which made him think of his own bedchamber. It was decidedly gloomy, cluttered and cramped.

It was not the master suite, of course. He had taken one look at his cousin's rooms and shuddered, shutting the door firmly on them. Now, having seen what could be done, he wondered whether they had possibilities.

The windows faced south-west with what would be

a fine prospect across the park and the new lower lake when that was completed and the rooms were probably spacious, once nine-tenths of the contents were removed, with a bedchamber, a dressing room and a small sitting room.

Tempting, if he could only remove all traces of Cousin Randolph. And, of course, the adjoining suite would have to be prepared for his bride.

Will mentally shied away from that thought. Presumably there were fashionable London decorators one could employ to give one's rooms the very latest touch. Let Wilmott find one of those and give him his head; he would probably enjoy it more than searching for drainage experts or tabulating crop yields.

Meanwhile, perhaps he should let Kat loose in the master suite. She would enjoy exploring the contents and perhaps retrieving some hidden gems in the process. In fact, now he came to think about it, that was the most likely place for the late Marquis to have secreted the jewels missing from their boxes, if they were special items he wanted to gloat over.

Which reminded him that there had been no sign of the pride of his cousin's collection, the Borgia Ruby. Randolph had shaken off the claims of that double-dealing agent, the one whose relations with Bonapartists proved his undoing, in order to secure the title to it. Or, rather, he had set Will on the case.

Kat had no need to warn him about the motives

of dealers—that one had the brass neck to maintain that he had merely received a deposit from Randolph when, clearly, the document that his cousin had shown Will had stated it was a sale, even though it was possibly at a bargain price.

But then, the man had been, if not a traitor, someone with very dubious connections and he had probably realised too late that he had been too eager and had sold at a low price. After that he had stopped at nothing, including perjury, to claim a higher return.

Strange that there had been no sign of that jewel yet, but if it was in the house, he could rely upon Kat to ferret it out. She might not be a jewellery expert, but she would find that a particularly interesting piece, he was certain.

He would tell her about the suite over luncheon, by which time she would, perhaps, have recovered from his clumsiness in the hallway. It had broken the magic of the charioteer and he was angry with himself about that. This might please her.

It did not occur to him until he was halfway down the stairs that it was not usual for marquises to worry about the happiness or otherwise of their librarians.

Will—*no*, Lovell. *Stop thinking about him like that!*—came in to the small dining room as Katherine was discussing tapestries with Elspeth.

Her companion seemed to have developed a passion for textiles that matched Katherine's mother's for lace. Having unearthed the hangings from under the stairs where Katherine and Lovell had been trapped, she was lamenting her lack of knowledge.

'I have been studying that book on tapestries you found for me in the library, dear, but it is such a vast subject, I feel most inadequate. The other fabrics are much easier—I can tell what material they have been made of and guess at ages from the designs and so forth, but tapestry is another matter.'

'I know they were exceedingly expensive when they were made, at least, the Tudor ones I have read about,' Katherine said. She broke off as Lovell took his place at the table.

'Is this something else that we need to summon an expert from London to deal with?' he asked.

'I fear so. Or even one from the Low Countries if these are Flemish,' Elspeth said, passing him the bread rolls. 'But for the moment I want to have them aired and hung up somewhere dry and clean so that the creases can begin to drop and we can see if there is any damage from the moth.'

'Might I suggest the chapel?' Mr Gresham said suddenly, from his place at the far end of the table where he had been quietly working his way through a large plate of cheese and cold meats. 'It is clean and dry now and has long expanses of windowless wall.'

Katherine helped herself to butter and left Elspeth to

enthusiastically engage with the chaplain on the subject of how the tapestries could be hung and whether they were of religious subjects and therefore suitable as a permanent feature in the chapel.

There was no sign of Giles Wilmott, which left her rather uncomfortably aware of Lovell carving himself slices of cold roast chicken with the air of a man who has not seen meat for a week. There was nothing wrong with his appetite after this morning's events, which was more than she could say about hers.

She broke her roll into small pieces and began to butter them slowly.

'I have been thinking where the missing jewellery might be,' he said casually as he poured himself ale from the jug by his place.

Katherine dropped her butter knife and thanked the footman who picked it up for her while she forced her expression into one of polite interest and reminded herself that several of the boxes had been empty, not just the one that contained the Borgia Ruby.

'Really? There is a safe or locked chest that you have recollected, perhaps?'

'No, none that I know of. But it occurred to me that if there were items my cousin wished to keep by him, his suite of rooms would be the most likely.'

'Surely you would have noticed them by now?'

'I am not using the Marquis's suite,' Lovell said,

adding pickled red cabbage to his plate before attacking the chicken.

'No?' Katherine reached for the water jug, gave a mental shrug and poured herself ale instead. She suspected she was going to need it.

'When you see it, you will understand. If you are not busy in the library, I was hoping you could deal with that suite next, as the ground floor is now in good order.'

When she hesitated, he added, 'I will be out all afternoon. I must start making calls on my neighbours or they will consider me as eccentric and unsociable as Randolph.'

'Certainly, I will have a look. I need to speak to Mr Arnley about paint colours in the library, but that should take little time, as only a small area of wall is exposed and the ceiling is very plain.'

'Thank you. You might also look at the Marchioness's suite next door as well, although I doubt my cousin ever set foot in there. It seems to be full of all the things he wanted moved to make way for his own acquisitions.'

'That could be very interesting.' Katherine looked up and met his gaze, smiled politely, then found herself unable to break the connection.

There was something in Lovell's eyes that held her, something she could not read. Not desire, she knew that look now. No, this was rueful, perhaps a little puzzled, as though he was looking at something he did not quite understand.

Perhaps it was simply that he was the archetypal male baffled by women and not understanding why she was not making a great fuss and to-do about what had happened between them that morning.

Or perhaps, she thought with a sudden stab of alarm, perhaps he could read something in her expression that betrayed her feelings for him. He had sensed her distrust at first, however careful she had been to hide it. Now could he see the opposite?

How ghastly if he realised she loved him. Was that better or worse than him thinking she wanted to marry him?

Stop thinking about marriage. Stop yearning for what you cannot have.

Katherine took a too-hasty gulp of ale, coughed, apologised, flapped her napkin and, by the time she had recovered, Lovell was assuring Mr Gresham and Elspeth that they could do whatever they wished with the chapel walls and the tapestries.

She indulged herself by studying his profile while he was distracted. Will Lovell was a good-looking man, she admitted to herself. He was not pattern-book-handsome like Quintus Gresham, but he had a more masculine type of beauty that relied on strong bone structure and underlying character and vigour. He would still be a striking figure when he was an old man, looking distinguished in a magnificent family portrait.

Along with his well-bred marchioness and their brood of fine children.

'What is wrong, Kat?'

'I—I was thinking that I haven't seen a family portrait gallery, which I'd have expected, given that this is the main seat,' she improvised hastily.

'The Long Gallery runs along the west side of the house. I had a quick look at it and was plunged into gloom by the sight of so many portrayals of the family nose. Or the chin.'

'Which do you have?'

'Neither, I am happy to say. My father inherited the nose, so I suppose it might appear in my offspring— hopefully the boys, not the girls. Randolph had both the chin and the nose. Go and look for yourself some time.'

'I will do,' she promised, intrigued and also depressed at the thought of Will's potential family.

Lovell, Lovell, Lovell, she chanted silently.

She dared not let herself think of him so familiarly in case she said the name aloud and somehow betrayed herself.

Lovell rode off after luncheon in elegant tailcoat, immaculate breeches and highly polished boots to make his calls. Giles remarked that Petrie, the valet, was smug because at last his talents had been utilised.

'He lives in hope that His Lordship will throw a dinner party and his genius with neckcloth and curling tongs will finally be appreciated.'

'Curling tongs?' Katherine stopped at the foot of the stairs, one hand one the newel post and stared at him. 'Lovell?'

'A valet may dream. I am off to discuss with Mrs Goodman where we can accommodate a landscaping expert and his assistant. They arrive tomorrow, along with the expert in water management and drains who will supervise the moat repairs. I only hope His Lordship appreciates the disruption we are heading for.'

'Do landscape and drainage experts eat *en famille?*'

'I imagine so, given how much they charge. I understand they rate themselves as highly as society portraitists. The assistants, I believe, are accommodated below stairs.'

'It should please Cook, at any rate. I understand she considers her talents as wasted as Petrie does and is pining for Lovell to throw dinner parties.'

They exchanged grins as Giles took himself off to the study and Katherine climbed the stairs in search of the master suite.

She found it after a few false starts. It looked like something from one of Horace Walpole's Gothic tales, hung with gloomy fabrics at the windows and around the bed. It made her shiver with its musty atmosphere and it gave her the uneasy feeling that she was in a nest of something dark and brooding.

Katherine pulled the bell cord by the bed, half expecting no response, but both Arnold and George were at the door within minutes.

'Strewth, thought it were a ghost, Miss Jenson,' George said. 'Nobody's rung from here since His late Lordship died.'

'Well, the current Marquis has decided that this is the next room to be cleared. Please can you fetch ladders and remove all these curtains so I can see what I am doing. You had best give them to Mrs Goodman and Mrs Downe, although whether they will thank me for them remains to be seen,' she added when Arnold shook out one curtain and started sneezing.

While they were away looking for ladders, she opened the windows wide and could appreciate why this was the main suite. The view was already fine and, when the lakes were cleared, would be delightful.

She turned as thumping and some muffled cursing heralded the return of the footmen with the ladders and stood aside as the curtains fell in clouds of dust.

'His Lordship never liked anyone coming in here, you see, Miss,' George explained apologetically. 'I don't know when it last got cleaned properly.'

Once all the fabric was removed she set them to taking down the pictures which she suspected might be quite good seventeenth-century Dutch and Flemish works.

'Where shall we put them?' Peter asked, eyeing a somewhat fleshy nude inadequately clad in a few inches of gauze.

'In the Long Gallery, please. Stack them carefully so the canvas isn't damaged.'

Left alone, and with some light to work by, Katherine began to explore properly. Where, if she was a collector and a hoarder, would she put the small articles she wanted to gloat over?

The bedside tables yielded nothing but some literature which made her raise her eyebrows and set to one side, a sticky jar of something labelled *A Sovereign Remedy for Congestion of the Lungs* and several auction catalogues. Tipping them up and removing all the drawers revealed no secrets.

She eyed the bed, a very fine half-tester which had, thank goodness, been stripped of its covering down to the mattress. No sign of slits in the side, nothing underneath as far as she could slide in a groping hand on either side. The pillows, when shaken, produced feathers but nothing else.

Would an elderly man want to be hopping in and out of bed to examine his treasures? The panelled headboard produced nothing, but the ornate tops of the posts at the foot, each just sticking up a foot above the height of the mattress, looked promising. She twisted and turned the one on the right. Nothing. The one on the left yielded immediately and lifted away, to reveal a hole down into the hollowed-out post and the top of a narrow drawstring bag.

Katherine pulled it out and upended it on the mattress. Necklaces slithered out, snakes of diamonds, emeralds and sapphires. A handsome Renaissance medallion fell on to them and then, flashing blood red in the afternoon sunlight as it flooded in through the window, the Borgia Ruby.

Chapter Nineteen

It lay in her palm, beautiful and strangely sinister, this jewel that had belonged to the lovely fair-haired daughter of a pope, a woman who had been labelled a poisoner and was probably no more than the pawn of the powerful, dangerous men around her.

Blood-red in its elaborate Renaissance setting, the twisted baroque pearls hanging from it like frozen tear drops, it seemed to pulse as the light hit it.

A living thing and, like so many great jewels, a thing of danger and desire.

There was a sound behind her and, without conscious thought, Katherine slipped the ruby into her pocket, then turned to see Lovell standing in the doorway.

I have done it now. I am a thief.

Or she would be in Will Lovell's eyes, never mind that his cousin had kept the pendant when all he had paid was a surety deposit.

'You have found them, Kat? The missing jewels?'

'Most of them, I believe,' she said, wondering at how calm she sounded. 'I didn't count the empty boxes. These are certainly finer than the pieces that were still in their cases—look at this pendant with its fabulous enamel work.' The ruby seemed to be growing heavier as she spoke. Heavier and hot, as though it was burning through her pocket with guilt.

It isn't theft. It is ours—mine and Mama's—and this man helped steal it and ruined Papa.

Somehow that no longer seemed enough.

It's because I love him, she thought miserably. *Now I have no idea where my loyalties lie, although I know where they ought to be.*

'Is something wrong?' Lovell came in and picked up the pendant she had indicated, but his attention was on her face.

'Oh, it is this room—so gloomy, it is enough to cast anyone into a depression. Taking the hangings down helped and let in some light and I had the paintings moved to the Long Gallery in case that revealed any secret cupboards in the walls. Some of the paintings are very good, I suspect.'

'And did it reveal any cupboards?' He looked around the room and she noticed that the wind had brought out the colour in his face and his hair was tousled from where he had carelessly removed his hat.

'I haven't looked. These were in the bed post. Did you have a pleasant afternoon?'

'The ride was stimulating, the calls, not so enjoyable.' He pushed his hand through his hair, disordering it even more, and she clenched her hands against the need to smooth it.

'I am not enjoying being the local lion and the target of so many hopeful mamas,' he added, walking away to scrutinise the nearest wall.

'An unmarried marquis under the age of ninety and in possession of both his wits and his teeth?' Katherine said over her shoulder as she went to scan the surface of the opposite wall. 'You might as well have a target painted on your back.'

The surface was plaster, not panelling and, other than the marks where the paintings had hung, there was nothing to be seen. She began to open drawers, finding folders of etchings and watercolours, some documents in handwriting that she thought might be Tudor and trays of coins.

'These are Egyptian.' Lovell had opened the cabinets on the other side of the room to reveal an army of small figurines, pieces of what looked like wall plaster painted with vivid birds and stylised plants and alabaster statues. 'More treasures.' He sighed. 'And what to do about this suite…'

'I haven't looked at the other rooms, but this could be lovely. Take everything out, paint it in pale blues and greens to reflect the park outside, have curtains and bed hangings just a little darker. Choose paintings that you like and just a few pieces of furniture. Buy a new mattress—this one looks as though it is an ancient Egyptian piece.'

He laughed at her attempt at humour and opened a door. 'Very well, you have convinced me. This is the dressing room. I'll tell Petrie to organise and decorate that as he wishes. And here's the sitting room. Hmm. I think we had better remove the mummy cases.'

Katherine came to look. 'Goodness. Six of them.' Aloof, ancient, unreadable faces stared back at her. The only furniture was an armchair facing the cases, as though the late Marquis had sat and conversed with them.

'Do you think they answered back?' Lovell said with a visible shudder, clearly thinking the same thing. 'They are beautiful workmanship and they are definitely leaving this house!'

Katherine tried the remaining door and found herself in another bedchamber. She wriggled past crowded furniture and flung open the curtains.

'Oh, how pretty.' It was a charming room in the style of the previous century, all white and soft blue and hung with light, flowery, embroidered fabrics at the windows and around the bed. All kinds of furniture of the same period had been jammed in, so it was like a lumber room, but the essential light-hearted elegance still shone through the clutter and the dust.

She heard Lovell come in and turned, facing him

across the width of the bed. 'See?' She ran a hand over the bed covering. 'It is all hand-embroidered. Exquisite.'

'Exquisite,' he echoed and she looked up to find him watching her with an intense look in those dark eyes. There was desire there, she knew him well enough now to see that, but there was something else—liking, perhaps, or affection?

The ruby in her pocket suddenly felt like a lead weight. Will Lovell trusted her, liked her—and she was betraying that trust, lying to him day after day. If she had known him for what he truly was, from the beginning, then she would have told him the truth, told him what had happened with her father and his cousin, trusted his integrity and judgement to asses her story fairly.

But it was too late now.

Kat stood by the elegant bed, vivid and interested, wanting to share her pleasure at this charming room with him. She looked so right there, naturally grace-ful, bubbling with an intelligence that he had never expected to find combined with such femininity.

So right.

What was the matter with him, gritting his teeth and forcing himself to plan for a Season negotiating the shoals of the London Marriage Mart in search of a suitable bride. He had her here.

The thought hit him like a blow and he sat down abruptly on the nearest chair.

True, he would be expected to marry an aristocrat, but, damn it, dukes married actresses, so why couldn't a marquis marry a perfectly respectable young lady who might be a commoner, but whose upbringing had clearly been perfectly respectable?

Kat would be a perfect choice for him. There was mutual desire; she was already taking an enthusiastic interest in transforming the house and estate; she was healthy, intelligent and would make a wonderful mother, he was certain of that.

Their eyes met across the width of the bed and he saw her change, the enthusiasm ebbing away as she turned a little pale, an expression that he was shocked to read as shame crossing her face.

For a second Will was confused, then he realised what Kat must be thinking. He had almost seduced her there on the grass that morning, he had made her uncomfortable by kissing her hand, and now he was staring at her across a bed with goodness knew what visible in his expression.

Kat was a virgin, a respectable young woman, and she had let herself be carried away for a reckless moment. Now she was ashamed, embarrassed and wary of him. It was his fault, his responsibility and, somehow, he had to make it right.

What could he say? *I'm looking at you with a view to marriage?*

She would imagine that his conscience had driven him to it after that passionate incident. Or perhaps that he was attempting to complete his seduction with false promises and would cast her off once he had succeeded.

Somehow he had to retrieve the situation. He stood and walked across to the window, pretended to be looking at the view when all he could see was that look of shame and hurt in her eyes.

'I am sure Mrs Downe and Mrs Goodman can restore this suite. It is, as you, say, charming. Perhaps you could have a word with them about it and instruct Arnley as you see fit about any works that are required. I am sure, with your combined taste, it will make a fitting set of rooms for a marchioness.'

'Certainly, as you wish,' Kat said, her voice colourless.

'And I will tell Wilmott to write to the trustees of the British Museum about those mummy cases,' he added. 'You have no need to trouble yourself about those.'

'Very well. I will continue the inventory for both suites and also move any books I find to the library and any more small valuable items to the strongroom.'

When he looked around Kat was already half out of the door and into the master bedchamber. There was not a great deal to be read from either the set of her shoulders or her businesslike tone.

'In that case I will leave you to it,' he said, opening the door on to the corridor. One thing was certain, he wasn't following Kat into any more bedchambers in the near future. 'Until dinner time.'

There was a vague mumble from the other room. He closed the door behind himself and leaned back against the panels. Now what to do?

Court her, of course. Court her in the most respectful, proper manner. Do not be alone with her, do not follow her into bedchambers, kiss her hand—touch her. Somehow convince her that your intentions are pure—

No, they are not, his conscience reminded him sharply. *You want her. You want her naked on that flower-strewn coverlet, her limbs relaxed into pleasure, her face soft with the aftermath of your lovemaking, her skin pale against that green silk.*

Very well, he must hide his intentions, Will resolved. This would be the most proper wooing in the history of courtship and Kat would never have to meet his gaze with that look in her eyes again.

Katherine wondered if she was going to be sick. She felt strangely hot and her stomach churned. She made herself go back into the Marquis's bedchamber and sat down on one of the heavy carved chairs until the wave of nausea passed.

What should she do? She fingered the outline of the ruby through the folds of her skirts. She could hide it somewhere and then 'discover' it—preferably with a witness. Or she could keep it until she had found the incriminating papers, the documents that proved it had been obtained by a deception and the court case that had ruined her father had been a fraud from start to finish. Or she could find it again, let Lovell have it and still seek the papers.

Whatever she did, other than pursuing this to the bitter end, would mean she was betraying her father and bringing more grief to her mother who was relying on her to clear his name. And anything other than walking away leaving Will Lovell with the gem was to betray the trust of the man she loved.

There really was no choice, she decided after half an hour of wrestling with her thoughts. She was nothing to Will other than a useful servant who had provoked some desire in him. There was nothing between them *to* betray, other than the duty of an employee to her employer, and she was not stealing, she reminded herself, simply retrieving what was hers.

He would be angry, annoyed that his actions on behalf of his cousin and client had been shown to be less than honourable, but that was all, surely?

She knew him too well to believe that he would harm her vindictively and what else could he do to her, after all?

Nothing, except break my heart, she thought with a shiver.

But she couldn't sit there all day. She got up and went to her room, wrapped the ruby in a large handkerchief and tucked it into the middle of a skein of knitting wool. She had brought her basket of knitting with no very firm intention of actually doing any, although ladies were expected to occupy themselves with some hand work in the evening, so Mama had added it to her bags. Now it served as the ideal hiding place—out in plain sight on the dresser.

'I wonder if you ladies would care to drive out with me tomorrow,' Lovell said when the soup plates had been cleared at dinner time. 'My coachman informs me that he has had the landau he found in the carriage house cleaned. It is rather an elderly vehicle, but he assures me it is perfectly roadworthy.'

'That would be delightful,' Elspeth said. 'Are you making calls, or perhaps visiting some of the tenants?'

'No, I propose merely an excursion for pleasure. Tompkins the gardener has a reputation as a weather prophet, apparently, and he forecasts a fine day. Wilmott, Gresham—why do you both not come, too, on horseback?'

Both men agreed and began to discuss possible destinations, but it seemed that Lovell had already made a decision.

'I propose driving westwards. There are fine beechwoods and some splendid views across the Vale of Aylesbury, I understand,' he said. 'We can take a picnic luncheon.'

Why is he doing this?

Katherine smiled and nodded and did her best to seem enthusiastic about the plan, but the thought of the ruby, hidden in her room, of the pressing need to find the papers that would prove the deception, nagged at her. She could not afford to waste time now, not when she had the incriminating gem in her possession.

It was an effort to look interested and to contribute to the discussion that Giles began about the study of rocks. 'There is so much to learn,' he enthused. 'I have been greatly interested in the writings of James Hutton, the Scottish geologist, on the formation of the earth. The fine view we will see tomorrow is due to the great ridge of chalk on whose slopes we are now. Mr Hutton proposes...'

'You were very quiet about tomorrow's expedition,' Elspeth said when they finally retired to their own sitting room.

'Was I?' Katherine asked vaguely. 'I do hope you were not offended by Giles's enthusiasm for Mr Hutton and his belief that the earth is hundreds of thousands of years old,' she added in the hope of turning the subject.

'Archbishop Ussher calculated it to have been created in the year 4004 before Christ,' Elspeth said. 'It has always seemed to me to be something impossible to calculate, especially as he was insistent that it occurred on the twenty-second day of October in that year. Not that I ever mentioned my doubts to Mr Downe, of course. He would have been most shocked.'

Katherine listened with half her attention to an amusing tale of the Bishop of Bath and Wells and his views on the likely fate of those blasphemous scientists. What on earth had possessed Lovell to propose an excursion? Sober lawyers faced with mountains of work and onerous new responsibilities did not take their entire retinue out for picnics.

Perhaps he was trying to throw her together with the two young men. Yes, that could explain it. Lovell was alarmed at the attraction for him that she had betrayed and was attempting to distract her by placing her in a relaxed, social situation with Giles and Quintus.

'Well, I am for my bed,' Elspeth announced. 'But first I will warn Jeannie that we will require light day dresses, our prettiest bonnets and sunshades. This September weather is still pleasantly warm and we must look our best as Lovell has devised such a pleasant treat for us.'

Yes, Katherine decided. She would make a real effort to look her best and she would gratify Lovell by flirting in the most unexceptional way with both young men, while treating him with solemn respect.

If he was beginning to suspect that her feelings for him went deeper than desire, that she had thoughts of entrapping him into marriage, then she must act decisively to quell those suspicions. And somehow she had to keep the love she felt hidden somewhere deep inside.

Chapter Twenty

'Ladies, how delightful you both look.' Lovell stood at the foot of the staircase as Katherine and Elspeth, who had breakfasted in their rooms, descended, followed by Jeannie.

The maid was laden with parasols, shawls in case of breezes, fans in case of overheating and a basket containing all manner of items that she considered essential for ladies venturing out into the uncivilised world of the English countryside.

The party had become more elaborate, it seemed. Jeannie would join them, to see to their comfort, and she and the footmen had already been despatched with hampers, rugs and cushions to establish the picnic site, guided by one of the grooms, a local man who could recommend the perfect spot.

There was even, Jeannie had reported when she brought their breakfast, a little tent containing a close stool and a washstand for the ladies' comfort and convenience.

'Why, thank you, my lord.' Elspeth preened a little as she reached the foot of the stairs. It was not unjustified, Katherine thought. Her friend was attired in a pale green gown with darker ribbons and a ruffled hem and was wearing a pale straw poke bonnet with matching ribbons.

Katherine was wearing a new gown in jonquil yellow with white trim and a Villager straw hat with a wide satin ribbon of golden brown, both ordered from the shops Elspeth had discovered in St Albans. If she said so herself, she thought she looked rather fine.

She bobbed a curtsy as she passed Lovell and kept on, out of the front door to where the landau was drawn up and Gresham and Wilmott waited, already mounted.

'My goodness, how fine we will feel in such a carriage and with such handsome outriders to escort us,' she exclaimed, attempting to sound like her youngest cousin, Elizabeth, who was a shocking, and very successful, flirt. Mama disapproved of her and, it was true, she had many admirers, but never a declaration that she felt inclined to accept, but her charming little tricks certainly appeared to make an impression on the gentlemen.

Both riders seemed about to dismount to assist her into the carriage, but Lovell ran down the steps and they settled back into their saddles as Elspeth exclaimed at the fine appearance of the landau.

It might have been an elderly carriage, but it had been polished to a high shine and two matched dapple greys were in the shafts.

'Are those more of your late cousin's horses?' Katherine asked as Lovell turned from helping Elspeth into the open carriage and offered her his hand.

'Yes. I kept them intending to buy a coach and then discovered I possessed this. Randolph's travelling coach is not fit for service,' he added, climbing in after her and taking the backward-facing seat. 'I must purchase a chaise and, I suppose, a town carriage.'

'Oh, yes, the Marchioness will certainly require those,' she said chattily. 'Although I imagine this landau is really a town vehicle, is it not? I suppose much depends on whether the hoods are still weatherproof.'

'Quite.'

She was not certain how to interpret that. It did appear that mention of his future bride was not a particularly welcome topic, but was that because he feared she was angling for the role, or because he was not looking forward to the effort of the Season or simply because he had no intention of discussing his private affairs?

Ignoring the nasty little pang under her left ribs, Katherine fixed a bright smile on her lips and waved to Giles Wilmott whose bay gelding was keeping pace alongside the carriage while Quintus Gresham had ridden ahead on a neat black hack.

Giles tipped his hat in response.

'What a very fine sight we must present. A fine carriage and horses, handsome young men as outriders,' she said. 'Just what the villagers expect from their new Marquis, I am sure.'

As she spoke, they began to rattle over the cobbles of the village street and Katherine looked around with interest. 'Several people have doffed their hats or curtsied.'

Looking profoundly uncomfortable, Lovell raised his hand in acknowledgment of the courtesies. Katherine kept her gaze firmly on the back of the coachman, not wanting to give the impression that she might be pretending that this was her carriage.

If it was... If I were the Marchioness, married to the man sitting opposite me...

For a moment she indulged the fantasy, mentally moving Lovell to sit beside her and furnishing the other seat with a row of children. Two boys and a girl? Two of each? They would have blue eyes and dark brown hair and, given their parents, would probably be thoroughly stubborn and a complete handful.

'The church appears to have a Norman tower,' Elspeth remarked, jerking Katherine out of her dangerous daydream.

'It does?' Lovell asked unwisely, earning himself a lecture on rounded arches and pointed Gothic arches and various infallible methods of dating churches.

Katherine, meanwhile, discovered that she could converse quite comfortably with Quintus Gresham who had fallen back to ride alongside the carriage.

'How have you found the Vicar here?' she asked. 'Is he a congenial colleague?'

'Oh, most welcoming, despite the fact that reopening the chapel has reduced his congregation. But he is a fount of information on local affairs.'

'I am so glad,' she said warmly, watching as he cantered ahead again as the road narrowed.

'About what are you glad, Katherine?'

Startled by the use of her full name, she turned and looked at Lovell. 'Why, that Quintus has found the local Vicar congenial. He is such a nice young man, it would be sad if he found himself isolated from the support of a more experienced cleric. I wonder if the Vicar has daughters.'

'You are inclined to matchmaking?' There was a sharpness in his voice as he put the question and something in his expression that made her think it was not a casual remark.

'One always wishes to see one's friends happy, although, of course, I am not so foolish as to imagine that matrimony is the answer for everybody's contentment.'

'You do not see yourself as a clerical wife?' Lovell said lightly.

'Why, what an idea!' She managed to looked confused, wished she could blush to order, but settled on fanning herself with her gloved hand. 'I am sure Elspeth would tell you that I would be a most unsuitable match for a man of the cloth, although perhaps a wife with scholarly interests....' She let her voice trail off as she looked at the riders ahead of them.

'Or perhaps your talents would best fit you for being the helpmate of a politician.' He still sounded as though he was intending to tease.

Puzzled, and vaguely suspicious, Katherine shook her head. 'I have no idea, nor do I have any strong political allegiances myself. But, as I am unlikely to encounter any politicians, the situation is unlikely to arise.'

There was just the slightest flicker of a glance to one side where Giles was now riding.

'You believe Giles has ambitions towards a government career, or taking a seat in the Commons? Goodness.' She did her best to sound thoughtful, but let a little smile curve her lips, as though she was tempted. Best not to be too obvious, perhaps. 'Who is matchmaking now?' she challenged lightly.

Lovell had the grace to colour slightly. 'I was merely jesting, although, naturally, if it is a question of the happiness of members of my staff, I would exert myself to assist.'

So, he thinks it would be a good idea to marry me off to his secretary or his chaplain, does he? Either it has not occurred to him that I would be constantly in his company if I did or he is intent on keeping me close at hand in order to... To what?

Katherine felt her smile harden. 'I have my work and I am Mama's companion,' she said, trying to sound just a little wistful.

The only man she wanted to marry was out of her reach and, apparently, amusing himself by teasing her with talk of matchmaking. It hurt, a little, but, naturally, she must be glad that Lovell no longer wanted to kiss so much as the tips of her fingers.

If she had been a more unprincipled and ruthless character, Katherine realised, she could have made an outcry about being ruined by him and demanded either marriage or a substantial sum in compensation.

No wonder Lovell had suddenly become so distant, had stopped called her Kat. This talk of marriage must mean that he had realised just how close to the wind he had been sailing in making love to her.

What is sauce for the goose is sauce for the gander, my lord.

She could be just as formal.

'What a charming drive, my lord. I had not realised how picturesque the villages were around here with their flint walls and little churches.'

As though sensing something wrong in the atmosphere, Elspeth began to talk, commenting brightly on the cottagers' gardens and the charming picture a young goose girl with her charges made on a village green.

Katherine sat back and silently watched the passing scene, responding politely to any remarks directed at her, or when Lovell offered to open her parasol in case the sun was too bright or fell to his knees to retrieve a dropped handkerchief.

They eventually reached thick beech woods, the tall, smooth greyish-green trunks rising to the thick canopy overhead. A ride had been driven through, edged by grass verges, and the carriage slowed to negotiate the uneven surface.

Fallow deer bounded away as they approached, dappled hindquarters and white tail scuts vivid against the undergrowth as the two riders cantered off in front of the carriage.

Then suddenly they were out of the woods on to short, rabbit-cropped grassland with a wide view over the Vale perhaps four hundred feet below the steep scarp they were on.

'The wagon has arrived, just ahead,' Katherine said, leaning out to look. 'It is certainly a marvellous place.'

'From what I heard, I thought it might please you,' Lovell said, then added, 'You ladies, that is.'

Was that an afterthought? Katherine descended from the carriage with Lovell's assistance and watched him thoughtfully as he handed Elspeth out. Was this a treat for both of them, or even the four, including the two men, or had he devised this for her alone and the others were some form of concealment?

But to what end? If Lovell was set on seduction, then taking his victim's chaperon and his own chaplain along was a very strange way to go about it.

She gave a mental shrug and decided to simply enjoy the outing. The sun was shining, the day was warm and the breeze that stirred the trees was soft enough to be refreshing, not cold.

Rugs had been spread out in the shade of some tall hawthorn bushes, cushions piled in abundance, the ladies' retiring tent was set up at a discreet distance and Cook herself had come along to supervise the food.

Or possibly, as Elspeth suggested in a whisper, to have herself a holiday because the footmen were certainly doing all the work while she supervised from her seat in the wagon.

Lovell established Elspeth and Katherine among the cushions, checked that they had the most pleasing view, opened parasols and went to fetch them lemonade.

'My dear,' Elspeth whispered, 'I do declare the man is courting you!'

'What? Nonsense,' she retorted sharply. 'He is paying you just as much attention and, besides, what man intent on courtship brings along the lady's chaperon and half his household?'

'A man who wishes to establish the complete honesty of his intentions,' Elspeth said. 'He impresses the chaperon with his restraint and observances of all the niceties and he impresses the lady with attentions that he hopes will be pleasing to her, while ensuring she feels quite safe from any, shall we say, *warm* behaviour.'

'And what I see is a man who wants a change of scene,' Katherine said. 'Lovell has been cooped up with all those ledgers and all the chaos that his cousin left him. If he ventures out socially, he is stalked by hopeful young ladies and their parents. He hears about this wonderful view and so what is more natural than to declare a holiday?'

She broke off as Lovell approached, a glass in each hand. 'Why, thank you.' She remembered her resolution to be formal. 'My lord.'

He quirked an eyebrow. 'Not at all, Miss Jenson. I had thought to have luncheon served in about an hour, if that would suit you, ladies?'

'Delightful,' she murmured. 'I wonder what Giles is about?'

Giles was lifting something from the rear of the wagon and called Quintus over to help him. They spent a few moments apparently unravelling something, then walked towards Elspeth and Katherine carrying something large and multi-coloured between them.

'Look what I found in a cupboard in the office,'

Giles said as he reached them. 'A kite and it is a beauty. It looks a good age—it must have been a childhood plaything of the late Marquis. I had to make a few repairs, but I believe it is sound now.'

They all stared at the thing, its slightly faded harlequin colours patched here and there with brighter coloured paper.

Quintus was carefully straightening its long tail of paper bows. 'We should try it now,' he said, suddenly sounding about twelve years old.

Both men took off their hats and coats, Giles held the roll of string and Quintus walked away towards the edge of the scarp, holding the kite above his head as the string unravelled.

'The wind is catching it now,' he called. 'Shall I let it go?'

'Yes!'

The kite soared, hesitated, then climbed again, Giles letting out the string and leaning back against the pull. It rose higher and higher and he began to run along the break of slope, making it swoop and soar, Quintus running with him, both of them laughing like boys.

Giles handed him the roll of string and they ran back, the kite climbing higher.

'Goodness, how fit and happy they look. Do you not want to try it, Lovell?' Katherine asked.

He was standing, hands fisted on hips, watching

the two experimenting, arguing noisily about the best way to gain height.

'Childish nonsense.' His eyes were fixed on the kite.

'Innocent fun,' she countered. 'Or perhaps you do not have the skill.'

As she suspected, at that Lovell took off his hat, stripped off his coat and strode down to the kite flyers. They surrendered the string at once, but their groan as the fragile kite plunged earthwards was audible to the two women.

Then Lovell found the knack and it climbed again, sending a buzzard that was soaring on the updraught swooping away in alarm.

'My mother used to say that all men are boys at heart,' Elspeth said.

'And mine says that if you want work done, one boy is worth half a man, but two boys are only worth half a boy. What three are worth, I cannot imagine, but we cannot expect much sense out of these lads until they have exhausted themselves.'

They settled back against their cushions to watch, sipping their lemonade. The three men were all under thirty, all tall and fit and full of energy and they made a sight that would gladden the heart of any young lady, Katherine thought.

Quintus Gresham was the best looking and, perhaps, Giles Wilmott, the more athletic, but there was no mistaking who had the most power, the finest figure.

The now-familiar tightening in her chest caught her again, a mixture of love, desire and depression. Will Lovell was all she would ever want and she could never have him.

'Are you all right, Katherine? That was a very heavy sigh,' Elspeth said. 'Is your head paining you again?'

No, my heart.

'I am quite well, thank you. I was just allowing thoughts of what remains to be done to oppress me. I should make the effort to forget work and enjoy this holiday.'

Giles had control of the kite now, making it swoop and loop. Then the wind must have changed in some way and it dropped, hitting the ground heavily. When Quintus ran to pick it up it drooped in his hands.

'One of the struts is broken,' he called and trudged back up the slope, a picture of despondency.

'Never mind,' Elspeth said when he drew level with them. 'I am sure you will be able to repair it when you get back to the Hall. And it will soon be time for luncheon, I imagine.'

All three men, looking slightly embarrassed at their demonstration of boyish enthusiasm, came and retrieved their coats and hats.

'Please do not feel you have to put those on again on our behalf, gentlemen,' Katherine said. 'We have no objection to your shirtsleeves or bare heads and it is very warm now. And, surely, the footmen can be excused their livery coats, too.'

That was greeted with smiles of relief all around.

The staff was laying out the picnic on a trestle table covered, incongruously in such a wild and natural setting, with a pristine white cloth. The gentlemen went to view it, then came back to report to Katherine and Elspeth for them to make their choices. Clearly, it was expected that neither should rise from their cushioned seats to serve themselves, Katherine thought with an inward smile.

'Cold chicken, a roll and some of the salad for me,' she requested, while Elspeth asked for the salmon.

That was duly brought, along with more glasses of cool lemonade, and the men settled themselves on a second rug in front of the ladies. As this was slightly downhill, Katherine had the sensation of being some Eastern potentate with her retainers at her feet. It was an amusing fancy, but it did not stop her wondering what, exactly, Lovell was about.

He was watching her closely, although subtly, and she was very aware of him. When she put down her empty glass he was on his feet at once, taking it to be refilled, rather than waiting for a footman to attend to it and when a wasp took rather too close an interest in the sweet liquid he produced a clean napkin to lay over it.

Could Elspeth possibly be correct and Lovell was

wooing her? But to what end? A man did not court a mistress in such a manner, she was certain of that, but the only alternative was marriage and he was a marquis, for goodness sake!

It was simply her friend's romantic soul and her own yearning for him to love her as she loved him that was making them both see something more than gentlemanly politeness in his attentions.

He had allowed himself to become too familiar with a member of his staff and now he was backing away, taking refuge in formal politeness, that must be the answer, she told herself.

Then he looked up suddenly, caught her gaze as she studied him and suddenly time stood still. The sound of Giles and Quintus bickering amiably over what village down in the Vale was the nearest faded away, her surroundings seemed to blur, and all that was left was Will Lovell's face, those intense blue eyes locked with hers, full of desire and something more. Something deeper and far more complicated.

Katherine knew she was returning that look without reserve, without trying to hide any emotion from him. Could he read her love in her eyes or was he as confused as she was at what he was seeing?

Chapter Twenty-One

'Oh, Katherine, do look at that enchanting little blue butterfly!'

Elspeth's touch on her arm jolted Katherine out of her trance and she pretended to follow her friend's pointing finger, although everything was still a blur.

'So pretty,' she agreed. 'I have never seen one like that before,' she added brightly when it finally came into focus.

'Those are butterflies of the chalk downlands,' Quintus said, twisting to look. 'We have them in plenty where my family lives, in Sussex.'

Elspeth immediately started asking him about his family and whether they knew her acquaintance, the Fanshaws, who also lived in Sussex.

Katherine let it all wash over her, pretending to follow the dancing flight of the little butterflies.

Had she just imagined that look? Will—she abandoned the attempt to think of him by his family name—was engrossed in a discussion with Giles about land drains, surely not a subject that a man with romance, of any variety, on his mind would think of.

Perhaps she wasn't well. Perhaps that blow to the head when she fell from the gig was causing her to have delusions, see things that were not there. But she had no headache, her vision seemed perfect.

'I think I will just rest my eyes for a little while,' Elspeth announced. She removed her bonnet, made herself more comfortable against the piled-up cushions and appeared to drop off to sleep immediately.

The two men stopped discussing drains and, with a muttered word to Will, Giles stretched out on his back, a cushion behind his head and tipped his hat, a woven straw, over his face. Quintus had strolled off. He appeared, from the way he kept crouching down and examining the turf, to be looking at wild flowers.

The footmen had cleared away the picnic and had retired to the shade of the wagon where they were playing cards and smoking while Jeannie looked over their shoulders at their hands and, from the occasional burst of laughter, was teasing them with suggestions on strategy.

When she looked around again Will was on his feet, one hand extended. 'A stroll to admire the view?' he said, his voice low. 'I believe we have a perfectly alert chaplain as chaperon, even if Mrs Downe is resting.'

Katherine stood up without taking his hand, no easy

thing to achieve gracefully on slightly sloping ground amid a scatter of cushions and a sleeping companion.

'I feel no need for a chaperon with you, W—er, Lovell,' she said once she was a few steps away. 'And a walk would be welcome.'

She had almost called him by his first name, he realised as he offered his arm, but all Will said was, 'Take care, this turf is somewhat slippery in places.'

Kat tucked her hand into the crook of his elbow and they began to walk, close to the break of slope.

'What fun for children to slide down this,' she observed, looking down the precipitous grassy scarp. 'Although rather dangerous, perhaps.'

They walked a little further in silence. The winds rising up that had sent the kite high into the sky was still blowing, sending Kat's skirts across his legs and making her clutch at her wide sun hat with her free hand.

What to talk about? How did one go about this courtship business? He knew how to flirt, but that was out of the question at this stage. Will cleared his throat. 'An amazing view, is it not? One was hardly aware of being at any height when we drove here and yet there is this virtual cliff. It must be almost five hundred feet at this point.'

Kat was still silent, then she said abruptly, 'I do not understand.'

'We are on chalk, which I believe, if I understand the writings of James Hutton on the science of geology correctly, is a rock that has been much bent and lifted by the movements of the earth over time. The same thing may be observed on the South Downs, in fact—'

'That is not what I mean,' she said, almost impatiently. 'I do not understand what this…this *formality*, is about. You used to call me Kat, now I am Miss Jenson, or you carefully avoid calling me anything. Before, you never cared about chaperons, now you make a point of it. And this outing—you have seemed committed to your labours with Giles and anxious that I continue my work in the house, yet you suddenly declare a holiday. You probe as if testing my attraction to Giles and Quintus.

'I am, my lord, confused.'

Damnation. He had been so concerned about moving slowly, being scrupulously careful, that it had not occurred to him that such behaviour would, in itself, appear strange. Now what? Laugh it off, pretend Kat was imagining things—or be honest?

Honesty, of course. This was Kat, too intelligent to have the wool pulled over her eyes, too important to lie to.

'I was attempting to begin a courtship, Kat. Apparently, I was not going about it the right way,' he confessed ruefully, wishing he could see her expression, but the wide brim of her hat hid her face completely.

Her reaction was unmistakeable. She jerked her hand free of his arm and took two abrupt steps away from him, up the slope.

'I will *not* become your mistress.'

Now he could see her face and there was more than indignation or shock there. She looked hurt.

'I am not asking you to,' he retorted, anger at himself making his voice harsh.

'Then what do you want?' Kat demanded.

Will shot a glance towards the picnic party, but Wilmott and Mrs Downe still appeared to be dozing and all that could be seen of Gresham was his distant figure vanishing into a clump of bushes, apparently still in pursuit of butterflies.

'I want you to marry me,' he said flatly, trying to keep his voice down and succeeding, he realised, in merely sounding exasperated.

Kat took two rapid backwards steps, stumbled and sat down on the grass with a thump.

'Is this your idea of a joke?' she demanded, tugging at the ribbons of her hat that had slipped. She jerked it free and tossed it aside.

'No. It is my idea of how to make an inept proposal,' he snapped back. 'Are you hurt?'

'Merely my dignity.'

Surely those were not tears he could see gathering in her eyes? Kat turned her head and stared out across the Vale, lips tight.

Will sat down, a cautious arm's length away. 'I may not be going about this the right way,' he admitted, 'but my intentions are serious and sincere.'

'You, *my lord*, are a marquis. I am a librarian from a gentry family. You require a wife who has been bred and raised to marry a man of high rank. An ability to set your library in order and an unfortunate physical attraction leading to an ill-judged episode in the long grass does not make me an eligible candidate.'

Will took a deep breath, let it out slowly and started to pick his way through the quagmire it seemed he had created.

'You are a lady. You are educated and intelligent. You have the skills and the interest to manage a large household and to be concerned for tenants and dependents. And, as you say, there is a certain attraction between us. I had thought to go to London to take my seat in the House of Lords and to participate in the Season, but—'

'But you have no desire for the tiresome business of attending Almack's and fending off matchmaking matrons and sorting through the ranks of young ladies on display in the Marriage Mart.'

'Well, yes,' he admitted. 'But—'

'How much less effort is required if you are already married. No simpering misses, trained to show not an ounce of the intelligence most of them undoubtedly possess. No need to be constantly alert for attempts to compromise you in the conservatory, no tiresome parties or overheated balls.'

'If I might be allowed to finish a sentence?' he enquired and received an icy nod.

'I do not deny that I was not looking forward to the Season. However, if I had not felt both liking and attraction to you, I would not have made this declaration.'

'You consider liking and attraction to be sufficient, do you?' Kat snatched up her hat, jammed it on her head and was on her feet before he could regain his and offer his hand.

'Yes, certainly.' Will stood, trying to read her face. Surely any young lady would be delighted to receive a proposal from a marquis? Or, at least, from one they were prepared to let kiss them, one with who they had co-existed with on an amiable basis for almost a month.

Although just how amiable *had* it been in reality? There had always been that edge, that uneasy feeling that Kat harboured some antagonism towards him.

'What do you consider sufficient?' he asked.

'Love,' she said flatly. 'Love and trust, as well as liking and attraction.'

Love? Aristocrats did not make love matches. Aristocrats made strategic marriages: blood lines, political influence, wealth, lands—those were the considerations. Everything else might, or might not, follow.

But then, he was not making a proposal with any of those things in mind. He was proposing because he wanted Kat. And Kat wanted something from him he was not sure he could give. Trust, yes. He trusted her already to have the run of his house and control of its valuables. He trusted her to say what she thought.

But love? What was that? His parents had enjoyed a happy, amiable and long marriage without, as far as he could tell, ever professing love for each other. None of his married friends ever rhapsodised about feelings of romance when they were courting—the young ladies were attractive, healthy, had the makings of excellent hostesses and had useful connections in the legal world. The lawyer's equivalent, he supposed, of what aristocrats looked for.

Love, he was given to understand, involved a burning desire to pen poetry to the beloved's eyebrows and a sensation of hopeless surrender to the emotion, including lack of sleep, inattention to anything else and an inability to find fault in the lady.

Will was sleeping perfectly well, was not aware of any absentmindedness and was as indifferent to poetry as he had always been. In addition, he was all too aware of Kat's faults—including, but not exclusively, stubbornness, a complete refusal to regard masculine pronouncements as infallible and a pair of perfectly ordinary eyebrows.

'I do trust you and I hope you feel you can trust me,' he said.

Her mouth set in the firm line he had come to know all too well.

'Perhaps if you were to allow me to court you, other…emotions might develop,' he suggested, wondering as he did so why he didn't simply wash his hands of the whole idea. Kat had refused him and London during the Season would be full of young ladies only too happy to accept a proposal from a marquis.

He opened his mouth to inform her that he would take *no* for her answer and would trouble her no more and found the words did not come. He didn't want those other, faceless, young ladies. He wanted Kat.

And, miracles of miracles, she seemed to be wavering. 'I… Yes, of course I trust you,' she said. 'But you do not *know* me.'

And that, Will realised, was true. There was something inside her that was hidden. Kat had secrets, even if they were only secret feelings.

'I would like the opportunity to do so. Can we not be Kat and Will? Can we not work together as we have been? I will stop trying to court you in proper form, I will forget about chaperons and formality. Give it a month, Kat—we may surprise ourselves.'

It was fascinating to try to read the emotions that she was trying so hard to suppress. Was he fooling himself that she wanted to say *yes*, but that something was holding her back? And that something was in her, not in him?

'Yes,' she said after what seemed like a year. 'Yes, let us take a month, Will. Then we may know what we truly feel.'

He held out his hand to her and she took it, her own soft and warm within his fingers, and they walked slowly back towards the others with nothing more said.

Katherine told herself that she had bought time. Time to assemble her evidence, time to think of a way to confront Will with it and somehow salvage whatever it was between them.

She owed it to her parents to clear her father's name, she told herself as the landau bumped its way slowly back through the woodlands. She owed it to herself, too. And she also deserved, surely, a chance at love? Whatever it was that had prompted Will to make that proposal, there was more to it than a man's lazy disinclination to face a London Season, she could tell that.

Men, her married friends had told her, were not sensitive to feelings, even their own. Often it took the emotional equivalent of a blow to the head to make them realise that what they were feeling was love.

She closed her eyes for a moment, imagining Will

in love with her, what that would be like, what it would mean.

'Are you all right, Kat?' he asked.

'Just a little tired,' she said with a smile. 'All that fresh air. And unlike some people, I did not take a nap after luncheon.'

'I was merely resting my eyes,' Elspeth said with dignity. 'I was quite awake the entire time.'

'Of course.' Katherine did not point out that when she and Will had returned it was to find Elspeth's soft snores making a strange duet with Giles's more robust contribution.

Her friend made no comment in the days that followed when Katherine called Will by his first name, nor did she mention her theory that he was courting or wonder why he suddenly seemed indifferent to chaperonage again.

Because Elspeth is matchmaking, Katherine thought as she threw herself into her work.

She finessed the library arrangement and spent every other spare daytime hour searching the upstairs rooms.

She found more small valuable objects, far too much furniture and clocks, even for a house of that size, and finally reached the Long Gallery and the family portraits a week after that disturbing picnic.

'I think the last room I have to look through is the Long Gallery,' she reported at luncheon. 'There is very little furniture, but there is any amount of panelling that might conceal cupboards.'

Will had spent every day shut in the study with Giles, wrestling with a crisis that had just blown up over leases which had been inaccurately dealt with in his cousin's time. In the evenings he and Katherine had been going through the library catalogue, discussing whether there were any items he wished to sell and identifying gaps where he might wish to strengthen the collection.

It had been a very amicable collaboration, although she had had a tussle to prevent him disposing of every book of sermons, arguing that many of his future guests would wish to read such books on Sundays. But, amiable as it was, it had not done much to advance their easy friendship further towards anything else and Katherine wondered if Will was regretting his stated intention of returning to the question of marriage after a month.

Now he put down his glass and remarked, 'I will come and search through it with you. We have finally beaten those confounded leases into submission and Giles deserves an afternoon off. It is time I confronted my illustrious ancestors.'

Will clearly felt like a boy let out of school and approached the serried ranks of his forebears in a frivolous spirit.

'What an array of stiff-necked bores,' he remarked.

'Oh, not all of them,' Katherine protested. 'Look, this little Tudor sketch is charming—it might be by Holbein. And there are some very good portraits among those that seem to date from late in the last century. Now, this gentleman looks like you, don't you think?'

'My great-grandfather,' Will said, coming to stand beside her. 'And the two small boys must be my grandfather and his older brother, Randolph's grandfather.' He took a step back. 'You think I look like him?'

'You are better looking,' Katherine said. 'He is too perfect and he knows it. Or perhaps the artist smoothed away all imperfections and gave him a suitably haughty look.'

'And I am not haughty?'

'You are not,' she said, smiling at him over her shoulder as she stopped back. 'You can look very forbidding when displeased, but—Oh!' Her foot caught in her hem and she staggered back.

'Kat.' Will caught her, turned her in his arms. 'What have I said before? Accident prone. Thank goodness there are no library steps, or steep scarp slopes in here.'

She laughed up at him and suddenly they were both still, arms around each other, eyes locked together.

'Kat?' he said again and this time it was a question.

It was not a proposal of marriage again, she knew that, but suddenly she did not care.

'Yes, Will. Oh, yes.'

Chapter Twenty-Two

There was a wide window seat, almost a day bed, made to look like a Roman couch, presumably so that a reader could lounge elegantly while perusing a volume, but there was little elegant about the way that they fell on to it, tangled together, mouths locked in a kiss that was almost desperate.

Katherine found herself on her back, Will's weight over her and him looking down at her, so close their noses were almost touching, so near she could have counted the darker flecks in his eyes.

'Are you sure, Kat?'

Sure that I love you? Sure that I want you? Sure that I know this is madness, that there will be heart-break—but I do not care?

'Yes,' she said. 'Certain.'

There was no hope for them, she knew that now. She would not, could not, betray her father and so Will would understand that she had been his enemy from the very first and that nothing would deter her from her vengeance.

It was not romantic, this coming together. The doors were unlocked, their need urgent. Neither made any attempt to undress the other and that, for Katherine, was a bitter loss. She wanted to feel Will's skin under her hands, learn the texture, the warmth of it, discover muscles and lines and those secret, sensitive spots that even a tough man must possess.

Then the heat of his mouth on hers blurred her thoughts and the caress of his hands over her breasts, even through layers of fine cloth and underwear, sent her own fingers exploring from the nape of his neck to the taut curve of his buttocks.

Her skirts were rucked up, he was reaching between them for the fastenings of his falls and they were both clumsy because they did not know each other's bodies yet.

Then Katherine felt the texture of Will's breeches against her bare thighs, felt the muscles bunch and slide against her softer flesh, and parted her legs to cradle him where he fitted so well.

She felt his fingers caressing her there where she was already so very ready for him, felt the pressure, curled her body up to meet it, rode on a wave of desire and new, surging, feelings and then they were joined and Will was abruptly still.

It had hurt, a little, she realised with what part of

her rational mind was still functioning, but that had gone now and she needed him more, needed something she could not define.

'Will, *yes*.'

And then they were moving together, as though they had always known the rhythm, understood how to be together.

I love you, she thought as the pressure and the need built and then suddenly broke apart, unravelled, throwing her into a whirlpool of feelings and emotions as she clung to him blindly.

Then he moved abruptly and she cried out at the loss of him as there was heat and wetness on her skin and the weight of his body, sprawled boneless, on top of her and then darkness.

'Kat?'

She was curled up against him, holding on tightly, quite still and quiet. Will was not certain whether that was a good sign or not, but they couldn't stay here, like this.

'Kat.' He pressed her shoulder gently, then took one hand in his. Under his fingers her pulse beat steadily.

'Mmm?' When her eyes opened he was caught in the look that seemed miles deep, centuries old. And then she smiled.

'Lie still,' he said, just touching her lips with his.

How did he feel? Will wondered as he carefully disentangled himself, did his best to restore his clothing to some sort of order.

His legs felt as though he had run ten miles, his brain didn't seem capable of focusing on anything but what had just happened and his body felt so good he could hardly believe it belonged to him.

He handed her the clean handkerchief that he found in one pocket, then tactfully turned away when she sat up.

She would marry him now, he knew that. It wasn't why he had taken her in his arms—that had been quite unplanned, utterly spontaneous—but it would result in her agreement, he was certain.

Kat had been a virgin and he knew her well enough to be certain that she would never be free with that virginity.

Behind him he heard her get to her feet. Lord, they hadn't even taken off their shoes…

'This does not mean I will marry you, Will,' she said, her voice just a little unsteady.

'What?' He spun around to confront her as she stood there, skirts smoothed down, pinning a few locks of hair back into place. 'You have to marry me now.'

'I do not think so.' She looked quite composed, if flushed, but he sensed she was holding on to that composure by her fingernails. 'You did not intend that in order to force me, did you? You would not have taken precautions against my conceiving if you had. We have just lain together because we both wanted to, very much. But that is all it was, all it can be.'

'Why?' He felt as though she had slapped him.

I love you.

'I… I cannot.' And she turned on her heel and ran from him, down the length of the Long Gallery, through the door. It banged closed behind her.

What could he do? He couldn't force her, although if his precautions failed and she was with child, he would have a damn good attempt at it.

Will paced slowly after her down the length of the gallery, conscious of the gaze of dozens of painted eyes on his back. Judging, pitying or sneering?

It was not until he was halfway down the stairs that it occurred to him that he had stated that Kat must marry him because he had taken her virginity. He had said nothing about his feelings for her, although he had demonstrated physical desire clearly enough.

Her pride, at the very least, must be hurt. Could he be honest with her? Dare he? That was rather closer to the truth. To admit that new-found love was to risk rejection, pity. Scorn, even.

But then, what was love if it did not hazard itself for the beloved? He had to tell Kat. Lay out his heart to be trampled on, if that was what it took. Trust her with the truth. But not yet, not while they were both reeling from what had just happened.

* * *

'Miss Jenson, excuse me.'

Katherine stopped dead in her headlong flight, composed her face into what she could only pray was normality and turned.

'Yes? Oh, it is you, Petrie.'

Will's valet stood outside what she realised was the old Marquis's bedchamber door. He was as serious and immaculate as usual.

'His Lordship asked me to put the dressing room in order, but I have found a cupboard full of papers and I believe that you are sorting those. I do not wish to overstep.'

She took a deep breath and smiled. He did not recoil, so she supposed it had looked all right. 'I can certainly look at them for you. Probably they can all be taken down to Mr Wilmott.'

'May I assist you?' he asked. 'Otherwise I have done all I can in there until it is cleaned and repainted.'

'No, thank you. I am sure you have a lot to be getting on with. I can always ring for a footman if there is more than I can manage.'

'Thank you, Miss Jenson. I am much obliged.' He made a prissy little bow and walked off.

She supposed she could go and look at this cupboard now. It was as good a place to hide as any and it would have to be cleared sooner or later.

Petrie certainly appeared to be efficient. The room

was neat, all the drawers empty and the cupboards and presses with their doors slightly ajar. To air, she supposed.

In one corner was a small cupboard, about eighteen inches deep and waist high. When she opened it she saw a far tidier arrangement than any other of the old Marquis's. It was empty except for the top shelf on which manila card folders were stacked neatly and when she pulled one out she saw it had a label written in a pinched hand: *Mummy cases.*

The next read *Manuscripts.*

Excited, she pulled them all out, scanning the labels. And there it was, on top of the second pile. *The Borgia Ruby.*

Her hands shook so much as she opened the folder that the papers it contained spilled across the floor and she dropped to her knees. Letters in her father's hand. Copies of the Marquis's replies. The draft of a letter to his lawyer. To Will.

And there, at last it was—the top half of the receipt, the part that showed clearly that the payment the Marquis had made to her father was a deposit, a surety, only. It had been cut neatly, but when she held it up to the light, there was the betraying watermark, sliced across: the two pieces would fit.

Katherine bundled it all back, slid the folder into the middle of the pile and carried the whole stack to the door, leaving the cupboard empty. There was nowhere better to hide something than in a mass of similar objects.

She carried it downstairs, through to the muniments room, and slid it on to a shelf next to some similar files.

Now she had virtually everything she needed to confront Will. All that was missing was the evidence that he had concocted the accusations against her father.

Her hand was on the door when she heard voices outside.

'Sir, the boxes have arrived from your legal clerk. They are in the study now, but shall I have them brought down to the muniments room?' That was Giles.

'Yes, do that. There is important material in there, so it is the best place for it.' Will.

Was it her imagination or did he sound strained, unlike his usual self when he was talking to his secretary?

It would be a wonder if he did not sound different after what had just happened.

'I'll have that done now, sir. They are taking up a considerable amount of room where they are.'

Will replied with a comment she did not catch and their voices faded away until she felt safe enough to look out. The passageway was clear and she left, closing the door behind her and turning the key.

Elspeth was very full of news at dinner, so excited that nobody appeared to notice that Katherine and Will were unusually silent.

She had discovered some wonderful embroidery, Elspeth explained, and she thought it might be Elizabethan, perhaps an altar frontal.

That, of course, greatly interested Quintus Gresham. It also provoked comment from the two new arrivals who had, apparently reached the house late in the afternoon—the drainage expert, a Mr Perkins, and the landscape designer, Cosmo Peronne.

Katherine did not believe that name in the slightest, but she was too grateful for the presence of two strangers to provide distraction from herself and to compel Will's attention.

Once Elspeth had talked herself to a standstill Will and Giles engaged the two men in an esoteric discussion on water management, discussing the moat, the stream and the silted-up lakes.

It all sounded exceedingly technical, with discussion about angles of slope, water pressure, sluice gates and depths, and Elspeth, Quintus and Katherine made no attempt to follow what they were talking about.

With the other two now exchanging comments on the latest Court news—something that never interested Katherine at the best of times—she was left to brood on what had just happened.

Her body was still tingling with the after-effects of their lovemaking and she still felt off balance. What had she been thinking of? Besides the obvious desire and love, of course... What had it been that had broken her determination to hold herself aloof until Will's month of courtship had expired?

It was almost as though something within her was determined to push this to a crisis, end it once and for all. Although quite how losing her virginity would achieve that was a mystery.

Then the discovery of those documents, the half of the receipt that proved beyond doubt the late Marquis's crime—it was almost as though she had somehow known that this was the end game, that everything was rushing towards the dénouement and she had snatched at the last chance to lie with Will, to somehow show him her love before she turned on him.

She did not linger and wait for the tea tray when she and Elspeth left the men to their port. 'If you do not mind, I will retire,' she said. 'I am tired and I really cannot face more discussion on drains and how to dispose of tons of mud, which they are sure to still be talking about when they come through,' she apologised.

Elspeth smiled and waved her off. 'Sleep well, dear.'

It would have to be tonight, Katherine thought as she sat at her dressing table while Jeannie brushed out her hair and put away her few items of jewellery.

The ruby was in her evening reticule, making the embroidered bag bulge more than usual, but she did not dare leave it anywhere. 'Leave that, Jeannie,' she said, putting her hand over it when the maid reached out. 'I want to look closely at the inside seams, I think one has split.'

Then she was alone with her thoughts. *Plan*, she told herself fiercely. Anything was better than feeling.

The sooner she searched the box of legal papers relating to the old Marquis, the better. She knew where they were and they might be moved later to somewhere she could not access so easily. And the sooner she had all the ends tied up, the sooner she could act.

The sooner I can leave here. Leave Will.

So, tonight. What to wear? She was in her nightgown with her robe over it and both were simple, practical garments. If she was seen, then wearing those meant she could pretend to sleeplessness and the need to go down to the library to find a book, and the slippers would be soundless on the stone floors.

She had the key to the room, but would the boxes be locked? She guessed that legal boxes would be, not because they contained valuable items, but as a simple act of preserving the privacy of the individuals they related to.

Fortunately her father had taught her to pick ordinary locks because so often the keys to items he had bought had been lost. Katherine sorted through her hairpins and selected three, each of a different thickness, and slid them into her hair. If the locks were more complex then she would be faced with the choice of trying to find the keys or breaking into the boxes and she did not want to have to do either.

She slipped the ruby into the pocket of her robe, somehow wanting to keep it, and everything relating to it, together and sat down to wait. The household kept country hours: by one o'clock all would be quiet. She would allow another half-hour to be on the safe side.

Will paced up and down in his bedchamber. He was still wearing his evening breeches and shirt, with a heavy silk banyan over the top. He wanted to appear at Kat's door decently clad because this was going to be tricky enough without appearing as though he wanted to come to her bed.

Which he did. But not tonight.

He hoped that Mrs Downe was a good sleeper—he thought she was from remarks he had overheard at breakfast time—because he was going to have to negotiate the ladies' shared sitting room before he could tap on Kat's door.

He could leave this until the next day, of course, yet he knew he would never sleep and he rather thought that Kat would not either.

He would tell her he loved her, sink every ounce of his pride if that was what it took, beg her to marry him, not because he had compromised her, but because he was certain now that they belonged together.

The clock stuck the half-hour and he glanced at it in the candlelight. Another half-hour. Two o'clock.

There were three of the big black tin boxes that lawyers used for their clients' papers to keep them safe from vermin and damp. Each had *Ravenham* painted in white on the lid, but it was possible to tell which was the newest because the paint was freshest.

She lifted it down, set it on the table and looked at the lock. Yes, just a simple mechanism designed to keep out the curious and secure the lid in place. A few minutes' work with two of the hairpins and it clicked open, the sound echoing in the small room.

Katherine took a deep breath and told herself to keep calm. The house had been silent and still as she had come downstairs, only the snores of whichever footman was on duty in the deeply hooded porter's chair in the hall disturbing the peace.

She delved into the box, lifting out thickly filled folders that were clearly to do with the Marquis's death and the inheritance of the title.

Below them was another labelled *Borgia Ruby*. Heart thudding, she opened it on the table and began to sort through it until she found what she was looking for, a letter from Will to his cousin.

Agents report that the man Jones purchased the gem from was a supporter of Bonaparte who had to flee France to evade the retribution of local loyalists. He has achieved this thanks to Jones's efforts and money.

One can only deduce from this act, which must have put Jones to considerable expense and involved some risk, that they were already confederates.

I can use this to demonstrate what a blackguard the man is and to undermine whatever sympathy the court might have for an apparent 'underdog' in conflict with a peer of the realm.

She spread the letter out, set the doctored receipt beside it, laid the ruby itself on top as a glittering paperweight. She had it all now.

A draught disturbed the papers, lifting one corner.

'What the devil do you think you are doing?'

Will stood in the doorway, staring at her. Then he looked at the table where the ruby glowed balefully in the candlelight.

Katherine reached out instinctively to cover the gem.

'And what are you doing with that?'

Chapter Twenty-Three

She looked the picture of guilt, Katherine realised. Beside her the legal box stood open, her picklocks beside it. Papers she had no right to look at were spread out in front of her and she was clutching a valuable jewel.

'That is the Borgia Ruby. Kat—'

'It is mine.' She found herself on her feet, confronting him, the ruby clenched in her fist. 'Your cousin stole it—see, here is the half of the receipt he cut off to make it look as though he had bought it, when instead of paying a security while he had it appraised.

'And here—' she jabbed one finger at the letter he had written '—here you are suggesting how a good man, an honest, loyal, *patriotic* man, might be cast as a traitor, a sympathiser with the enemy, in order to make his word in court worthless.'

Will had not moved. 'Who are you?'

'Katherine Jones, his daughter. And this ruby belongs to me and to my mother. She is a widow. Did you know that? The story you told in court broke my father, ruined him, killed him.'

'I trusted you. I—'

'Papa trusted the court for justice. I worked hard for you. I have done everything you employed me for.' She made her voice cold. 'And do not think I have robbed you. Not one item that does not belong to me has been taken. Only this, which is mine.'

'You could have told me.' He looked bleak and somehow...empty.

'Yes? Told you what, Mr "We Can Use This" Lawyer? That you cousin was a liar and a cheat? That Papa helped that pathetic little man escape because that was part of the price of the ruby? The war was over—what harm could he do? You had not one scrap of evidence that my father conspired with Bonapartists before that, because there was none to be found.'

'It was my duty to present my client's case in the best light,' Will said.

'It was your duty to tell the truth!'

'So you came here hating me. But then... Are you such a good actress, Kat?'

'Yes, I came here hating you.' Something forced the truth from her. 'And then I started to like you, to desire you. It still did not make anything right, even when I—' She almost said it. *Loved you.*

'I wanted to marry you,' he said. 'What did you want?'

'For you to clear Papa's reputation. To tell the world that he was not a traitor, not a confidence trickster. To have the ruby's ownership clear so Mama can sell it.'

'Give me that receipt. Both pieces.' He held out his hand, those long fingers that had held her, caressed her.

She should not trust him with it. All he had to do was snatch it away, set the candle flame to it and her proof was gone. She could read in his eyes that he knew what she was thinking, saw the bitter twist of his mouth.

'Here. Hold the pieces up to the light and you will see that the watermark matches.'

He took them, read them, then held them together between finger and thumb of one hand while he reached for the candle.

Katherine held her breath. All it would take is one touch of the flame…

But he held it behind the paper and looked closely at the point where the two parts joined. There was a long silence, then, 'Keep it.' Will dropped the two parts next to the ruby. 'Keep the receipt. Keep the damn jewel. Be gone from this house at daybreak—a carriage will be ready for you.' He raked her with a look that left her feeling scorched and turned to the door. His hand was on it, then he looked back.

'I was searching for you because… No.' He shook

his head. 'I had not thought myself quite the fool I clearly am.' Then he was gone.

Katherine found she was sitting again, although she had no recollection of it. In front of her, on the litter of papers, lay the ruby, glowing like a malevolent eye.

There were always tales about the great historical gems, stories of spells and magic, of love affairs and murders. Katherine had dismissed them as amusing romantic nonsense.

Now, for the first time, she believed them. This stone was cursed and it had ruined their lives. It had killed Papa, plunged Mama into deepest grief and now it had ruined whatever was between her and Will.

Why was he looking for me? Does he feel something, something more than desire? If he did, he doesn't now. Not any more. Not now he knows I lied to him, deceived him, did not trust him even when we had become so close.

Katherine stood up, steady suddenly with a kind of frozen calm. She returned the legal papers to their box, used her hairpins with a steady hand to snick the lock closed, returned it to the shelf. Then she folded the receipt and Will's letter into the ruby's box and placed the jewel on top, touching it only with her fingertips, and closed the lid.

She would take it home and sell it as soon as she could find a buyer. With the receipt intact at least it would be clear that Mama had title to the thing, even if dealers knocked the price down as a condition of handling something from the daughter of a ruined man.

Then she locked the door behind her and climbed the stairs to her room to pack. They would be ready at first light: she had no desire to face Will Lovell ever again.

'I still cannot believe he gave it up,' her mother said two days later when Katherine was at last able to tell her what had taken place. Not all of it. There were no mentions of kisses, of her lost virginity, of marriage proposals and her broken heart.

'Nor can I,' Katherine agreed wearily. 'I think he just wanted to be rid of me—and of it.'

'Will we be able to sell it now?' Her mother was eyeing the box with the same wariness she might have shown a small unexploded mortar.

'I think so. I will start to make enquiries.' Just as soon as she had shaken off this clinging lethargy, the feeling that she would never smile again, never find anything amusing or pleasant or worthwhile.

'...it must have been so unpleasant for both of you,' Mama was saying and Katherine forced herself to pay attention. 'Poor Elspeth was most distressed by having to leave in such a clandestine manner. I do wish she had stayed on with us for a while.'

'So do I. She was a great support and I feel I haven't thanked her enough,' Katherine admitted. 'Neither of us was in a fit state for long conversations on the journey home.'

'The morning papers, ma'am.' Jeannie came in with the three they normally took and laid them on the table, then went straight out again instead of stopping to relay any gossip she had gleaned from the newspaper sellers that morning.

'Jeannie is not happy either,' Katherine observed. 'I rather suspect a dalliance with one of the grooms. I only hope it was not serious because—'

'Katherine! Oh, Katherine, look!' Her mother thrust the copy of the *Morning Post* at her. 'See? There. Read it out loud.'

There was a full column in the legal section headed *Jones v the Marquis of Ravenham*.

'"...*as the lawyer acting on behalf of the late Marquis of Ravenham I can disclose that the evidence presented on behalf of the Marquis was incomplete and lacking an essential element which proves, beyond doubt, that the jewel known as the Borgia Ruby was the lawful possession of Mr Arnold Jones and remains that of his heirs. Further, it is indisputable that the suggestion raised during the case that Mr Jones was in any way in league with Bonapartists, or was in any manner disloyal to his country, is entirely false and based on erroneous evidence. William Lovell, Third Marquis of Ravenham.*"'

Breathless, Katherine turned the pages of the other two papers. 'It is here, too—*The Times* and the *Chronicle*.'

She realised her mother was drying her eyes. 'Mama?'

'You did this. You brought that dishonourable man to realise what he had done. My darling Arnold's name is cleared.'

No. It was Will's sense of honour that led him to do this. He had no need to.

To find that she could think like that after all that had happened surprised her, confused her. Katherine realised that she should be delighted, happy beyond words that she had achieved what she had set out to do—to have her father's good name restored and, less important, to secure the return of the ruby.

But I am not. I feel hollow, as though my chest has been an echoing void.

'Mama, I am going out for a walk. I need to clear my head.'

'Of course, dear.' Her mother was still dabbing at her eyes. 'I will write to Elspeth—if she has not seen the newspapers she will be so glad to hear our news.'

Will spread the previous day's *Times* out before him. His communication had been printed exactly as he had written it, he saw, checking carefully. Beside lay a furious letter from his partners in the law firm, demanding to know whether they should expect a suit for damages from the family of Arnold Jones.

He picked up his pen and wrote across the bottom of the letter.

No. They are honourable people. R.

He folded it and tossed it across the desk to Giles who was radiating tact to a painful extent. 'Readdress that to the Chambers, please.'

He had been furious with Kat. Hurt and furious. She had lied to him, betrayed his trust and yet...

He looked down at the newspaper again, at what he had written. What else could she have done? If she had arrived on his doorstep claiming that his cousin, a peer of the realm, had deliberately falsified a document in order to steal a valuable jewel, what would he have done?

Thrown her out, of course.

And that matter of her father and the Frenchman. That had been badly done. He had thought his cousin's case was fully justified and that he was dealing with a rogue and a thief. What was more likely than that Jones was disloyal into the bargain?

I should have checked. I should have dug more and Kat owed me absolutely nothing but her hatred.

Yet she had worked hard to do what he had employed her for. That was honest and she had been that. There had been endless opportunities for her to have robbed him blind, but she had not.

What hurt, he realised now, was that as she had come to know him, as they had grown so close, she still had not been able to trust him with the truth of her mission, because that was what it had been, as much as any intelligence officer infiltrating behind enemy lines.

But I am not the enemy, Kat. I love you.

There was a scratch at the door and Giles got up to answer it.

Behind him Will heard murmuring, a muffled exclamation and then his secretary went out. A tenant at the door, perhaps.

If I go to her now, tell her that I understand her deception, that I honour her devotion to her father, that I love her—what then?

He could not hope she would forgive him, let alone return his regard in any way, but he knew he could not live with himself if he did not at least hazard it. Hazard his heart, hazard his future.

The door opened and closed again. 'Giles, I am going to London. This afternoon. Bring me anything that must be dealt with immediately.'

'There is only an ex-employee to deal with, my lord,' said the person behind him as he became aware of a faint scent of jasmine, of a tingling down his spine. 'I fear she must be dealt with now, as she has something to say.'

He came to his feet as he turned. It was not an hallucination brought on by sleepless nights. It was Kat.

It was not encouraging. Will's face was blank of emotion, his body tense. Katherine swallowed and launched into her carefully prepared speech.

'I have come to thank you, my lord, for the notice in the newspapers. My mother and I are deeply relieved that Papa's good name has been restored. After the way in which we parted, I realise that you could well have done nothing.'

'I thought it was the only honourable thing to do when I realised that your father was innocent and that, therefore, his supposed connection to the French needed further exploration,' Wil said, very formally, very much the Marquis of Ravenham.

'And I am sorry that I deceived you when I sought employment here,' Katherine added.

'You performed everything I hired you for to an excellent standard. I can hardly fault you on that. In fact, I realise I owe you your wages.'

They were both so stilted, formal. So very correct— an armour to get the through this.

'Don't! Don't make this about money,' she burst out. 'Not after...'

Silence, then Will said, 'I am curious. How had you intended to play this out once you had the ruby and the evidence?'

'I would have come to you, told you what I had dis-covered, demanded that you did what you have just done.' She gestured towards the open newspaper.

'And if I had simply taken it all back from you, dared you to do your worst, countered your accusations with the story that you were a discarded and spiteful mistress?'

'You would never have done such a thing. You are a man of honour.'

'You think that now, perhaps.' In his turn he indicated the paper. 'But were you so certain then?'

'No,' she admitted. 'But I would have risked it. Lo—' Katherine froze.

Will closed his eyes and she saw him draw a deep, shuddering breath. 'One of us has to say it,' he said, almost to himself. 'One of us has to risk it all.

'Kat, I had decided to drive to London this afternoon and, when I was there, I was going to call on you.'

'Why?' she whispered, her heart beating too hard.

'To tell you that I understood. To tell you that I was sorry. To tell you that I love you. I don't even know if you heard me before. I can't imagine that you would have believed me.'

She sat down, hard. Thankfully, there was a chair just behind her.

'You love me? I thought perhaps you would feel you had to make a declaration after we had lain together.'

'It is why I was looking for you that night. To tell you that I love you and want to marry you. Not because we made love, not because I had in any way compromised you or that I thought I owed you something. Because I do not think I can ever be happy again without you and I suspected that perhaps you felt the same, despite your denials.'

'I realised that I was falling in love with you after that morning at the temple,' she confessed.

Is this a dream? Is Will really telling me he loves me, just as he does over and over in my dreams?

'It was…dreadful. I felt I was betraying Papa *and* you. It was a struggle to know where my loyalties lay. I didn't dare trust you,' she concluded miserably.

'You were right to choose as you did,' Will said. 'I couldn't understand you, how what I sensed from you was so changeable. Now I see what you were struggling with.'

Then, at last, he smiled and there was so much love, so much tenderness in his face that Katherine gasped.

He held out his hand and came towards her and she stood, took it in her own, felt the emotion that flowed between them and was suddenly, and completely, happy.

Will stooped, scooped her up in his arms and somehow opened the door.

'Will? *Will!*'

He strode across the hall towards the stairs, passing his butler, his chaplain, the landscape designer and the drainage engineer.

'Grigson, the lady's suite is to be made ready. Perkins, I want that moat pond finished and a rowing boat on it by the end of the week. Gresham—see about a special licence, will you? The name of the bride is Katherine Jones.'

'Katherine Amanda Jones,' she said, breathless, over his shoulder as she was swept up the stairs.

'Rowing boat?' she added as Will reached the landing.

'This house is going to have everything you want. You said you wanted to make a boating pond out of the moat and you will have it.'

'Will, the house already has all I want—you.'

'My lord?'

'Petrie, out.'

As the door closed behind the valet Will lowered her to her feet beside the bed. 'I love you. I want very much to show you how much. May I? This time without our shoes, on a proper bed and with no disapproving ancestors looking on.'

'I cannot think of anything I would like better,' she admitted, pushing his coat back from his shoulders.

They undressed each other, urgently and then, when it was the last few garments, slowly, carefully.

Katherine had expected to be shy when she stood in front of him naked, but she was too much in wonder at the sight of him to be self-conscious.

Will lifted her on to the bed, followed her and lay beside her, caressing her, kissing her, and she let him for a few moments, then began boldly to stroke and kiss him in turn, revelling in the way his body reacted to her touch, gasping in pleasure at the magic his hands were weaving.

When he came over her and she cradled him against her body, where he fitted so well, she felt no fear. They had joined before and this time would be even better.

'Love me, Will,' she whispered as he entered her.

'Always. Fly with me, my lady.'

'For ever,' she promised and let him take her soaring up into the fireworks and the velvet darkness and, finally, to rest.

A long time afterwards she turned her head on the pillow. 'What did you just say, my love?'

'*"Who can find a virtuous woman? For her price is far above rubies. The heart of her husband doth safely trust in her,"*' Will said. 'It's in the Bible. I looked it up when I realised that I didn't care about rubies, or my title or anything else. I just wanted you, needed you. That I could trust you with my heart.'

'Always and for ever,' she promised and kissed him.

* * * * *

MILLS & BOON ®

Coming next month

ONLY AN HEIRESS WILL DO
Virginia Heath

Book 1 of **A Season to Wed**
The brand-new regency series from
Virginia Heath, Sarah Rodi, Ella Matthews and
Lucy Morris

Gwen laid down her quill and steepled her fingers. 'This is a surprise, Major Mayhew—although I must say, a timely one. I've been thinking about earlier and—'

'So have I. Incessantly. But I'm in. Obviously I am in.' He suddenly smiled and that did worrying things to her insides. However, if his smile made all her nerve endings fizz, what he did next made them melt. 'I would have been here sooner but I had to collect this.' He rummaged in his waistcoat pocket—this one a vivid turquoise peacock embroidered affair that shouldn't have suited anyone but did him—and pulled out a ring. 'This was my mother's. I hope it meets with your satisfaction.'

She stared at it dumbstruck. Shocked that he had thought of it and yet unbelievably touched that he had. 'You brought me a ring…' She had assumed, when her engagement was announced, she would have to buy her own and that it would be a meaningless trinket—not an heirloom. Not something that meant something to someone. Something pretty and elegant, a simply cut oval ruby the size of her little fingernail surrounded by diamonds, that she probably would have chosen for herself before she talked herself out of it for being too bold.

He shrugged awkwardly. 'It seemed the very least I could do after you proposed.' Then to her utter astonishment he reached across the table, grabbed her hand and slipped it on her finger. 'It fits perfectly. Perhaps that's an omen?' He held her hand while he stared at it, twisting it slightly so that the lamplight caught the stones and made them sparkle. Gwen barely noticed the gem, however, as his touch was playing havoc with her senses.

He let go of her finger and, for a fleeting moment, common sense returned, warning her to yank the thing off and hand it back to him. Except...

It felt right on her finger and she couldn't formulate the correct words to tell him that she had changed her mind. That he wasn't at all what she was looking for, but she hoped he found another, more suitable heiress, to marry as soon as possible. Instead, there was another voice in her head overruling that of common sense. One that was rooting for Major Mayhew, no matter how wrong she already knew him to be.

Continue reading

ONLY AN HEIRESS WILL DO
Virginia Heath

Available next month
millsandboon.co.uk

COMING SOON!

We really hope you enjoyed reading this book.
If you're looking for more romance
be sure to head to the shops when
new books are available on

Thursday 27th February

To see which titles are coming soon, please visit
millsandboon.co.uk/nextmonth

MILLS & BOON

LET'S TALK
Romance

For exclusive extracts, competitions and special offers, find us online:

- **f** MillsandBoon
- **X** @MillsandBoon
- **⊙** @MillsandBoonUK
- **♪** @MillsandBoonUK

Get in touch on 01413 063 232

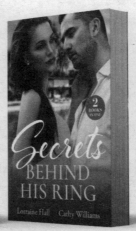